ACCLAIM FOR ANDREW KLAVAN

"Edgar Award–winning Klavan's well-orchestrated fantasy thriller features . . . an imaginative mix of gaming action with real-life stakes. With just the right cliff-hanger ending, this trilogy opener shows promise."

—*BOOKLIST* (ON *MINDWAR*)

". . . the focus is on action, and there's just enough left unresolved to tempt readers onward."

—*KIRKUS REVIEWS* (ON *MINDWAR*)

"A fantastic read. Fast-paced and wildly imaginative, *MINDWAR* is a cinematic cyber thriller with more twists than a circuit board."

—JOHN DIXON, AUTHOR OF *PHOENIX ISLAND* (INSPIRATION FOR THE CBS-TV SHOW *INTELLIGENCE*)

"Klavan retains his James Patterson–like gift for keeping pages turning, and the mystery behind it all . . . is a juicy one, and well handled."

—*BOOKLIST* (ON *NIGHTMARE CITY*)

"This book will appeal to anyone who is looking for a fast-paced adventure story in which teens must do some fast thinking to survive."

—*SCHOOL LIBRARY JOURNAL* (ON *IF WE SURVIVE*)

"Klavan turns up the heat for YA fiction . . ."

—*PUBLISHERS WEEKLY* (ON *IF WE SURVIVE*)

"The original plot is full of twists and turns and unexpected treasures. Klavan's writing is quick, tight, exciting, and intense. The adrenaline-charged action will keep you totally immersed."

—*RT BOOK REVIEWS*, 4 1/2 STARS (ON *CRAZY DANGEROUS*)

"A thriller that reads like a teenage version of *24* . . . an adrenaline-pumping adventure."

—THEDAILYBEAST.COM REVIEW OF *THE LAST THING I REMEMBER*

"Action sequences that never let up . . . wrung for every possible drop of nervous sweat."

"[Klavan] is a solid storyteller with a keen eye for detail and vivid descriptive power . . . The Long Way Home is something like 'The Hardy Boys' crossed with the 'My Teacher Is an Alien' series."

"I'm buying everything Klavan is selling, from the excellent first person narrative, to the gut-punching action; to the perfect doses of humor and wit . . . it's all working for me."

"Through it all, Charlie teaches lessons in Christian decency and patriotism, not by talking about those things, or even thinking about them much, but through practicing them . . . Well done, Andrew Klavan."

HOSTAGE RUN

HOSTAGE RUN

THE MINDWAR TRILOGY
BOOK TWO

ANDREW KLAVAN

THOMAS NELSON
Since 1798

NASHVILLE   MEXICO CITY   RIO DE JANEIRO

Published in Nashville, Tennessee, by Thomas Nelson. Thomas Nelson is a registered trademark of HarperCollins Christian Publishing, Inc.

Thomas Nelson titles may be purchased in bulk for educational, business, fund-raising, or sales promotional use. For information, please e-mail SpecialMarkets@ThomasNelson.com.

Scripture quotations are taken from the Holy Bible, New International Version®, NIV®. Copyright © 1973, 1978, 1984, 2011 by Biblica, Inc.™ Used by permission of Zondervan. All rights reserved worldwide. www.zondervan.com

Scripture quotations are also taken from the KING JAMES VERSION is in the public domain.

Publisher's Note: This novel is a work of fiction. Names, characters, places, and incidents are either products of the author's imagination or used fictitiously. All characters are fictional, and any similarity to people living or dead is purely coincidental.

Library of Congress Cataloging-in-Publication Data

Klavan, Andrew.
  Hostage run / Andrew Klavan.
    pages ; cm. -- (The mindwar trilogy ; Book 2)
  Summary: "Rick Dial is faced with an impossible choice: save the life of his best friend Molly. or save the free world. Rick Dial's career as a superstar quarterback ended when a car accident left him unable to walk. But his uncanny gaming ability caught the attention of a secret government organization trying to stop a high tech terrorist attack on America. He's been to the fantastical cyber world called the MindWar Realm. and returned to Real Life victorious. But the stakes have just gone up. Another attack is imminent and Rick is the only one who can stop it. How can he, though, when terrorists have kidnapped his best friend Molly and are threatening to kill her if Rick returns to the Realm? As Molly uses every resource of mind and body to outwit her brutal captors, Rick races against time inside a nightmare video game where a fate worse than death may bewaiting for him. Hundreds of milesapart, both will have to test the power of their faith and the strength oftheir spirits. They are being forced to a moment of sacrifice. one thatcould cost them everything"-- Provided by publisher.
  ISBN 978-1-4016-8895-0 (hardcover)
  I. Title.
  PS3561.L334H67 2015
  813'.54--dc23

                        2014037034

Printed in the United States of America

15 16 17 18 19 RRD 6 5 4 3 2 1

LEVEL ONE:
THE GAME BEGINS AGAIN

1. GIRL FIGHT

MOLLY WAS JUST finishing up her jog when the killers came for her.

It was finals week. Five days until the Christmas break began. A quiet had fallen over the university. Students were at their tests during the day or grinding away at the books in their dorms and in the library at night. The undaunted party crews were now confined to Greek Row and a few venues off campus where no one would complain about their loud music. A lot of kids had already headed home. By five or so every evening, when the last dusk light had faded and the winter night came down, there was no one walking on the lamplit pathways and the majestic stone buildings were dark.

That was when Molly liked to hit the gym. The other athletes had cleared out by that time and the after-dinner amateurs hadn't shown up yet, so she usually had the place to herself. She used the locker room to change into her black workout outfit. Pulled on a black elastic band to keep her hair out of her eyes and clipped it in place with a couple of bobby pins. Took her phone, headset, and key card and headed into the workout room.

It was a long room with ellipticals and treadmills lining one wall and weight machines and free weights against the other.

Molly was a volleyballer, the setter on the school team. Her workout was tough. She ran through a brutal hour-long weight routine to keep her core and upper body strong. Coach Nasty—an iPhone workout app—shouted encouragement in her earbuds as she sweated through the reps. When she was done, she paused only long enough to switch over to her JogHard app. Then she pushed out through the gym's metal side door and took off running into the chilly darkness.

She did five miles, out to the edge of the campus, up Library Hill, through the residential streets of NorthSide, then along College Avenue until she cut into the campus and followed the winding paths back to the gym. All the while she was running, her jogging mix was slamming jock-beat music into her ears, interrupted only by the occasional location, speed, and distance stats droned at her by JogHard: "You're at College Avenue and Fourth Street. You have run 3.5 miles east at a pace of 5.2 miles per hour!" Very little of this noise broke through into her consciousness, though. Mostly, as her sneakers slapped the pavement, as her breath came out of her in short bursts of wintry steam . . . mostly, she was thinking about Rick Dial.

He'd been gone two months now. She didn't know where. His whole family had left town. He e-mailed her now and then, but he never told her much, never told her where he was or what he was doing. It was all hush-hush, some secret government thing his dad had gotten him involved in. Rick's father and hers were close friends, both professors here in the Physics Department her father ran—but even Molly's dad didn't know what Professor Dial was doing or where he'd gone. It seemed no one did.

Slowly, Molly was beginning to accept what she already knew in her heart of hearts: Rick wasn't coming back.

What did that mean to her? Was she in love with Rick? If she had a dollar for every time she had asked herself that question during one of these evening jogs, she'd have a whole lot of dollars by now. She probably could've bought a Porsche outright with singles alone. Rick and she had been friends since they were kids. They were just starting to become more than friends when Rick's car was broadsided by a panel truck. His legs were smashed up. His career as a football quarterback was over. His college scholarship was gone. He locked himself away in his room to play video games for hours on end—his way to avoid accepting the bitter change that had come into his life.

And he wouldn't talk to Molly anymore. He wouldn't answer her calls or return her e-mails. So she never really got to find out how far their romance was going to go. It was as if she had started falling for him—and then been frozen in midfall. And *then*, before she could break through his depression and get him to talk to her, it was all over. He was gone.

She cried when he came to her house to say good-bye. She cried off and on for a few days after that. She still cried sometimes in bed at night when she thought about him. But was she brokenhearted or just disappointed? Had something irreplaceable been lost forever, or was it just one of those things you forgot about over time? Was she in love with him? Congratulations, Mol: another dollar.

So that's what she was thinking about when the killers came. She never saw them until it was too late. With some Kelly Clarkson

5

survival anthem drilling into her brain through her earbuds and the computer voice of JogHard offering up her final stats, with her body exhausted from her workout and her mind returning obsessively to the same old memory—that sweet, sweet moment when Rick had kissed her and everything had changed—(*I never expected this, Molly!*)—she really didn't have a chance.

She was just reaching the gym again. Slowing down to a walk as she came up on the PE Building's side door—the one that led straight into the workout room. She had her key card out of her tracksuit's pants pocket. She swiped it through the slot with one hand while she pulled her earbuds off with the other. She shouldered the door open—and the first thug barreled into her, shoving her through.

Molly was a big girl. Her face was elegant, even delicate—with light brown hair framing gentle brown eyes and a small nose dotted with faint freckles—but she was almost six feet tall and broad-shouldered, and her legs, belly, and arms were hard with muscle. As the surprise blow sent her stumbling into the workout room, she turned on her attacker, ready to fight. Then she got a look at him. The sight made her sick with fear. She could tell at a glance he wasn't just some street thug. Dressed head to foot in black—black jeans, black T-shirt, black windbreaker—he was rangy and graceful. His head was thin, pointed top and bottom like a diamond. His smile was tight and confident. And there was death in his eyes.

She knew at a glance she couldn't fight him. She had to run. But even as the thought came to her, the other thugs grabbed her.

There were two of them, waiting in the gym. They came up

behind her and locked her arms in theirs. At the same time, the first thug, the smiling Death's Head, drew a syringe from inside his windbreaker and stepped toward her.

In high school Molly had taken classes on self-defense for women. They'd been taught by a gruff female ex-Marine named Stella. Stella told the class: the first rule of girl-on-guy fighting is that the girl's going to lose in a straight-up brawl. Those scenes in the movies where the lead actress punches some guy in the jaw and he goes somersaulting backward across the room—doesn't happen this side of reality. Hit a guy like that offscreen, and you'll break your hand and then he'll kill you. Best bet: hit the guy once, somewhere where it counts—in the throat, in the eye, in the groin—then run like your butt's on fire, screaming as loud as you can.

Good plan—except the two thugs who had hold of her arms were stronger than strong, their grips like steel bands that locked her helplessly in place. And here came Smiley McDeath with that syringe. Another second and he was going to stick that thing into her neck and knock her out. And what then? Cart her off into slavery like one of those girls she sometimes saw on the news? Or worse: use her and kill her so that her dad had to identify her body at the morgue?

Well, it might go down like that, she thought. But win or lose, it wasn't going to happen without a fight.

Fear and determination gave her strength. She lifted her right leg high and drove the edge of her sneaker down hard into the ankle of the man beside her. He cried out and staggered, loosening his hold on her arm. She used the moment to drive her elbow into him, knocking him back. Then, with her right arm free, she let out a high yell and drove her palm into the other thug's nose.

The blow struck home hard. Thug Two's face was covered with a splat of blood as his nose broke, flattened under her palm. He fell back, and Molly spun away. She staggered across the gym, trying to escape the man with the syringe. If she could make it into the locker room, she thought, she might be able to break out of here . . .

But there was no way. The three men had already recovered and were coming after her. The first thug—the one she'd kicked—wasn't hurt at all. He was moving toward her in a low, fighting crouch, ready for anything. Thug Two—the guy whose former nose was now just a fond nose memory—was swiping the blood off his face with the back of his hand and stalking her with eyes that had gone white with rage.

As for Smiley McDeath, he had paused to put the protective cap back on the syringe needle. In fact, he was doing this with such deliberate calm and confidence that it sent a chill through Molly's heart. A moment later, he, too, was closing in on her, cutting off the path to the locker rooms, backing her up against the wall.

Molly had seen scenes like this on television shows, but nothing like this had ever happened to her in real life. She was shocked by the fear she felt. So much fear. It seemed to sap the energy right out of her muscles, seemed to drain the will out of her heart. Still short of breath from her run, she almost wanted to surrender right then and there, just to get it over with, just to end the terrible suspense.

Almost.

But she couldn't help noticing that the wall the thugs were backing her up against was the wall with the free weight shelves. And hey, if they were going to give her something to fight with, well, then she was going to fight until the fight was over.

She turned fast, grabbed a dumbbell—five pounds—and flung it at the Nose Guy with a whipping twist of her wrist. She was so quick, Nosey never saw it coming. The dumbbell hit the dumbbell smack in the center of his face, right in his ouchie, poor thing. His childish squeal of agony would have made Molly laugh in triumph if she hadn't been busy fighting for her life. But even as Nose Man reeled backward, gripping his face with both hands, the other two kept coming at her.

Molly grabbed a second dumbbell off the wall—another five-pounder. She didn't throw it this time. They were too close. She swung it back and forth in the air, so that the two thugs had to duck out of reach to keep from getting brained. That gave her a second to think.

She thought: *Scream!*

She kept swinging the dumbbell at one thug then another as she let out the sort of shriek she hadn't shrieked since her fifth birthday party. A silent prayer flew from her heart to heaven: *Let there be some football guys in the locker room. And Lord, if you could make them defensive linemen weighing about 280 pounds apiece, so help me, I will give, like, every penny I have to charity.*

The thugs ducked her wild swings and cursed. Her screaming was getting to them.

"Shut her up!" shouted Smiley McDeath, no longer smiling.

"I can't reach her!" the other thug shouted back.

For that one moment, Molly began to hope she was going to get out of this.

Then the side door opened and the Troll came in.

That's what he looked like: a troll. Not one of those cute plastic trolls with the stand-up purple hair either. But an evil fairy-tale troll, the kind of green-skinned, pimply midget muscleman who hits unsuspecting travelers over the heads with his club. And all right, he didn't have green skin, not quite. And he was dressed rather stylishly in gray slacks and a black turtleneck and a corduroy jacket. But he was about four feet tall with bulging arms and legs. He had a huge head with thick red hair. He had tannish cheeks with sickly pink patches. He had big round eyes full of pain and rage. Even his friends would have said he looked like a troll. If he'd had any friends. Which he didn't.

The other thugs all stopped in their tracks as he entered. Even Nosey stopped sobbing and dropped his hands from his bloody face.

Molly paused, holding the dumbbell over her shoulder, ready to strike. She went on screaming as loud as she could. Someone had to hear her somewhere.

The Troll crossed the workout room quickly with a rolling, crippled gait. His hate-filled eyes took in the scene: the Noseless Wonder, bleeding and mewling; Thug One panting with his useless efforts; Smiley McDeath all out of smiles and looking right well ashamed—and, of course, Molly, brandishing the dumbbell at them all and screaming like a banshee.

The Troll gave them all one look. Then, in a voice like a landslide of gravel, he said, "What's taking so long?"

Whereupon he reached quickly inside his corduroy jacket, drew out a gun, and shot Molly in the chest.

It was a stun gun: it hit Molly with an electric charge that turned her arms and legs to water. The next thing she knew, she was lying on her back, her mouth open in a soundless cry of agony. The smiling man with death in his eyes was leaning over her, his syringe lifted again.

After that, there was only blackness.

2. MANHUNT

"FIND HIM!" MISS Ferris said. "Now!"

She never raised her voice. She never changed her tone. The expression on her face didn't even flicker. It was as flat and unemotional as ever. She wasn't a big, imposing figure either. She was a small woman, in fact, and young, only in her thirties. She had short black hair that made her hard features seem almost boyish. She wore a dark pantsuit that made her body seem all straight lines and angles. But as unimpressive as she might have seemed to an outside observer, everyone in the room knew she was in command. The moment she gave the order, the security team of enormous and muscular tough guys—Victor One and Bravo Niner and the hilariously named Juliet Seven and all the rest of the letter-and-number crew—scattered, on the hunt.

Her face set—it was always more or less set—Miss Ferris turned away from the retreating hulks and faced the thin microphone that snaked out of the Control Room wall on its gooseneck wire.

"Don't make them hurt you, Rick," she said, her tone still cold and impassive. "Give yourself up while there's still time."

"Fat chance," Rick Dial muttered to himself. And he continued to drag himself along the narrow air vent.

This was his plan—not much of a plan, he had to admit, but

13

the best he could come up with. The compound that housed the MindWar Project was largely underground. And the thing about an underground compound, Rick had realized, is that it needs air. And the thing about air is that you have to bring it from above ground and pipe it through the whole facility. Rick had spent the last six weeks pilfering the compound's specs, mapping out the air circulation system, and stealing the security cards and codes he would need to gain access to the vents.

But of course the place was so well guarded, so locked down, so wired up with security features, that the alarm had gone off mere minutes after he'd entered the ventilation system. Miss Robot Face Ferris was probably tracking him on sensors even as she broadcast to him through the compound's loudspeakers.

"Really, Rick," he heard her deadpan voice droning to him now. "You're being childish. You know you can't pull this off."

Why didn't she ever change her tone of voice? She sounded like a GPS giving directions. *Turn left in five miles—and give yourself up.*

Something about the emotionless woman really got under Rick's skin. He wanted to shout at her: "Where's Mariel? Who's Mariel? How can I save her?" He had to bite down hard to keep his mouth shut so he wouldn't give his location away.

But even though he said nothing, Miss Ferris knew what he was after. Her monotonous drone continued over the speakers: "This isn't helping anything, Rick. We're doing everything we can to help your friends. I know it's frustrating, but you can't just act on your own like this."

"Watch me," Rick muttered. He ignored the throbbing ache in his legs and continued to drag himself down the metal shaft.

Miss Ferris didn't understand, he thought. She didn't know how he felt. How could she? With her stony face and metallic blue eyes, empty of all emotion. She didn't understand that he couldn't just wait around hoping she and Commander Mars might one day decide to send him back into the Realm. He had to get back there—soon, now. He had to find Mariel, to rescue Mariel. She had saved his life. He owed her. And maybe more than that. He wasn't sure yet, but he thought it was possible he had fallen in love with her. Even though he had no idea who she was. Even though he wasn't even sure she was real.

It had happened like this. Two months ago, Commander Mars, the leader of the MindWar Project, had sent Rick into the Realm. The Realm was a bizarre country in cyberspace, a projection of the imagination of a mysterious terrorist named Kurodar. Kurodar had created the Realm by wiring his brain into a number of supercomputers. Through the Realm, he was hoping to infiltrate America's defense systems, its electricity grids, its business exchanges—infiltrate them through pure thought, unstoppable, and so destroy them and bring the country to its knees.

Until Mars and Miss Ferris had tapped him for this mission, Rick had been a broken man: his football career over, his legs crushed, his spirit in ruins. For months, he had locked himself in his room to play video games endlessly. And weirdly, it was that—his gaming skills, linked with his quick quarterback reactions and leadership ability—that had turned him into the perfect MindWarrior. Mars and his techs had projected Rick in avatar form into the online world of Kurodar's sick imagination. There, Rick had been able to stop the cyberterrorist from slaughtering thousands.

15

But it wasn't the success of the mission that had revived Rick's soul, that had inspired him to start working his legs back into shape, that had reignited his natural drive and ambition, and his pure macho fighting ferocity. No. It was Mariel.

How to describe her? She was a silver nymph who traveled through the MindWar Realm's metallic water; a mysterious Lady of the Lake who had armed and armored him for battle, who had taught him to marshal the power of his spirit so that he could sometimes change the very nature of reality in Kurodar's online world. She was brave and wise and, yes, majestically beautiful.

And she was trapped in the Realm. And she was dying.

Bit by bit, hour by hour, while Rick remained here in this stupid compound, helpless, Mariel's energy was slowly bleeding out of her. Soon—maybe even now—she—and her friend Favian—would sink into the Realm's nightmare version of death, a living decay from which their souls could not be released until the Realm itself was destroyed.

Mariel was dying—and Commander Mars would not let Rick go back into the Realm to save her. Mars and Miss Ferris wouldn't even tell him how she had gotten into that place or who or what she was. Was she a human being like himself, who had been sent into the Realm to battle Kurodar as he had? Was she someone he might one day meet in RL—in Real Life? Or was she just some strange manifestation of the Realm itself? Or . . . what?

Rick didn't know. But he thought the answers had to be in the compound's files somewhere. And he had decided to find them.

Over the last few months, Rick had been getting strong again, working his body back into gridiron shape. His legs still hurt like pins were being stuck into them, but his arms were growing powerful. They pulled him along the narrow air shaft quickly. When he craned his neck, he could see the vent up ahead. He had studied the compound specs a long time. He knew that was the exit he wanted.

"Listen to me, Rick," Miss Ferris said to him now over the loudspeakers. "I haven't told you this before, but we've been making plans to send you back in. We're almost ready."

"Yeah, right," Rick muttered to himself.

And as if she heard him, Miss Ferris droned back, "Think about it, Rick. I've kept a lot of secrets from you. I've had to. That's my job. But I've never lied to you—and I'm not lying now."

Sweat was pouring into Rick's eyes as he pulled himself painfully the last few yards to the vent. It was true, he thought, Miss Ferris hadn't lied. But she hadn't helped him much either. And she didn't know what it was like for a guy like him to just sit around helplessly while Mariel drifted into the grip of an agonizing living death. Rick was an action guy. A fighter. Even a hothead sometimes. He couldn't just do nothing. He couldn't turn himself to heartless stone like Miss Ferris.

The vent. He reached it. Struggling to move in the narrow space, he wrestled his Swiss army knife out of his jeans pocket. This wasn't going to be easy. There were only two bolts holding the vent in place, but the heads were on the outside. He had no way to reach them. He was going to have to use the knife's wrench to loosen their shafts.

He knew he had only minutes, if that, before the security team caught up with him. He drew on his quarterback mind, that laser-like focus that allowed him to throw a football accurately while huge linemen thundered toward him for the sack. His hand never shook, his eyes never wavered. He loosened the bolts. He shoved out the vent. As it clattered to the floor, he slid through after it, headfirst.

He clattered to the floor himself—and, oh boy, the pain that shot up through his aching legs gave him a Venti-sized jolt of wake-up. He cried out but immediately rolled over and stood up on the Persian rug, ignoring his agony. A telescoping walking stick hung from his belt and slapped against his hip, but he didn't use it. He could walk pretty well now for short distances.

A Persian rug? he thought suddenly. What was up with that?

He looked around him. He was in a small room, very small, and very different from the other cold, bare, mechanical rooms throughout the compound. This was more like a gentleman's study in a suburban home. The rug. A studded leather chair behind a mahogany desk with a sleek laptop on it. Shelves of leather-bound books on every wall. A flat-screen monitor with a scene of the outdoors: it stood in for a window down here below the earth.

This, Rick knew, was Mars's office. Rick had chosen to come here because it was at the compound's center, far away from the security stations around the perimeter. He figured it would take the guards a while to reach him here. Also, he figured the commander's computer would have the greatest access to the project's secret files. That's what he was after: the file on Mariel.

His breath short with anticipation, Rick limped to the desk and dropped into the leather chair, grateful to get off his aching legs. Stealing Mars's password had been no small feat. Unlike his dad, Rick was no computer genius. He'd simply had to maneuver himself into position to read the commander's flying fingers as he entered the word into his machine. It had helped that Mars was distracted at the time by the fact that Rick was yelling at him, demanding to be sent back into the Realm.

Now Rick tapped the computer's keys and waited for the machine to come to life so he could enter the password himself.

I'm coming for you, Mariel, he thought with ferocious intensity.

But neither ferocity nor intensity helped him here. Nothing happened. The computer stayed dark. Rick tapped the password into the keyboard again. *Come on, come on.* He checked the power cord. Checked to make sure the thing was on.

Nothing. Dark.

Rick's hopes began to curdle in his stomach.

"Wrong fingers," said a voice from the doorway.

Rick jumped to his feet, his eyes rising quickly. There, framed in the suddenly open door, was Victor One, his father's personal bodyguard.

Victor One was a little older than Rick, twenty-six. He was a little taller and more muscular, too, with short-cropped brown hair, a weather-beaten face, and witty blue eyes. He wore jeans and a U.S. Army sweatshirt. He'd been some kind of special forces hero in Afghanistan, and while he was an easygoing kind of guy, nowhere near as intense as Rick, he was plenty tough. Rick knew he was ready for action.

Rick pulled his walking stick from its holster and pressed the button so that the stick shot out full length. He didn't have much hope of beating Victor One in a straight-on duke-out, but hey, a nice stick could be a dangerous weapon in the hands of a man who had survived sword fights with two-legged alligators in the Realm.

"Just stay away from me, V-One," Rick said to him. "I've gotta do this."

"Fact is, you *can't* do this," the bodyguard said calmly, leaning casually against the doorjamb. "There's no way. This computer only wakes up when it feels Mars's fingerprint pressed to the screen. What will they think of next, right?"

Rick tried not to show it, but he was silently cursing himself for being an idiot. No computer genius—that was an understatement. He'd never even thought of a fingerprint-sensitive computer lock. Mars probably let him steal his password just to make him feel stupid. It had worked, too. He felt stupid-plus.

"Bring him back here, Victor One," came Miss Ferris's monotonous command from the loudspeakers. "Bring him back here right now."

Rick raised his stick threateningly, but Victor One just went on leaning in the doorway.

"Does that robot voice of hers annoy you like it does me?" he asked.

"Oh man, does it ever," said Rick. "It drives me bats."

"I want him back here right this minute," said Miss Ferris—but though her words were growing angrier, her tone remained unchanged.

"See, she thinks I'm going to rush at you," said Victor One with a shrug. "Slug it out or something. You hit me with that stick. I hit you back. And so on. I don't know about you, but that sounds really painful to me."

"It does," said Rick. "I have to agree with you there."

"And here's the thing," Victor One went on. "You really can't get into that computer, so we can stand here all day if you want to and it's not gonna get you anywhere. Better idea? I happen to know Lady Ferris is telling the truth. They *are* about to send you back into the Realm. Do what they say and you can get everything you want without all the hitting stuff. Personally, I always prefer to skip the hitting stuff."

Rick looked at the useless computer. Looked at Victor One in the doorway. He sighed. The man was right. A fight would get him nowhere. There was nothing more he could accomplish here.

"Are you sure they're planning to send me back into the Realm?" he asked Victor One.

Victor One opened his mouth to answer—but it was Miss Ferris's automaton voice that came through the loudspeakers instead.

"It's true," she told him. "We're ready to send you back into the Realm. But there's something you're going to have to do first . . ."

3. TEST-DRIVE

THE CREATURES CHARGED over the hill in droves: an army of fanged demons, sweeping the air with axes, maces, and claws like swords. Some could fly on gray, leathery wings, and these shot heat beams from their eyes that scorched the grass below them. A cacophony of weird, hollow, nerve-jangling shrieks rose like a cloud from the midst of the horde.

Rick had only ninety seconds left before the ticking device in the earth exploded. He had only a minute or so before the horde of demons reached him. He was armed with nothing but a small, dagger-like blade. He had used the blade to pry the front panel off the bomb. Its printed circuits were now displayed in the open, but there was no way for him to tell which line in the maze of metal would disarm the device and which would set it off. He was pressed close to the edge of a cliff. Beyond it was a sheer fall of a thousand feet onto jagged rocks. The bomb was planted deep in the ground. There was no way to budge it. If it exploded, it would scorch the plain and Rick with it.

"We're going to have to tell him about Molly," said Rick's father quietly. Lawrence Dial—code-named the Traveler—was a small, balding bespectacled man. He looked nothing like his son, but exactly like the physics professor he was.

"No. It will only distract him," said Commander Jonathan Mars.

The two men were sitting together in a small amphitheater in the underground compound, a high-ceilinged room with arcing rows of movie-style seats descending to a large screening area above a platform. Rick—Rick's body—lay on the platform inside a glass box the size of a coffin. His avatar—the living embodiment of his imagination—was projected in 3-D holographic images in the screening area. There he was, life-like, fiddling with the bomb while under attack by the demon army. He now had only forty-five seconds left until the demons overran him. He had about a minute before the bomb went off.

"This mission is going to take every ounce of focus he has," Mars went on brusquely. "We hoped when Rick blew up Kurodar's fortress, the Axis Assembly would withdraw their support of MindWar, but somehow Kurodar has convinced them to double down. He's strengthened the Realm and refined its interface with RL. I need a hundred and ten percent of Rick's attention. That's why I won't even send him in—or anyone in—until they can pass this test."

Mars continued to watch as the holographic drama unfolded. He was a man in his fifties. Silver-haired, craggy-faced. He had bushy white eyebrows that hung like cliffs over humorless, deep-set eyes. Whereas Rick's dad was dressed casually in slacks and a button-down shirt, Mars wore a black suit with a red tie. He made a fitting companion for his second in command, the prim Miss Ferris, who was sitting next to him, stone-faced.

"No one's passed the test yet," said Miss Ferris flatly. "We've brought in two professional gamers, three Green Berets, and several Navy SEALs. Each one has been either torn to shreds by the demons or blown up by the bomb."

"Except one of the gamers—he committed suicide by jumping off the cliff," Mars added. "But the point is: If they'd really been in the Realm, they'd have been dead. Worse than dead. What dies in there is trapped forever."

The Traveler unconsciously lifted his hand to touch the small metal cross he wore beneath his shirt. "Not forever," he began to murmur—but Mars silenced him with a lifted hand, leaning forward to watch the 3-D images more closely.

Rick was at the crisis point.

The demon hordes were so close now, they filled Rick's vision when he cast a frightened glance their way. It was hard to think with the sight of so many hideous red, twisted, fanged faces swarming at him. It looked like there were about a million of them. And those flying ones—the way their eye-rays burned the earth with white-hot fire; very bad news. The minute one of those babies touched him, he'd be smoke and ash.

This wasn't like the Realm. His life wasn't really in danger, not in RL. But Mariel's life very much was. If he flunked this test, they would not send him back into the MindWar. And if they sent someone else, there was no guarantee he would care enough to try to bring Mariel back with him.

Rick had to solve this puzzle. He had to figure out a way.

He looked at the bomb wedged into the earth. Its timer ticked steadily down. Forty-two seconds left. The demons swarmed toward him, filling the air with their shrieks. Rick felt sweat streaming out from under his hairline, streaking his cheeks like tears. For the life of him—for the life of Mariel—he could not figure out how to defuse this thing. Cut a circuit at random and he'd almost surely blow himself to kingdom come.

He looked up again at the demon army, a wave of screaming evil. He couldn't very well fight them off either.

Some problems have no solution, he thought miserably. *Some stories have no happy ending.*

He had only recently started praying again, and he didn't find it easy. Deep in his heart, he was still angry at God for all that had been taken away from him: his football career, his scholarship, the strength of his legs. All the same, he breathed a quick prayer now: *Please help me out here! I don't know what to do. For Mariel.*

God didn't answer—at least, Rick didn't think he answered. But his own voice now spoke in his mind with a different tone.

He thought: *If the problem has so solution, solve a different problem. If the story has no happy ending, tell a different story.*

He gripped the small blade in his damp palm. He turned to face the oncoming demons. He felt his throat closing with fear. He had an idea—but man oh man, it was a dangerous idea.

"Well, he's brave at least," Commander Mars muttered. "You have to give him that. The SEALs turned to fight, too."

"Yes," droned Miss Ferris. "Just before the demons killed them."

"Watch," said Rick's dad. "My boy knows how to fight—but he knows how to think, too."

In fact, though, the professor sounded a lot more confident than he felt.

Now, as Rick looked on, the leader of the demons gave a wild, high cry and broke from the pack. Racing forward, he swung a flaming mace above his head, a whiplash of fire, snapping out into the air in front of him. The flames were whirling in the direction of Rick's face.

Rick watched the Demon King come. He felt an old familiar rush of excitement go through him, the adrenaline of the football field. It washed away all fear, washed away anything but his ferocious will to win. There was no leg pain here. He could move as quickly as he used to when he was at his best. He bared his teeth with determination. His eyes blazed as they focused on the motion of the onrushing Demon King.

The flaming mace whipped straight at his head. Closer. Closer. Then, just as it was about to snap out and strike him dead, Rick ducked quickly. He dropped to the ground. He rolled forward, under the spinning lash of fire. Then he leapt to his feet right in front of the Demon King and rammed his blade into the creature's belly.

The Demon King's death shriek was deafening. Hot green blood gushed out of him and spilled over Rick's forearm, burning like acid. Rick kept the dagger buried deep and used his other hand to grab the demon by the throat.

At the same moment, a flying demon swooped down at him, shooting red beams from his eyes. Rick had seen him coming all along. He was counting on it, hoping for it.

Holding the knife in the Demon King's belly with one hand, gripping the Demon King's throat with the other, he used his powerful arms to lift the evil being off the ground.

The flying demon dive-bombed, its face a twisted red mask of terror. Its eyes flashed—then the heat beams shot out of them.

Rick hoisted the Demon King's body in the air and held it up above his head like a shield. The heat rays hit the Demon King—and good thing for King-Boy he was already dead, because he wouldn't have liked it much when his body burst into flames.

At that, Rick bent his knees, gave a deep growling shout, and hurled the flaming demon corpse at the winged attacker.

The winged demon screeched and twisted to the side to avoid the fireball. His wings corkscrewed and lost their lift. He plummeted to the earth, smacking down so hard Rick felt the ground tremble beneath his feet.

Or maybe that was the thunder of the onrushing demon army, who could say? They were mere yards away, seconds from sweeping over him, tearing him to pieces. The bomb in the earth was counting down its final seconds.

Rick looked to the winged demon.

Dazed for a moment, the creature was shaking the dust off itself like a dog shaking off water. Then it crouched, ready to spring into the air again. It lifted its red-hot eyes to the sky.

It lifted off—and Rick grabbed it, wrapping his free hand around its leathery ankle as its huge wings flapped above him. Letting his sword hand dangle by his side, Rick let the flying demon pull him off the ground. He was surprised by the strength and speed of the thing. His weight didn't seem to slow it down at all. It carried him high and then higher into the air. With a hoarse, puzzled scream, it twisted its neck and saw him. It clearly wanted to blast the unwanted burden off its leg with its fire rays. But it couldn't get the angle, couldn't take the shot without setting itself aflame. It had no choice but to carry Rick even higher, hoping to shake him off and drop him onto the sharp rocks below.

Rick flew up and looked down. He saw the earth—and the horde of demons covering the earth—become smaller and smaller below him. As the flying demon carried him impossibly high into the sky, Rick watched the demons wash like a red tide over the surface of the cliff. Even the other flying demons were far beneath him now.

Rick was counting down in his mind. *Three—two—one* . . . He reached zero and flashed a wicked grin.

Bye-bye, Demon Guys, he thought.

And just then—as if he'd given the command—the bomb went off below him. The sea of red creatures was engulfed in an even greater flood of fire. The flames spread swiftly over the entire plain. They boiled up from the earth to challenge the very vault of heaven. The sight was so spectacular that Rick crowed in triumph—even though he could feel the heat of the fire through his sneaker soles, even though he was dangling above certain death, his sweaty hand desperately gripping the flying demon's leg.

"That's it," said Mars. "Pull him out. He solved the puzzle. We're sending him into the Realm ASAP."

Rick's dad—the Traveler—turned to Mars quickly, blinking behind his spectacles in surprise.

"But he hasn't gotten out of the situation yet," he said, gesturing to where his son's 3-D image dangled precariously above the sea of fire. "He hasn't proven he can survive!"

Mars had already risen to his feet, was already following Miss Ferris along the row of seats toward the exit aisle.

"We don't need him to survive," the commander barked to the Traveler over his shoulder. "We just need him to win. He passed the test. He's ready."

4. PRISONER OF WAR

MOLLY OPENED HER eyes on darkness. Panic shot through her. She couldn't move. She couldn't breathe. Images flashed in her muddy brain. Memories. The thugs in the workout room. The Troll. His gun. For a second, she actually wondered if she might be dead—dead and buried. Or even worse: buried but not dead, left to smother in a narrow coffin six feet beneath the earth. In terror and panic, she began to cry—which made it even harder to breathe. She was strangling on her own tears . . .

She had to steady herself. Had to get control. By pure force of will, she made herself draw a long draught of air in through her nose. She was gagged—some kind of tape over her mouth—that's why she couldn't get enough air. But her nose was clear. She could breathe if she tried. If she quit crying and really tried.

She did. She fought down her tears. She breathed. She stared into the darkness. Was she blindfolded? No. There was a faint— very faint—line of gray light just visible in front of her. She had a sense of motion, too. She could hear motion. Cars. Cars on a highway.

Understanding washed over her like nausea. She was locked in the trunk of a car—that's what it was. Her hands were bound behind her. She was gagged. The Troll had stunned her with some

31

kind of electric jolt, then the Smiling Death Guy had injected her. She could still feel the aching pain in her neck. Her arms and back ached, too. She sensed that she had been unconscious for hours.

Tears welled up in her eyes again, but she forced them back down. She had to keep breathing. Keep steady. At least she was alive. Start with that. And pray.

Molly's faith was a secret thing. Her father was an adamant atheist. He thought religion was unscientific. Molly could remember her dad and Rick's dad having friendly arguments about the subject long into the night. Rick's dad was just the opposite of hers. A devout Christian, he thought that science made no sense without God. "The odds that an accidental universe would accidentally create a creature like us who could understand it," he argued, "well, it's like a random wind blowing through a junkyard and accidentally assembling a jet plane."

Molly had never told her father that she agreed with Rick's dad more than him. Her father had strong feelings about it, and she thought it might upset him. But it wasn't Dr. Dial's arguments that convinced her. The fact was: Ever since she was a little girl, she had known God was there. She had felt him with her. She had talked to him. She had felt him guiding her, and comforting her. Whenever her father explained his philosophy to her, she had always nodded respectfully. But in simple truth? It had never really occurred to her not to believe.

Now she said a prayer in her mind. Asked God for help. Guidance. Then she went quiet inside, just breathing, just trying to feel God there, feel that he loved her, was with her, hated to see this happening to her. The prayer didn't get her out of the jam (as her father would've been quick to point out), but it calmed her down and gave her strength. And that's what she needed. Strength. Otherwise the tears and panic would take her over.

Okay, better; she was calmer. She could think now. The panic was still urging her to thrash and fight: *Have to get out, have to get out!* But she could see that wouldn't help any. When she tried to struggle against her bonds, there was no give at all. Her wrists were taped so tightly together she could hardly budge them. All the same, she began to work them back and forth what little she could, hoping she could get enough leverage eventually to slip free. Not much hope of that, though. What else could she do?

Listen, she thought. Listen and look. Try to figure out where she was, where they were taking her. At least that way, if she got the chance to call for help, she'd be able to direct her rescuers.

She breathed steadily through her nose. Lay very still, straining to listen, to hear anything she could. Yes: there were voices. The men in the car. They were talking. Laughing. Harsh masculine laughter. Probably discussing what they would do with her. She couldn't hear the words. Part of her didn't even want to.

The car slowed and then the road got rougher. That meant they had left the highway and were traveling over side roads, Molly figured.

The men's laughter grew louder. Now one of them spoke so sharply, she actually understood him:

"Hey! Listen to this!"

Molly listened as hard as she could. There was a new noise. Music! And wait! Not just any music. That was Kellie Pickler singing "Don't You Know You're Beautiful?" Then more male laughter.

Molly's pulse sped up as she understood. No bunch of guys were getting down to Kellie Pickler. That wasn't their music. It was hers. It was her running mix! They were fiddling with her phone, with her JogHard app!

Which meant they had made a terrible mistake—terrible for them, that is. Good for her.

They had taken her phone and left it on. The phone had a GPS in it. It could be tracked by law enforcement. As soon as people realized she was missing, as soon as her friends or her mom and dad called the police, the first thing the police would do would be to try to locate her phone. If her kidnappers would just keep it on until they reached their destination . . .

But just as she thought that, the music was interrupted by the voice of JogHard.

"You are at Highway 313 and Cooper Road!" JogHard announced. "You have run 157.4 miles west at a pace of 74.8 miles per hour!"

The electronic voice was immediately followed by an angry male growl. Molly couldn't make out the words, but she didn't have to. JogHard had reminded these clownish thugs that keeping her phone was a dumb idea. Another moment and the music stopped altogether. They had probably shut the phone down or thrown it out the window. There was no more laughter after that.

Too late, Molly thought. JogHard stored her workout info in the cloud so she could keep records of her exercise. If the police just knew to look for the app, they would find her.

Highway 313 and Cooper Road. 157.4 miles to the west, she repeated in her mind. *Remember that.*

They kept on driving. Not long—half an hour at most. Molly tried to keep track of the turns. Left, right, right again . . . It was difficult. She was still working her hands in her bonds. Not getting very far with that. Getting tired. Nauseous from the drug and the motion. Bathed in sweat. She needed to go to the bathroom, too. Still she tried to stay focused. Another turn. Left, right . . .

Now the car began to slow.

What happened next happened very fast. The car stopped with a jolt. Molly heard the car doors squeaking open, thunking shut. Men's voices, muttering. Then the trunk popped—and the men were peering in at her where she lay bound and helpless.

It was night, dark. Their faces were bathed in the hellish red of the taillights. She saw the man she'd busted in the nose. His lopsided honker and swollen eyes made him look grotesque, like a demon.

Without a word, two of the men grabbed her by the arms and hauled her out into the night. Clean cold winter air washed over her: a relief after the suffocating trunk. Her legs, cramped in the tight space for so long, had fallen asleep. When the men set her on her feet, the pins and needles were paralyzing. She nearly folded; nearly collapsed.

They didn't give her a chance to fall, though. They frog-marched her across a short space of open ground. When she stumbled, they dragged her so that the toes of her running shoes scraped over the dirt. Molly looked around wildly, trying to see where she was, to get any clue that might help her locate herself. Confused, she took in everything. Night sky. Stars. Naked branches. Towering pines. There was a broad building up ahead, four stories tall. She couldn't figure out what it was. Couldn't make sense of its rambling shape.

Then they were inside. Deeper darkness. A flashlight beam shot chaotically over chipped, dirty white walls. The men held her arms tight, their fingers digging painfully into her flesh. They growled at her, "Let's go. Move it." She stumbled along in their grasp.

It was all happening so quickly she couldn't think. Where were they taking her? What were they going to do to her when they got there? There were no pleasant answers. Tears of fear flowed from her eyes, but she stayed silent, praying in her mind: *Comfort my mother and father and brother. Give them strength. Give me strength. Help me.* Nothing out loud. She wasn't going to beg these lowlifes for mercy. She wasn't going to give them the satisfaction.

She tried to keep her feet under her as they hauled her upstairs. She cried out behind her gag as she stubbed her toe on a step, then banged her ankle. Up one flight. Around a corner. Down a dark hallway, the flashlight picking out broken light fixtures, more scarred walls.

A door up ahead. The thug with the flashlight opened it. The other two—the two who had her by the arms—hurled her through.

Molly staggered forward several steps. With her arms bound behind her, she couldn't keep her balance. She stumbled and went down, twisting as she fell so that she landed on her shoulder. It was a hard fall. It jolted her. She felt the ache in her bones.

It was even darker in here than out in the hall. The flashlight beam careened this way and that, picking out one thug's face then another's. She remembered them from the workout room. There was the Nose Guy and there was Thug One and there was Smiley McDeath and—Molly took a sharp breath—he was holding an ugly-looking combat knife, suitable for murder. The blade glinted in the flashlight's beam.

Is this it? Are they going to kill me? Comfort my family . . .

Holding the knife, the smiling man crouched over her where she lay on the floor. Her mind went blank with fear. She stared through the dark at the thug's thin, skeletal face. Caught in the outglow of the flashlight, it looked like a Halloween mask.

He leaned in close to her. She expected to feel the blade of the knife drive into her body. The agony. The life pouring out of her. But the next moment, with a sharp, violent movement, Smiley McDeath cut the tape that bound her wrists. Her hands were free. Smiley grabbed the tape on her mouth and yanked. Burning pain shot over her face. Her lip started bleeding. But it felt good to take a full breath. She gasped greedily at the air.

The smiling man leaned close to her, filling her vision with his deadly stare. "You're useful to us alive for now," he said. He had a hoarse, strangely high-pitched voice. "But we'll kill you if we have to. Make a noise and we'll kill you. Try to escape and we'll kill you. Annoy us and we'll kill you. Just keep quiet—keep still—and who knows? You might just stay alive. You get me?"

Before Molly could even nod in answer, the narrow face was gone. The flashlight turned away from her. She lay where she was on the floor and watched as the shadows of the three men walked to the door.

The tears were still flowing down Molly's cheeks and when she called out, her voice was thick with crying. "Why are you doing this to me?" she said.

They didn't answer. They didn't even turn back. They went out. The door shut behind them.

Molly lay on the floor in the dark alone.

Highway 313 and Cooper Road. 157.4 miles west, she thought, crying, gasping for breath.

157 miles from home.

5. MISSION CRITICAL

A HELPLESS TERROR flooded Rick's heart. He knew that something awful was about to happen to him. He felt it first as a tingle in his fingers. He looked down and his worst fears were confirmed: his hand was beginning to dissolve!

First his fingertips went, then the stumps of his fingers, then his knuckles, then his palm. It was awful! His hand was pixilating in front of his eyes, the flesh transforming into foggy, colored squares, like a video going wonky when the Wi-Fi isn't fast enough. He tried to call out for help, but his voice wouldn't come and he realized with horror: he was dissolving on the inside, too, his lungs turning into pixels, and his stomach . . .

A silent scream filled his mind . . .

Then there was loud, rapid knocking on a door and he woke from the nightmare, breathless.

He looked around, his pulse hammering. He was in his bedroom, in his bed. He saw the Orange Empire football poster through the morning shadows. The New England Patriots calendar . . .

The knocking was coming from the bedroom door.

"Yeah," he said sleepily.

The door came open and his father poked his head in.

"Almost time for the briefing," he said quietly. "Better get up if you want some breakfast."

When his father had withdrawn, Rick sat up on the bed. He pressed the heels of his palms against his brow. His head was throbbing. The headaches weren't getting any better. And the nightmares—they were definitely getting worse. That last one— wow!—like a horror movie being shown inside his brain. His hand pixilating. His insides dissolving. Not good. Not good at all.

He knew it was because of the MindWar. He had gone into the Realm too much on his first mission and he had stayed in there too long. His consciousness had started to come apart, just as Miss Ferris had warned him it would. She had told him: if you remain in the Realm more than an hour and a half or so, you will lose your mind and turn your RL self into a vegetable. He had nearly done just that, and the aftereffects were still with him.

Over the last weeks, he'd convinced himself he was recovering, getting better. And in a lot of ways, that was true, he was. His broken legs were so much stronger now. His whole body was stronger. But the nightmares continued to haunt his sleep, and the headaches continued to dog his mornings. He hadn't told anyone about them because he was afraid Commander Mars would take him off the project. He couldn't let that happen. He had to get back into the Realm to rescue Mariel and Favian. But the nightmares and headaches weren't going away, and it was beginning to worry him.

He got up and washed up and limped down the hallway to the kitchen.

The MindWar Project had installed the Dial family in a

pleasant little green-and-white wooden house in a quiet corner of the forest compound. The apple and oak and maple trees that surrounded the place made for nice views from the windows: the branches obscured the barbed-wire fencing and guard towers that ringed the compound. Indoors, Rick's mom had made the place as homey as possible. Family photos hung on the walls and the furniture was warm-looking and comfortable. And now there were Christmas decorations, too: fairy lights on the windowsills, a crèche on the lampstand, and a substantial pine tree standing untrimmed in the living room. Rick and his brother, Raider, and their dad had left the compound and gone out into the surrounding forest to cut the tree down themselves. And the five guards armed with automatic rifles who had gone with them on their outing had added just that necessary touch of Christmas spirit!

Mom had taken special care fixing up the kitchen. The yellow tiling on the wall and the fake wood tiling on the floor, the orange curtains on the windows, the breakfast table in a nook beside the stove—it looked almost like their old kitchen back home. In fact, despite the rigors of living in a fenced-in compound surrounded by armed guards all the time, Mom herself was looking brighter and more cheerful than she had in months. And Raider—who'd turned nine years old a few weeks ago— well, he always looked bright and cheerful, but he looked even more cheerful now if that was possible. His round freckled face was flapping as he chewed his cereal, all the while chattering away in his high, excited voice. It seemed like nothing could depress the kid.

It was all because Dad was back. That's what made everything

seem all right again, even here in the middle of the woods, surrounded by barbed wire and guns. There he was at the breakfast
table again, absentmindedly paging through the *Wall Street
Journal*, only half listening to Raider's chatter, letting his coffee
get cold, forgetting even to eat his eggs unless Mom reminded
him. It made their home seem almost normal.

Having everyone back together again, having everyone act so
loving and cheerful, Rick wanted to feel nothing but happiness.
But his emotions . . . they were complicated. It was great that his
dad hadn't really deserted the family for good, but it still rankled
Rick that he had left at all. Worse, he had pretended he had run
off with an old girlfriend, Leila Kent. He had let them believe that
about him for months, leaving Rick bitter and angry that whole
time. Rick knew his father was trying to protect them, trying to do
the work he needed to do to end Kurodar's MindWar against the
U.S. But was it right to sacrifice his family's happiness—even for
a little while—just to go off on some secret mission? It still made
Rick angry when he thought about it, and he thought about it a lot.
He didn't want to be angry with his father anymore, but he was.

Still, for now, he tried to join in with the general good cheer.
Despite the throbbing in his head, he gave them all a hearty "Good
morning, team!" as he scored a mug of coffee from the machine on
the counter. He dealt his brother a friendly head noogie as he sat
down at the table. And for the next fifteen minutes, he dutifully
shoveled cereal into his face, listened to Raider yammer, and even
made a couple of jokes and laughed with the others.

It was only when he and Dad got ready to go that the mood
shifted. Then Mom stood in the foyer watching with a forced

smile as they went to the door. Her eyes, Rick saw, were full of fear, and her hand rested protectively on Raider's shoulder. Raider pressed his lips together in a show of determination and pumped his fist at his big brother by way of encouragement. But even the Happy Face Kid looked pretty fearful himself.

Outside, in the clear, crisp, cold morning, Rick and his father walked across the compound together. Rick was still limping a little on his aching legs, but he was much bigger than his father, his strides much longer, and he managed to keep up. Yet, even though they moved along shoulder to shoulder, they were silent. With all the unspoken feelings between them, they'd had a hard time making conversation with each other these last couple of months. They went past the compound's barracks and its main building, each lost in his own tense thoughts. Their footsteps, crackling on the frosted earth, were the only noise they made.

They came to a nondescript bungalow at the compound's center. It was little more than a shed of wooden boards and glass. An armed guard was posted at the door. He nodded to the elder Dial as they entered. Another armed guard waited inside. He watched them, stone-faced, as they walked into the big elevator that took up maybe half the bungalow's interior.

"It's weird," murmured Rick as the elevator door closed and the box began to sink quickly. They were the first words he'd spoken to his dad since they'd left the house. "At home, everything seems so normal. The Christmas stuff and Raider chattering and Mom making breakfast . . . Then this."

His father nodded. "I have a feeling it's all going to get a lot weirder before it's over, too," he said with a sigh.

Back again in the underground amphitheater, Rick sat beside his father and Commander Mars. Miss Ferris (in yet another dark-colored pantsuit) stood on the platform before the holograph screen and raised a pointer toward the three-dimensional image of a factory building.

"I'm sure you remember the explosion and fire at the fertilizer plant in southern Arkansas last month," she said flatly. "Nine people were killed in the blast."

Rick sat up sharply as the 3-D factory exploded, sending a holographic fireball up toward the ceiling. It looked so real, he almost expected the flames to engulf Miss Ferris herself. Not that that would make her change her tone of voice or anything!

"The explosion was officially ruled an accident caused by a friction spark that ignited some poorly secured chemicals. And that may in fact be what happened," she went on. "But about forty-five minutes prior to the event, a Spartan combat drone disappeared from a nearby facility owned by General Aerodynamics, one of the country's leading drone manufacturers. The Spartan is a miniature radio-controlled flying device, but it's capable of carrying and firing powerful missiles along with other weapons."

The first billowing three-dimensional flames were subsiding into the scorched factory as Rick said, "Wait, wait, wait. Are you saying you think an American drone may have opened fire on an Arkansas fertilizer plant?"

"I'm saying it's possible," said Miss Ferris.

"That doesn't make any sense."

"No. It doesn't. Unless the drone's controls were taken over from an outside location."

Rick felt something like a cold wind go through him. *Outside location.* He knew what that meant. The MindWar Realm: the world created through the interface of computers and Kurodar's imagination. In theory, it could allow him to simply think his way into any computer system in the world and take it over. That included the system that controlled a weaponized drone.

"So you think this was some kind of test," Rick said, thinking it through out loud. "Kurodar wanted to see if he could take control of our warrior drones. If he could, then he could use our own weapons to launch an air attack on the U.S. from inside the country. He could strike anywhere he wanted. He could massacre . . ."

"No one knows how many," said Miss Ferris without any emotion at all. Rick found himself wondering if maybe she was a drone herself.

"But if it was a drone that attacked the warehouse," Rick asked her, "wouldn't there be, like, a computer trail? Pictures? Radar? Satellite images? Don't we have that stuff covered?"

"That's exactly what worries us," said Miss Ferris, gazing up at him with an expressionless face. "When I say the Spartan disappeared from the manufacturer, I mean it disappeared completely. No radar. No satellite images. Nothing. It was just suddenly gone—and forty-five minutes later . . ." She gestured at the burning building again.

As if he not only took control of the drone, but somehow managed to blind security to the attack, Rick thought.

"It shouldn't be possible," said Miss Ferris. "But apparently, it happened. And it may not be the only time."

Rick opened his mouth to echo her, "It may not . . ." But he fell silent as the ramifications occurred to him.

"We think it's possible—even probable—that other drones have gone missing from their storage facilities. A lot of other drones."

Rick let out a snort at the idea. "Well, don't they have inventories?" he drawled sarcastically. "I mean, doesn't the government or the factories or somebody keep count of exactly how many deadly drones we've got? Seeing that they're, you know, deadly. I mean, if Kurodar stole enough untrackable drones with enough firepower, he could destroy an entire city! Shouldn't our security systems be able to prevent that?"

"You would think so," said Miss Ferris without cracking a smile.

Rick blinked—but before he could speak again, Miss Ferris turned back to the holograph screen and the images there changed.

The burning factory faded away and in its place there appeared a weird, abstract, diagrammatic map. It was, Rick knew, a map of the Realm. The MindWar engineers had downloaded it from Rick's brain while he was immersed in Kurodar's online world. Rick recognized parts of it. He remembered the Scarlet Plain, the Blue Wood, the Sky Dome Fortress—or what was left of it after he had blown the place to the cyber version of kingdom come. And, in the distance, he saw the Golden City that was supposed to be the heart of the place, its power center.

But between the areas he had already explored, and the city to which he had never been, there was a great black area with a huge silver ring placed in the center of it.

"Because the MindWar Realm emanates directly from

Kurodar's imagination," Miss Ferris said, "it's impossible to diagram it accurately without an actual presence on-site."

Meaning me, Rick thought, eyeing the silver ring warily.

"But once you've been through an area, you leave traces of your avatar consciousness and we can continue to monitor it for changes. We can't be a hundred percent certain, but we think we've detected a new structural anomaly beyond the area where the Sky Dome Fortress used to stand. We believe this may be the new facility Kurodar has been testing, and it may have something to do with his ability to completely circumvent our defenses. Given the size and shape of it, we think it's nearly complete and might be fully operational in as little as three days."

"Three days! You think . . . whatever that thing is—it'll be able to take control of our warrior drones and use them against us—three days from now?"

Miss Ferris faced him directly, her expression as blank as ever—although Rick imagined he saw something especially grim in her eyes. She had just opened her mouth to answer when an angry shout came from beyond the amphitheater door.

"Forget it! That's just not going to happen!"

Startled, Rick realized that while he had been wrapped up in Miss Ferris's monotone lecture, his father and Commander Mars had quietly slipped out of the theater.

Even more startled, he realized it was his father—his quiet, bookish, religious, absentminded-professor father—who was shouting at the top of his lungs.

"Keep your voice down!" said Commander Mars in a harsh whisper. He gestured brusquely, trying to get the Traveler to move away from the amphitheater doors. Underneath that absentminded-professor routine, the man was as stubborn as a stone mule, Mars thought.

The Traveler—Lawrence Dial—dutifully followed Mars a little ways down the hall. It was true: despite his mousey, professorial looks, he was a man with a good deal of inner fortitude. For instance: as flaming angry as he was, he'd already gotten his temper under control, never an easy thing to do. Now he managed to bring his voice down. He didn't want Rick to hear them arguing. Within hours, his son would be returning to the Realm, and he was going to need all the confidence he could get. He didn't need to know that the two leaders of the MindWar Project—the two men most responsible for keeping him safe during his immersion—pretty well despised each other.

"It's just not going to happen," the Traveler repeated in a voice as low as he could manage. "I held off breaking the news to him to give you time to make a plan. But No Plan? That's not going to cut it. We are not—repeat not—abandoning Molly to those killers."

"I said we would go and get her as soon as the mission is over."

As a devout Christian, there were certain words Lawrence Dial didn't like to use out loud. But let's face it: he was thinking them. This Mars, after all, was the man who had once pointed a pistol at his chest, completely ready to kill him to save his precious mission. Dial could not be surprised by Mars's cold-blooded attitude now, but he sure wasn't happy about it either.

"That's not good enough, Mars," he said. "They could kill

Molly by the time Rick gets back. They might well have killed her already."

"Well, that would be a shame," said Mars coldly. "But it's better that one young woman die than the entire country be destroyed."

The Traveler drew a long breath, trying to keep his temper in check. He knew that Mars disliked him intensely. He knew that Mars wanted to walk away right now. There was only one reason the commander was listening to him at all: the MindWar Project needed the Traveler in order to succeed. It was Lawrence Dial who had developed the system that injected Rick into the Realm. It was he who had developed the energy burst that had been programmed into Rick's avatar so he could deliver it to Mariel and Favian and keep them alive a little while longer. And if anyone was going to create the sort of weapon they needed to win the MindWar once and for all, it would be him, the Traveler, Dial. Mars needed him, and so he would listen for a while. But Dial would have to stay calm if he was going to make his case.

"Listen to me carefully," the Traveler said, lifting a finger and leveling it at Mars's face. "Molly is a fine young woman and the daughter of my best friend . . ."

"Don't make it personal," Mars said.

"It is personal. I'm not going—"

"We don't bargain with terrorists—" Mars interrupted.

"I'm not talking about bargaining," Lawrence Dial interrupted back.

Mars's craggy, frowning, Mount Rushmore of a face turned red with rising fury. He raised a stiff finger and poked the smaller man hard in his narrow chest. "I expect loyalty from you, Dial."

The Traveler could not help himself. He had not lifted a hand in anger since he was a little boy, but he swatted the commander's finger off him. "I've got nothing but loyalty," he said. "I'm loyal to my God. I'm loyal to my family. And I'm loyal to my country."

"I *am* your country!"

"No, sir. You are my government. That is in no way the same thing. My country is the collection of free and sovereign individuals who make up the United States of America and the Constitution under which they live. You just work for them. And so do I. And that means we have to behave as they would have us behave."

"That's ridiculous. The people don't know anything about this! It's a secret operation, remember?"

"All the more reason for us to do what's right," said Dial.

Mars's face turned even redder. He stepped up close to the Traveler, as if he meant to intimidate him. He did mean to. Mars intimidated most of the people he dealt with. But he didn't know Dial.

And he didn't get to know him any better now. Because before he could start talking, the door to the amphitheater opened and Dial's son Rick was standing there. There was a look in the big kid's eyes that said he was ready to tear Mars's head off and use it for a basketball.

The apple doesn't fall far from the tree, Mars thought with disdain.

"What's going on?" the kid said.

Lawrence Dial turned to Rick. He gave a curt nod of his head down the hall.

"Come on, son," he said. "We're getting out of here."

6. OUTLAW VOLLEYBALL

RICK KNEW FROM the look on his father's face that this was serious business. But what business? That, he couldn't guess.

He stood in his dad's office in the low-ceilinged attic of their house. Normally, the house would have been empty around this time. Mom and Raider would've been at the small schoolhouse at the far end of the compound where Mom helped tutor Raider and five other kids whose parents were on the compound staff. But the school's Christmas break had begun just the day before, and Rick could hear the bink-bank-bonking music of *Super Mario Brothers* filtering up to them from Raider's room on the second floor. Mom was busy with some sort of Mom-thing on the floor below.

About ten minutes ago, Victor One—Dad's pet tough guy— had appeared on their front step as if summoned by some kind of secret Victor One signal. Now he and Rick and Dad all stood shoulder to shoulder in the cramped attic office, gathered around Dad's desk and his computer.

"What's going on?" Rick said.

But his father didn't answer. Leaning over his keyboard, his fingers flew over the numbers and letters rapid-fire.

"This entire compound was built for cybersecurity," he explained as he tapped away. "It was constructed over the course of months to my specifications, fashioned to be the one place where I could modify our defense systems without any danger of Kurodar breaking into my computer and stealing or destroying my work. So far, that security seems to be holding up well. But the minute I explore beyond the systems here . . . well, there are vulnerabilities. Every morning, for instance, I visit an information sharing site to keep up with the latest discoveries in my field. When I went there today, I found a message waiting for me. The message was written in a code that only a very few people could have understood. I understood it, and I followed its links through a series of further security blocks so complex they would have eliminated pretty much anyone but two people on earth—me and Kurodar. Finally, I was able to unlock what you're about to see."

He pressed one final key and stepped back. As Rick and Victor One watched the monitor, an image appeared, the image of a man.

"Who's that?" said Rick. "He looks like a troll."

His father held up a finger to silence him.

But it was true: the man on the screen was definitely troll-like. His flaming red hair somehow emphasized the spotty pallor of his face, which in turn emphasized the enormity of his head, which in its own turn made his small but muscular body seem even more misshapen than it was. Even before the Troll spoke in that sliding-gravel voice of his, Rick could see the rage and agony in the man's huge eyes.

"Professor Dial," he rasped, "I'm speaking to you as a messenger from your colleague, the man you call Kurodar. He sends you his compliments. He was very impressed with your cleverness in inserting your son into the MindWar Realm—and with your son's ability to avoid the security bots designed to stop him from causing damage. In fact, Kurodar was so impressed, he respectfully requests that you not repeat the effort. From now on, he wants you and your son to stay completely out of the Realm."

Rick snorted. "Yeah, right. We'll be sure to do that."

Again, his father held up a finger: *Listen!*

"In return for your restraint," the Troll continued, "we will restrain ourselves as well. We will refrain from bringing this young lady's life to a premature and very painful conclusion."

The scene shifted—and Rick felt a weight drop inside him like an elevator with a broken cable.

Molly!

She was kneeling on a hard wooden floor. She was dressed in a black running outfit, her light brown hair held back with a band, her gentle face so pale the soft freckles stood out darkly. She was in an empty room. The room was shadowy, harshly lit by the camera's spotlight. There was a grate on the window behind her and tree branches visible through the glass. There were black scratches gouged into the chipped paint of the walls. Rick could tell Molly had been crying, but she wasn't crying now. She was looking directly into the camera, her eyes fierce, her arms bent out from her sides, her hands braced on her thighs.

"Go on," a high-pitched male voice prompted her from behind the camera.

Molly licked her lips nervously, but her voice was strong and steady. "Professor Dial. Rick, if you're watching this. These men took me from the university after my jog," she said—and Rick noticed she gave her thigh an angry little tap with one hand on that last word. "They want me to tell you that I'm all right. For now. I'm being held prisoner. Which is hard," she continued, giving her thigh another angry tap. "But they want me to tell you that they won't hurt me as long as you do what Ku . . . Ka . . ."

"Kurodar," prompted the voice behind the camera impatiently.

"What Kurodar wants you to do," Molly said.

Molly hesitated, and the high-pitched voice offscreen was thrown at her like acid: "Tell them the rest. Go ahead."

"Oh, right," said Molly. She looked straight into the camera. Something dry and ironic about that glance, Rick thought, as if, even now, Molly's typical tongue-in-cheek sense of humor was still in play. "I'm supposed to tell you how scared I am, and then I'm supposed to cry and beg you to do whatever they said."

Rick felt a warm wave of admiration wash through him. Molly was speaking the words they told her to speak and making a mockery of them at the same time with her brave, unflinching tone. Kneeling there, helpless, under threat of death, she was totally defiant, practically spitting in her captor's eye. And the thug behind the camera knew it, too: Rick heard him let out an angry curse of frustration before the picture suddenly went black. Rick's admiration turned to fear and he prayed silently that the thug wouldn't hurt her.

Now the Troll returned to the screen. "She is a brave girl. It would be a pity for her to die so young. But she will die. If the police come after her, we'll kill her. If you try to rescue her, we'll kill her. And, most importantly, if you make any further attempts to interfere with the Realm, we will kill her—very slowly and very painfully. So do her a favor, Professor Dial. Keep quiet. Keep low. Stay out of the Realm. You and your son both. The MindWar is over. We win."

With that, the video ended.

In the silence afterward, Rick raised a hand to his mouth. The hand was trembling. Thoughts and emotions were crashing together inside him like a forty-car pileup on the highway.

Molly. His Molly. He could barely believe it, barely take it in. She and he—they were so alike, they had so much in common, she was almost like his second self. They were both athletes, both fierce competitors, both the unlikely children of brainy professors. And they'd been on the verge of becoming more than friends when everything went wrong . . . the truck crashing into his car . . . his broken legs . . . his bitterness . . . the MindWar . . .

And Mariel.

There had never been any promise between him and Molly, but, all the same, Rick knew that something important and deep between them had been interrupted by all the trauma and adventure of these last months. It was as if they had been two vines growing side by side, slowly twining together into one—and they had suddenly been ripped apart. Even so, maybe they would've gotten past that interruption, maybe they would have started to grow together again, but now . . . ?

Now there was Mariel. It made Rick feel confused, not to mention rotten. He felt as if he had betrayed his friend, turned away from Molly because he had developed a crush on . . . on what? What was Mariel, anyway? Was she even human? He didn't know. When he was in the Realm, her silver, spirit-like appearance was so real, so captivating. And his desperate desire to rescue her from Kurodar's slow death compelled him to think about her all the time, kept her image in the forefront of his mind. But what was she really?

Now Molly was in danger, too. She was definitely real! And the thought of her overwhelmed everything. The desire to help her was like a fire in his spirit. It suddenly reminded him just how much he cared about her.

He came out of his thoughts and noticed that both his father and Victor One were looking at him. They were waiting for him to speak.

"I've got to help her," was all he managed to say. "I've got to find her."

His father shook his head. "You can't. Kurodar has the means to launch a devastating attack on this country. He may be only a few days away from pulling it off. And you're the only one who can stop him."

"But . . . if I go into the Realm, they'll kill her. They said so."

"The Realm is a big place. Kurodar's mind can't be everywhere at once. We don't think he'll even know you're there at first."

"But . . ."

"And if you don't go in, thousands, maybe millions, will die," his father said.

Rick tried to think but he couldn't. The storm of emotions gathering inside him pushed every thought away. "It doesn't matter," he said. "I can't go into the Realm. I have to find Molly."

"Listen to me—" his father began.

The storm of emotions broke. Rage flashed through Rick. Before he could stop himself, he snarled, "Maybe you're willing to hurt the people you love for the sake of a mission, but I'm not!" The moment the words were out of his mouth, he was sorry for them. He knew full well his father was only trying to do what was right. And even he himself wasn't sure what the right thing was. All the same, the anger still boiled in him and he couldn't bring himself to apologize.

But his father didn't seem to need it. His voice remained steady; his eyes, blinking behind his glasses, remained calm.

"I have a better idea," he said—as if Rick hadn't spoken at all. "If we try to contact anyone outside—the police or any federal agencies—Kurodar will know and they'll kill her. Also, there's Mars. He's not with us on this. He's likely got law enforcement holding back."

"What?" Rick nearly shouted.

"I know. He doesn't want anything to jeopardize the mission."

"Why, that lousy—"

"So that leaves it up to us," Rick's father said, cutting him off.

"That's why I have to go find her," Rick insisted.

"No," said his dad firmly. "You go into the Realm. Victor One will go find Molly."

Rick drew a breath. His eyes shifted to the bodyguard. Victor One was standing slumped on one hip, his hands in the pockets of his jeans. He looked relaxed, but all the wit was gone from his expression. His blue eyes flashed like gemstones.

Rick shook his head. "No," he said. "I'm Molly's friend. I'm the one who—"

"You're the one who's trained to go into the Realm," said Victor One. "Me—well, the Army taught me how to kill people and break things. I'm good at it. Very good. And I move quiet. No one will see me coming. I'm trained for this, Rick. You're not. Trust me. I'll find her. I'll set her free."

Rick's lips moved, but no more words came out. He didn't know what to say, didn't even know what to think. He was haunted by the image of Molly forced to kneel on that hard floor—and by the image of Molly crying when he said good-bye to her the last time. But even awash in anger and fear and guilt, he knew deep down that Victor One was right. Rick's hours and hours of video-game playing had been a sad and stupid response to his accident, but by some work of providence they had turned him into the one person who could best do battle in the Realm. When it came to a search-and-rescue mission in RL? Rick's legs were still weak, plus he had no real fighting or weapons training. Victor One, a former special forces hero, was a better man for the job.

"All right," Rick said. It was hard to get the words out, but he did it. "You go. But how are you going to find her?"

At that, Victor One and the Traveler exchanged an uncomfortable glance. With a sinking feeling in his gut, Rick realized: they didn't know where to begin.

Victor One gestured at the computer. "Run her part of the video again," he said.

Rick nearly groaned aloud when he saw Molly's image reappear on the monitor. He couldn't stand to see her—even to think of her—held captive like that by thugs without a conscience. Brave as she was, strong as she was, she couldn't defend herself against them. Why had he ever left her behind? Why hadn't he realized she'd be vulnerable? Why wasn't he there to protect her?

"Look at her hands," Victor One said. "Tapping her legs like that . . ."

Rick looked. He had noticed it before but had thought it was just an angry tic. Could it be more than that?

"She's a volleyballer," Rick murmured. "That's what they do. They signal each other with their fingers before the serve so they know where the ball is going."

"That's what I was thinking," said Victor One. "Before they serve, they point. But what's she pointing to?"

Rick shook his head. "She only does it twice. When she says the word *jog*, and when she says the word *hard*. Could she be pointing to the words?"

"We thought of that," said his dad. "It would have to be something simple like that, but . . . well, it doesn't mean anything. Jog hard? That doesn't tell us anything."

Rick shook his head. Jog hard. His dad was right. It was just random nonsense.

His father started to go on. "We thought maybe she was giving some kind of directional signal, but—"

"Wait, I know what that is!" came a piping voice behind them.

The Traveler, Rick, and Victor One all swung around together, startled to see Raider standing in the office doorway. For a moment, they could do nothing but gape in surprise at the nine-year-old's eager, pie-plate face.

Raider blinked at them. "Well, I do!" he said.

"What is it, son?" Lawrence Dial asked him. "What do you think it is?"

"It's an app. JogHard. You put it on your phone and it tells you how far you ran."

The three men continued to stare at him.

"Well, it is!" said Raider.

In spite of all the dark feelings swirling inside him, a bleak laugh broke from Rick's lips. "You know, I think the kid's right. Molly does have an app like that on her phone. Nice going, Raider."

Raider beamed like the sun, delighted to have helped.

"Molly's phone has been turned off . . . ," the Traveler murmured.

Rick raised his eyes to his father's. "But maybe the app feeds location info to the cloud for storage."

Rick's father nodded and quickly swung away from him, his fingers moving to the keyboard of his computer.

As the Traveler tapped away, trying to work his way into Molly's cloud account, Rick's gaze moved to Victor One.

Victor One lifted his chin to him. It was as if he knew the trouble raging in Rick's heart.

"I'll find her," said Victor One again. "Put it out of your mind, Rick, as best you can. Do what you have to do. Go into the Realm. Fight the MindWar. Stop these fools before they unleash red hell on the lot of us. Just trust me. I will find her. I will bring her back. Alive."

The two men's eyes locked for a long moment. Even with

the guilt plaguing him, eating at him, Rick knew there was no other way. He was going to have to trust Victor One to make this happen.

He nodded. "All right," he said. "Let's get it done."

7. THE SECRET OF SPACE OCTOPUSES

THE MAN WHO looked like a troll walked quietly through the forest. His hands pushed deep into the pockets of his overcoat, he shivered with the cold. All around him, visible through the naked branches of the winter trees, deep stretches of stagnant swamp shimmered. Small patches of ice flashed in the gray light. The Troll Man's breath turned to small puffs of fog in front of his lips. He bowed his large head and pushed on.

The Troll's name was Ermias. Once an enforcer for an international gang of drug dealers, he had spent a lifetime bringing death to the enemies of his bosses. Now death had come for him. The strange little man was sick. He was dying. At best, the doctors told him, he had only months left to live.

And he was afraid. Ermias was an evil man, but he was not an atheist. He had been raised a Christian, and he had never lost his faith. He believed that when he died, he would stand before the throne of God and face eternal judgment for the things he had done. The thought filled his sleepless nights with terror.

He might have repented, of course. He might have confessed his sins, and changed his ways, accepted his punishment on earth and hoped for forgiveness in the next life. He might have, but he wouldn't. He felt there was no point in telling God he was sorry. He wasn't sorry, not at all. He had enjoyed his work all these years. He had enjoyed wielding the power of life and death. He had enjoyed making people afraid. He had enjoyed making them suffer. He could pretend to repent, but it wouldn't be real, and God would know. There was no point in repentance.

And anyway, he thought he had a better idea.

How much easier it would be, he thought, simply to live forever. No death—no judgment, right? Easy as that. It was with this clever plan in mind that Ermias had accepted the job of kidnapping Molly Jameson. He had brought her to her prison here in the forest. He had made the video to send to the Traveler. His work was finished. And now he was going to accept his reward—his eternal reward, so to speak—from Kurodar.

Kurodar, the god of MindWar, was going to make him a creature of MindWar, unchanging and eternal. In the Realm, Ermias would never die.

Up ahead now, through the trees, Ermias saw the barn. It seemed little more than an old lopsided structure. Its paint was gone and its wooden boards were bare and brown and splintery. Now that the swamps had reclaimed the land around it, no one was likely ever to find it sitting here in the middle of nowhere like this. If they did find it, no one would suspect what was inside it. If they did suspect, no one would be able to enter it before they were gunned down by the four men hiding in the trees all around, each holding a machine gun.

The four guards wore thick black snowsuits and balaclavas against the cold. The masks hid their faces but not their dark, brutal eyes. When they heard the branches crackling under Ermias's feet, those eyes shifted toward him, and they brought their rifles up in front of them, ready to fire.

Then they recognized Ermias and lowered the guns to let him pass.

The Troll went by the guards silently. He reached the barn. He shifted a panel on one of its unpainted, splintery boards and revealed the pad underneath. He pressed in a ten-digit code, then pressed his thumb against the pad's sensor. The heavy steel door hidden behind the barn's wooden planks slowly slid open.

The Troll stepped inside.

At first he could see nothing in the interior shadows. But slowly his vision adjusted. With his abnormally big eyes, he had always been able to see well in the dark. He could make out the drones arrayed on the stone floor, row after row of them: a miniature air force ready to lift off on its mission of destruction. He moved among them until he reached the back wall.

This wall was not made of steel like the others. It was fashioned out of some unique and changeable polymer. Indestructible and black as night, it was a key element of Kurodar's latest invention: the Breach.

The Breach was something entirely new: a living link between the MindWar Realm and RL. It was through the Breach that Kurodar had taken control of the drones; through the Breach that he had hidden them from the American defense systems to move the stolen mini-planes invisibly through the sky. The Breach opened the border between Kurodar's mind and reality. It gave him the power to change the world with but a thought.

He truly was like a god, thought the Troll.

Ermias stood before the Breach, breathing deeply, waiting. This was where it was going to happen. This was where he was going to beat death and escape judgment.

"My job is done, Kurodar," he said aloud. "I've come for payment."

For a moment, nothing happened. Then, first, the wall began to vibrate. Next, it became transparent. Ermias could see right through it, could see the forest outside the barn. And now, amazingly, the wall seemed to dissolve completely. Ermias could feel the winter chill wash over him as if he were standing outdoors again.

He stared at the forest. And what happened next defied belief. The entire wood, all the winter trees and stretches of swamp, began to flicker and grow dim. It was as if the light of the world were failing . . . fading . . . fading . . .

Then—*flash!*—there was nothing! The forest was gone. The swamp gone. The world—RL itself—was completely gone. A night of absolute blackness had fallen over everything like a great stone. Stretching out in front of Ermias was an immensity of nothingness. Space. And yet more than space. This emptiness somehow lived. It lived and breathed and . . . pulled at him, called to him. It was drawing him into itself.

Yes! thought Ermias. And for the first time in months, his fear of God's judgment lifted off him.

He spread his short but powerful arms and let the power of the darkness sweep over his small misshapen body. The darkness took hold of him and suddenly he knew what it was. It was

Kurodar. Kurodar himself. It was Kurodar's mind, the force and power of Kurodar's imagination. It was in the dark, it was taking control of him, taking control of his flesh, his cells, the very fabric of what he was.

It was like a new creation. Ermias felt his body begin to transform. He was becoming larger, much larger. His already oversized head was expanding and becoming the center of his body. His arms were extending into snapping, rubbery tentacles, stretching out across a vast distance. His chest felt as if it were about to burst—and then it *did* burst as even more tentacles grew out of the core of him. At the same time, he could feel himself being lifted up, up, out of the living world. He was being drawn into the center of that utter blackness of unending space, drawn into that utter blackness of Kurodar's imagination.

With a thrill of excitement, Ermias felt his dying body replaced—replaced with something monstrous, yes, but with a monstrous shape that was impervious to disease and decay, a monstrous shape that would overcome human weakness, overcome time, overcome death itself.

I'm becoming immortal! he thought in raging triumph.

The next moment his enormous octopus form was sucked into the farthest reaches of nothingness and the man who once was Ermias became the Great Octo-Guardian of Kurodar's massive WarCraft.

8. WARPATH

RICK DIAL WAS still thinking about Molly as he stepped into the Portal Room. His mind and heart were in utter confusion.

He knew he had to do this thing, to return to the MindWar. Kurodar was planning an act of terrorism that could wipe out a whole city's worth of people, maybe more. Rick had to go into the Realm to stop him. What else could he do?

But what if Kurodar saw him or sensed him there, what then? Would he order his thugs to kill Molly on the instant? Would Victor One be able to find her and rescue her before they did?

He felt guilty about putting Molly at risk like this. And he felt guilty about something else as well. He felt guilty because he was eager: he was eager to enter the Realm again. Partly because he wanted to stop Kurodar from killing people, sure. But partly, he knew, it was because he wanted to see Mariel. To find Mariel. To bring her back to RL . . .

Was he doing the right thing? Was he doing it for the right reasons? Was he going to cause the death of a woman he cared about, one of the best friends he'd ever had, maybe *the* best?

A lot of questions. Zero answers. Not one. He just didn't know.

The Portal Room was the heart of the MindWar complex. It was large but crowded close with machinery and people. On every wall, on every countertop, there were screens and flashing graphs, keyboards and e-charts and microphones—and there were operators stationed in their chairs to work them, so many operators they were practically sitting shoulder to shoulder.

Then, at the far end of the room, embedded in the center of the wall, there was a transparent box. It was the size and shape of a coffin. Its bottom was lined with a sheet of some kind of flexible metal. This was the portal, the doorway that would send Rick into the MindWar Realm.

The tech operators in the room looked up as Rick moved past them. He approached the portal slowly. He had worked so hard to get the strength back in his legs that he walked with only a slight limp now, but there was always enough pain there to keep him from any overly quick or sudden movements.

Miss Ferris stood beside the portal, waiting for him. Juliet Seven stood beside her. Juliet Seven was Miss Ferris's personal security man. Despite his name, he was a towering blocky monster of a fellow who seemed to Rick like a comic-book figure drawn by someone who only knew how to make rectangles and squares. He stood with his enormous arms crossed over his enormous chest. He was smiling to himself as he watched Rick come forward. There was something about Rick and Rick's grim intensity that always seemed to amuse the big man.

Rick's pulse sped up as he approached them. He was eager to get on with the immersion, but he was also nervous. That is, he was scared.

"You have ninety minutes," Miss Ferris told him. No words of encouragement, of course. She didn't even say hello. "The timer will be visible in your right palm as always. Pay attention to it. After ninety minutes in the Realm, your consciousness will start to disintegrate. Stay in there too long, and you'll spend the rest of your life without a working brain."

Rick gave a quick nod, eyeing the portal in the wall above him. "Thanks for the pep talk," he said. He wondered what she would say if she knew about his headaches and his nightmares. She probably would've called off the whole mission, sent in one of the other gamers they had tested for the job. Well, it didn't matter what she would've done if she knew. She would never know. He would never tell her.

"We've installed a fresh energy pod in your left hand—that is, it will be programmed into your avatar's left hand," she continued in her robotic voice. "If you should find your friends, feel free to give the energy to them. But always remember, that's not the mission. The mission is to find Kurodar's new outpost and stop him before he launches a drone attack." When Rick didn't say anything, she added, "Am I making myself clear?"

"I know why you're sending me in there," said Rick, annoyed at the way she always badgered him. "I'll get it done or die. One or the other."

"Remember, we only have . . ."

"Three days. I know."

"We can't afford to have you waste your time . . ."

Saving Mariel, Rick finished her sentence in his mind. But out loud, he only repeated more forcefully, "I know!"

Miss Ferris pressed her lips together. He could tell she wasn't satisfied with his answers. He didn't care. He was risking Molly's life just by going in there, but he didn't have much choice about that. It had to be done. But no matter what happened, he wasn't going to leave Mariel to die as well. Or Favian. One way or another, he would find them both; get some fresh energy to them; keep them alive until he could bring them out of the Realm for good.

"All right," Miss Ferris said finally. "You should emerge at the last portal point you found, right where the fortress was. Remember: without a portal point you can't get home, so don't stray too far from one without locating a new one. Ninety minutes is all you've got."

Rick drew a deep breath. "Are we gonna do this or just chat all day?" he asked her.

Miss Ferris's only response was a glance at Juliet Seven, a slight lifting of her chin. In response, the big man held out an arm like a girder to help Rick up the three stairs to the portal. But Rick ignored the arm. He didn't need the help anymore. He climbed the stairs on his own, climbed into the box, and lay down.

The next moment Miss Ferris was there above him. She touched the lid of the portal and it slowly lowered over him, closing him inside.

This was the part of the immersion process Rick liked least of all. He was a little claustrophobic; not too much, but being shut up in this coffin-like thing made him sweat. Even worse, he now felt the box's metal lining come to life beneath him. It began to rise and wrap itself around him like a cocoon. It closed tighter and tighter around the sides of his face and over the top of his head. Soon he felt the familiar sting of it, as if a thousand tiny needles were injecting something through his skin.

RL—Real Life—began to fade into darkness. And at the

center of that darkness was a corridor of light. Rick knew he had only to will it, and his spirit would fly through that corridor like liquid through a straw. The next thing he knew, he would appear inside the mad world of Kurodar's digitalized imagination, like a living character injected into a video game.

He hesitated only a moment. He thought of Molly. He thought of Victor One. He thought of Mariel. He thought of Kurodar and his stolen drones. He didn't know if he was doing the right thing. He didn't even know what the right thing was.

But he had to do something. He had to try.

The words came into his mind, it seemed, on their own.

God help us, he thought. *God help all of us.*

Then he entered the MindWar.

LEVEL TWO:
THE ENERGY WRAITHS

9. SWORD 2

THE FIRST TIME he had ever entered the Realm of MindWar, it had been . . . well, incredible. The bizarre colors—the scarlet grass, the blue trees, the bright yellow sky—and the sudden strength that flowed through his then-shattered legs . . . He remembered he had whooped like a madman, running here and there just from the sheer energy and excitement of his first arrival.

It was nothing like that this time. He stepped into a world of death and ruin. The only thing that seemed to have any color at all was the purple diamond of light that pulsed and glowed beside him: the portal through which he had come. Everything else was black and brown and gray, fallen and dead.

This was where Kurodar's fortress had stood, a grandiose castle full of immense statues and stained-glass windows and topped, in its central room, with an enormous dome that mapped the heavens. It was from here that Kurodar had commandeered several aircraft, had threatened to crash them into a city in order to blackmail the Traveler to turn over his work. Before Kurodar could succeed, Rick had managed to blow the place up. It had crumbled into rubble and flame. Rick himself had barely escaped with his life.

Now, where that fortress had been, there stood only jagged

walls of stone, hollow archways leading not into grand halls, but to open fields covered with broken rocks. There were corridors going nowhere and roofless rooms. And over all of it there was silence— silence, except for a weird electrical whisper that was very much like the rising and falling whisper of the wind.

What was once the bright red grass around the fortress had been scorched by fire to sere gray ash. And while the sky above was still yellow, all the vibrancy had somehow drained out of it. The color seemed swampy, sickly, like the color of jaundiced skin.

Worst of all—most disappointing to Rick—the moat was empty. Before, it had been filled high with flowing mercurial water, silver and bright. That—that water—was the element through which Mariel moved and in which she lived. This was the place where he had seen her last, her hand reaching up out of the silver flow to take back the sword she had given him. Now the moat was just a long trench, its walls and floor thick and brown and fluid like mud. There was nothing living in it.

Rick lifted his eyes from the moat and looked off into the distance. Far away, he could see the misty skyline of the Golden City. That, Mariel had told him, was the heart and battery of this place, the core from which Kurodar's imagination spread out, dreaming new portions of the Realm into existence. Somewhere between here and there, according to Miss Ferris's map, stood Kurodar's new outpost. But strangely, though there wasn't anything to block his view, Rick could see nothing like an outpost anywhere. From this ruin to that golden skyline, there was only a level plain that started gray and then steadily grew brighter and redder as it spread away from the center of destruction.

What should he do, then? Where should he begin? Should he just start walking in the direction of the city? He tested his legs—walking, then jogging, along the edge of the moat. Once again, he couldn't help but feel a surge of joy at the strength in them, the absence of pain. It was a little taste of the old days, when he was a high school football hero, when his biggest worry was how to win the next game.

After a few steps, though, he stopped. As his breathing slowed, he heard that strange wind-like silence again—and he heard now that it was more than silence, really. There almost seemed to be voices in it, an eerie high-pitched singing. Rick thought it had been there all along, but it was louder now. Closer.

He glanced at his right palm where the timer was embedded. The seconds were rapidly counting down: 88:47 . . . 88:46 . . . He raised his eyes to the ruin again and saw that he was standing by a collapsed gateway, two brown walls of stone that had tilted into each other, the low point in the middle where the gate itself had been. This, he remembered, was the spot where he had emerged from the fortress as it fell. This was where he had seen Mariel for the last time and promised to return for her. This was where he had hurled the sword to her, and her hand had reached up out of the moat to catch it.

He missed her. He missed her presence, her voice, her face. He feared he had already lost her, that he would never see her again. The thought made him melancholy. He turned his gaze to the empty moat again as he remembered that final moment . . .

And he saw something! There, at the bottom of the moat. Something buried in the mud.

He moved to the very edge of the pit. He squinted as he stared down into it. What was it? Something small, only about the size of his hand. It was green with flashes of silver in it.

Rick caught his breath. *The sword!* Though the moat was deep, and the thing on the bottom was half covered with mud, he thought he could just make out the image of the woman that was carved into the hilt of his old sword. The carved woman looked like Mariel herself. He remembered how, when he had wrapped his hand around the hilt to wield the sword, he had felt her strength and her wisdom flowing into him, giving him extra power and guidance. He had even heard her voice in his mind.

As he stood there, looking down at it, the wind—or the sound of the wind—or whatever that weird sound was—rose higher for a moment. It really did seem like some sort of wordless singing now. A high-pitched musical cry that almost seemed . . . *hungry*, was the word that went through Rick's mind.

The noise sent a chill through him. He quickly glanced over his shoulder at the ruin behind him: the dark, toppled stones and half-shattered structures silhouetted against the jaundice-yellow sky. His eyes flicked to a broken archway at the ruin's farthest edge. Had he seen a flicker of motion there? Something darting behind the stones? He stared in that direction for a moment. Nothing moving now. He must've imagined it.

He turned to the moat again, looked down again at the sword hilt buried in the mud. He glanced at his left palm, where a red light flashed on and off beneath his skin. That was the energy pod that would give fresh life to Mariel and Favian. Before he had left the Realm the last time, he had used the sword point to lance his hand, and the energy had flooded out of him into the sword's blade. That was why he had thrown the sword to Mariel, to transfer that energy to her. She needed it to stay alive. Had she taken the energy and left the sword for him to find and use when he came back? Or was it maybe a message of some sort?

He knew he had to hurry. He knew he had to find Kurodar's outpost before the madman launched an attack. The time on his hand was counting down, and there were only three days until the new outpost was ready.

But the hilt seemed to beckon him from the moat bottom. He had to find out why it was there.

Even as a quarterback, he had always been an intense macho man who charged ahead on instinct. That hadn't changed, even with his injuries. Without further thought, then, he lowered himself to the ground. He turned and lowered his legs over the side of the wall. It was a long way down, too far to jump. But by sliding over the edge, hanging on to the rim of turf above, he found that the wall of the moat was as soft and muddy as the bottom. He kicked his toes into the dirt, creating a foothold first for one foot, then the other. He let go of the earth above with one hand, his left hand, and jammed his fingers into the mud as well. They went in deep, giving him purchase, a handhold. He brought his other hand down and jammed that in another place. Yes. He could do this. He could climb down, gripping the soft earth.

He started his descent. Above him, he heard that sound again—that high, hungry musical cry. It swirled above his head, sending another chill down the back of his neck. He told himself it was nothing. Just the wind. He kept climbing and sliding down the wall.

His arms were strong. And here in the Realm, his legs were strong, too. It did not take him long to reach the bottom. As he landed, his sneakers sank into the damp earth. He felt mud squeeze up over his laces and soak his socks with clammy cold. The suction slowed him down as he waded out away from the wall to reach the flashing object buried in the ground.

He stood above it. It was the hilt, for sure. He could see it clearly now: the twining lines rising to the image of that majestic face he remembered, the face that had haunted him every day since he had been in this place, a queenly and imposing face and yet tender, compassionate, and wise.

Rick crouched in the mud. His hand slippery with grime, he reached down and wrapped his fingers around the hilt.

He heard himself gasp. It was like sticking his fingers into an electrical outlet: the buzz that went through him, the instant surge of energy.

I am here.

"Mariel," the word came out of him in a whisper. The jolt of energy inside him blossomed and spread into a flowering sense of joy and well-being. He almost seemed to see her standing there before him.

She was still alive!

With a tug, he drew the hilt out of the mud. The blade was all but gone. There was only a broken fragment of it, a few jagged inches of steel protruding from the handle.

Slowly, he stood up out of his crouch. He straightened. He

lifted the broken sword and turned it this way and that in the sickly light.

Live in your spirit, Mariel had told him once. He could almost hear her saying it now. *If you focus it, your spirit can transform the substance of the Realm itself.*

It was true. He had proved it. Learning to focus the very self of himself, he had been able to change his entire body here, to take on the form of the alligator security bots who protected the place. He couldn't do it for long—it was just too hard to keep up that level of focus—but whatever that core piece of himself was, he knew he could use it here. He knew it could make even this shattered weapon into something powerful and deadly.

Help me find you, he thought, trying to concentrate on the sword, trying to contact Mariel through the sword.

There was no answer, and yet he sensed that she heard him. He sensed that if he kept hold of this thing, it would lead him where he needed to go.

He slipped the weapon into his belt and tromped back through the mud toward the wall.

He began to climb up. It was much tougher going than the descent. The wall gave way and the mud slid down each time he tried to rise. By the time he was halfway up the moat wall, he was out of breath and he felt the muscles in his arms growing weak. A fearful little part of his mind spun out a whole fantasy about how he could slide down to the bottom and get stuck down there, far away from any portal point. He would languish in the empty moat while his ninety minutes ran out and his mind went to pieces.

But one of the things that Rick had learned playing football—and it was just as true here as it was in RL—was that courage is all about turning off that fantasy machine, silencing that part of your imagination that spins out images of disasters that haven't happened yet and may never happen if your luck holds good. It was like something his father had told him once: *Don't worry about tomorrow; tomorrow can worry about itself.* Probably a Bible quote, he thought sardonically. Just about everything his father said was.

He felt a flash of anger thinking about his dad, and then a flash of guilt.

He went on climbing, grunting with the effort. He gripped the wall—and the mud gave way in his hand. The wall slid down and he started sliding with it. He cried out. Pulled his hand from the sucking mud. Drove it back in, trying to get fresh purchase.

His slide stopped. He clung to the wall, panting. He had to stop thinking about . . . well, about everything, about anything but this. He had to pour his mind into the task before him. *Don't worry about tomorrow . . .*

He took up the long, slow, frustrating climb again. He rose. He didn't fall anymore. He wouldn't fall. He wouldn't let himself fall. He just determined it was not going to happen.

Sure enough, slowly, sliding, muddy hand over muddy hand, foot above foot, panting, gut-wrenching step-by-step, he clawed his way back to the top of the wall. Almost there, he reached up—up—touched the sere and ashen grass above and felt the hard earth of the surface underneath it. He gritted his teeth and let out a last loud grunt as he dragged himself up over the rim. Then, panting for breath, he rolled over onto the surface and lay on his back, exhausted, staring up into the weird yellow sky.

Tired as he was, he managed to lift his hand and stare at it. The timer embedded in the palm was covered in mud. He wiped it more or less clean against his black sweatshirt, held it up again: 73:16 . . . 15 . . . He had to get up, get moving. There was no more time to lie around.

He gave another loud groan as he pushed himself up on one hand—but the noise of his groan was washed away by the sudden rise of that noise, that noise like the wind. It was shockingly loud now, but filled with the same high-pitched song of hunger. The closeness of it made Rick's heart race.

He leapt to his feet. That wasn't the wind, he thought at once. That was . . . a creature. A living thing—or what passed for a living thing in this bizarre, digital place.

He looked around—looked all around him. There! Something. Another movement, a sudden darting behind the fallen stones off to his right. And *another* movement off to his left: something ducking behind an arch.

There was something here. Something in the fortress ruins.

Rick stood still, eyes wide, watching. His pulse was beating so hard in his head it nearly drowned out every other sound. That high, hungry song had dropped again to a low wind-like whisper. His glance shifted quickly, left, right, back again, as he tried to catch out in the open whatever it was that was hiding among the stones.

He started moving cautiously toward the fallen fortress, toward the archway where he had seen the movement, seen something out of the corner of his eye darting away. His hand went to the hilt of the broken sword in his belt, ready to draw the weapon, such as it was. He stepped up to the pillar of stones. The shadow of the archway fell across him, cooling him. He leaned forward very carefully until he could look around the corner. Nothing there.

He felt his body relax a little. His hand came away from the sword hilt.

And that was when the high song rose again, almost a shriek now, and right behind him.

Rick spun and saw the thing: a glowing, globular shape floating in midair. Somewhere in the white mist of its form, there were red eyes, and sharp, vampire-like teeth. For one second he caught the scent of its raw animal craving.

And then—with shocking speed—it leapt at him.

10. WRAITHS

NOTHING COULD HAVE prepared Rick for the horror of it. The floating creature did not seize or slash him: it engulfed him, swallowed him, all in an instant. Despite its blobby appearance, it moved with panther-like quickness. He was immediately surrounded by it, captured inside its glowing presence like air inside a bubble. The creature's red eyes were pressed so close to his they seemed to touch. He stared at them in mesmerized terror.

Then he felt the thing's teeth sink into him—and his life began to drain away.

The white luminescent blob pulsed all around him. Its song of hunger—that ghostly high-pitched song—was everywhere, filling Rick's mind, sapping his will, hypnotizing him into submission while the creature fed off his very life. With every moment, Rick could feel the beast getting stronger. And he was getting weaker as it drew his energy out of him and into itself. He knew instinctively that it would be less than a minute before he was sucked dry, transformed into a husk of lifeless nothing, left to live out his non-death in endless torment until the MindWar Realm should pass away and his spirit was freed.

Sickened by the thought, and by the slimy glow pulsing and

bulging as it sucked him dry, he swallowed his disgust and fought off the weakness already infecting his will. He shut his mind to the creature's hypnotic song. He focused on his hand, fought to move his hand. The fingers were already trembling with weakness like an old man's. But he forced the hand down blindly to his belt, to the sword hilt there. With their last strength, his fingers closed on the metal. What a relief! Some remnant of Mariel's power immediately shot through him, giving him a fresh bout of energy.

Willing that energy into electric motion, Rick drew the broken sword from his belt and wildly thrust it forward, jabbing its few inches of steel into the living, sucking glow that surrounded him.

At first, he thought the attack would have no effect. How could you stab something that had no substance, a creature of mere mist? But no, the being did seem to have a paper-thin body of some sort. The jagged point of the broken blade pierced it—Rick felt it tear through. And with all his remaining might, he dragged the steel edge across the length of the creature, slashing the beast open.

The hypnotic song that filled Rick's mind was instantly transformed into a wrenching scream of agony. The glow that surrounded him, that was feeding off him, grew brighter for one moment and seemed to expand like a balloon.

Then, in a red flash, the wraith exploded. Rick felt the damp on his face as its mist sank down to the earth in a thin rain the color of blood.

The dead wraith stained the earth dark red. Rick gagged and coughed thickly as he stared down at what was left of the thing—the thing that a moment before had been leeching his energy away. Sick to his stomach, he reached out his hand to support himself on the pillar of the arch beside him.

And with wild keening musical cries, two more wraiths darted out of the ruins and rushed at him.

A flood of fear gave Rick more strength than he thought he had. He ran—and he ran fast. The wraiths had appeared out of the tumble of stones to his right. He ran to his left—toward the collapsed gate where he had once exited the fortress. Rick was amazed at how swiftly his feet flew up over that rubble, how quickly he climbed to the top of that low point in the center, and how fearlessly he threw himself off into the plain of broken stones beyond. *There is no telling what you can do with a couple of energy-sucking vampire wraiths at your back*, he thought.

He hit the ground and tripped on a broken stone. He stumbled a few feet forward and then pulled up short, frozen, the sword hilt still gripped in his hand.

They were everywhere.

On this side of the wall, he could see them clearly. All throughout the ruins, among the jagged walls, the standing pillars—coming through the roofs of the roofless rooms and darting through the archways—the glowing, floating white shapes were racing toward him. The air was filled with their music—that high, hungry sound. It vibrated and snaked its way into Rick's head and made him feel dazed and disoriented.

He looked back. The two wraiths that had been chasing him were already drifting up over the wall. The others all around him were steadily approaching through the ruins from every direction.

They weren't moving as fast as that first one had. That was probably their attack speed, Rick thought. But they were closing in without stopping, and there wasn't a lot of room to run.

But what choice did he have? He took off, fast. As soon as he did, the high songs of the wraiths grew louder. The air rang with them. And the circle of glowing shapes began closing in faster.

Rick had always been a passing quarterback, cool in the pocket with a deadly accurate throwing arm, but he could run when he had to and he had to now. He leapt over stones. He dodged around a pillar. He reached a section of wall with two wraiths like bookends moving in from either side. He grabbed the top of the wall and vaulted over it, his feet barely touching the rocks as they flew across.

He landed on the other side and more wraiths swept toward him, singing. He picked out the spaces between them and ran for daylight.

He passed a hollow pile of rocks: a collapsed doorway. A shocking sting of cold went through him, and then a shocking pain. He turned and saw a smaller wraith wrapped around his arm, its teeth sunk into his flesh. He slashed at it with the broken sword, nearly cutting himself open. But he got the wraith: it shrieked and pattered to the ground in a red rain.

The wraith-song grew louder and louder until it was a steady scream, deafening. Rick was now so disoriented that the world around him just seemed to be a jumble of stones and shapes and darkness and oncoming ghosts. He felt gripped by a kind of madness. Not half an hour ago, he had been in the world of men and women. He had been annoyed at Miss Ferris and worried about

Molly and jealous of Victor One . . . and now he was in this bizarro universe of ruins and wraiths, where the only worry he had was how not to be engulfed by a hungry blob and sucked dry of life itself.

He felt dizzy, sick. He had to slow down. He had to look around, get his bearings, even if it gave the things a chance to attack.

He stopped running. He turned frantically this way and that. The wraiths were close—so close—and still steadily floating toward him from every side, pulsing, ready to pounce at any second. But he had crossed a good part of the ruined fortress now. He could see the far walls, see where the fallen piles of stone thinned out, where the gray grass ended and blended with grass that grew softly pink, then scarlet red as it ran off into the distance toward the Golden City. There were wraiths coming from that direction, too, but they had not closed ranks; there were gaps between them, gaps through which he could run.

A wraith to his right let out a scream and leapt at him—but too late. Rick was already running again. The thing missed him and went flying past.

Rick dashed for the fortress's rear walls. They had crumbled and burned like the rest of the place, but they were still tall, still formidable. The wraiths seemed to see where he was headed. Their song grew louder as they came after him. Rick cried out as the noise invaded his head, as it tried to reach into him and steal his mind, his will. He roared as he ran, trying to fight it off.

Twenty yards to go, a red-zone run in football. There was no giving up. There was only success or death.

Help me! he cried out to God in his mind. The oldest prayer of all, bursting up out of his heart before he even had time to think about it.

The wall. Just ahead. He could now see crevices and gashes in the broken stone: handholds; footholds. Out of the corner of his eye, he saw the white glowing blobs sweeping through the air to close in on him for the attack. He reached the base of the wall and didn't stop. He just leapt for it. Grabbed a crevice. Pulled himself up. Reached up. Grabbed the top of the wall. Hauled himself onto it.

And a sudden shriek deafened him. A sudden agony shot up his leg. He looked down to see that a wraith had grabbed his right foot and swallowed his leg to the knee. The white glow was seeping up toward his waist like a deadly stain. The hungry song was filling Rick's mind, obliterating his thoughts. The energy was draining out of him.

Precariously balanced on the wall, he drew Mariel's blade and slashed down at the glow. The creature screamed so loudly it made Rick's ears ache. But the blow told. The thing turned to red rain and spilled down the side of the wall, painting the stones bloody.

Rick took one last look at the army of ghosts flying toward him. Then he shoved the blade back in his belt, lowered himself off the wall with both hands—dangled—let go—and fell to the earth beneath.

The drop was so far he stumbled to one knee. But there was no time to rest. The song of the wraiths was muffled by the wall for only a moment. The next moment it rose again as the white blobs flew up over the top of the wall and came down after him, their red eyes burning.

Rick ran—ran across the open plain. It was the oddest thing. As he left the ruins behind, the world around him became more colorful. It was like running out of one of those old black-and-white movies they show on TV and into a modern color movie. As he put some distance between himself and the ruined fortress, the ashen grass beneath his feet turned a richer and richer red. The jaundiced sky became brighter, a yellow more like butter than sickness. He caught sight of blue tree lines off in the distance to his left, and the gold of the faraway city before him winked and glittered in the Realm's strange, sourceless light.

Rick ran faster. The ground rose up in front of him. He didn't let it slow him. Even as he climbed the little hill, he managed to pour on speed.

He looked back over his shoulder. The wraiths were following him, but they were losing ground, falling away behind him. He was escaping. He laughed out loud in triumph.

Then he looked forward. Just in time. Just in time to stop himself from falling off a sheer cliff into . . .

. . . into nothingness.

He had reached the end of the world. There was nothing but black space in front of him.

The wraiths were closing in behind him, and there was nowhere left to run.

11. DARK FALL

EVERYTHING INSIDE RICK—heartbeat, breath, thoughts—stopped cold. He felt as if he were suspended, lifeless, on the very brink of reality. Well, in fact, he was.

The red grass ended at the tip of his toes—ended in an unnaturally straight line. Beyond that spot, between him and the distance, there was nothing. Just nothing. The incline in the earth had hidden the drop from view as he was approaching it, but now he saw the place where the world suddenly ended, and beyond that place: blackness. There was a broad canyon of absolute blackness, with red grass far, far away on the other side.

Rick had just barely managed to bring himself to a halt before he flew off the precipice into the abyss. He tottered there for a second before he was able to regain his balance and pull himself back. He stared down into the unimaginably black blackness, and the wind rose behind him, and the song of the wraiths rose, too.

He looked over his shoulder. Oh yes, they were still coming, relentless. And so many of them. They had joined together now into a single legion, an army of glowing white blobs with red eyes and dripping teeth, sweeping up the hillside to overwhelm him.

Funny: it was just like the test they had given him back at

the MindWar compound. The oncoming demon army. The cliff. Except here there was no bomb and no flying demon to help him destroy his enemies and escape. Here there was a riddle that might not have an answer—or whose only answer might be Rick's destruction. Well, maybe *funny* wasn't exactly the word to describe it!

Rick stared down at the oncoming wraiths, turned and stared down into the Canyon of Nothingness. The emptiness of that canyon was so complete that it overwhelmed his imagination. He could hardly stand to think about it, hardly look at it for more than a moment.

He raised his eyes to the red grass on the other side. About a hundred and fifty yards away, it looked like to him: a football field and a half. As the song of the onrushing wraiths grew louder and louder, as their high-pitched hunger began to jangle inside his head again, he stared across that black distance. With a hollow feeling at the pit of his stomach, he saw a small purple glow over there. Another portal point. A way out, back to RL. But what good did it do him? There was no way to get to it. No way across the black canyon.

He turned his back on the dark. He gripped all that was left of Mariel's sword. Instantly, he felt her spirit rush up his arm and spread all through him. He drew the weapon from his belt again. He stared down at the onrushing wraiths. Their song swirled around him, filling the air, filling his mind.

After he had taken the MindWar test and escaped the demon army, his father told him that some of the others who had taken the test, some of those who had taken it and failed, had done just what he was doing now. The soldiers especially. They had stood and turned and faced the demons head-on, and they had been swept away and died. He knew that was going to happen to him here and now. He was going to be overwhelmed by the wraiths, drained to a death that was worse than death itself.

He knew. And yet he could think of nothing else to do.

The sword hilt seemed to radiate courage into him. More than courage: faith. It was Mariel's faith, steadfast, unwavering. But somehow, as he stood there, it became his faith, too.

Some stories have no happy ending, he thought. *In the Realm, just as in RL, sometimes it's all about having the courage to face whatever comes.*

He felt something let go inside him, something he had been holding on to tightly, some sense of control. He released it, and he knew, without really putting it into words, that he was giving himself over to God.

He braced himself for the final attack. The wraiths came closer. Their song grew overwhelmingly loud—so loud, he almost didn't hear that other voice—that familiar hollow echoing voice that had been calling to him for the last few moments.

"Rick! Rick! Rick Dial! Over here!"

The wraiths—and death—were less than thirty yards away when the voice finally broke through to him. He turned. He stared across the Canyon of Nothingness.

He saw Favian on the far side.

He could barely make out the sparkling figure at that distance, but really, how could he mistake him? The gangly, anxious sprite was made of shifting light and energy: who else was like him?

A starburst of fresh hope exploded in Rick's core. Was there some way . . . ?

And yes. As he stared across the black canyon at his old friend, Favian extended one hand to the drifting, glowing purple diamond of the energy portal beside him. Rick saw the purple lightning as Favian drew the portal's energy into himself. Then Favian extended his other hand toward Rick. There was a bright, dragon-toothed burst of violet light and a narrow band of energy shot from Favian's extended hand across the canyon, shot all the way from where Favian stood to the cliff's edge at Rick's feet.

A bridge! A thin purple, wavering bridge of energy now lay across the Canyon of Nothingness.

"Hurry!" Favian shouted. His hollow voice carried to Rick like a distant echo. "I can't hold it for long!"

Rick took one last glance back at the wraiths. They were so close now their red eyes seemed bright as fires. Their song was so loud it seemed to obliterate everything else.

Rick knew what he had to do. He slipped his broken sword back into his belt. He faced forward. He tried to test the energy bridge. He tapped the sole of his right foot gingerly on the fizzing line of purple light. He felt nothing. It had no substance. Everything inside him told him he would fall through it. And the prospect was more terrifying than falling from a height to certain death on the earth below. To fall into this canyon where reality itself came to an end, to fall and fall into an eternal darkness: the thought turned his very cells to ice.

"Hurry!" Favian shouted—even at this distance, Rick could hear the strain of effort in his friend's voice.

The wraiths sang louder as their attack came on.

Rick held his breath and stepped off the edge of the world.

He set his right foot down. Somehow, miraculously, the bridge held him. Without thinking—if he had thought about it, he would never have been able to do it—he put his left foot directly out in front of the right. And now he was on the bridge with death behind him and all the world before—and nothing, nothing at all, below.

And yet the bridge did hold him. It was narrow, chillingly narrow. Almost like a tightrope. As he began the slow walk forward, he had to set the heel of each foot smack in front of the other's toe, and then quickly bring the next out in front of the first. He had to stretch his arms to either side to keep his balance. And most of all, he had to keep himself from looking down. Even the slightest glance into that blackest of all blacknesses took the heart out of him, made him quail at the sheer impossibility of what he was trying to do.

He went forward, one step on the thin energy bridge, then another. Already he was too far to turn back and yet so far from the other side, he felt he could never make it. And now, too, the wraith-song washed over him. Were the creatures following him? Were they going to swarm him even here, on the bridge? How would he fight them then? He didn't dare look back to check. His balance was too uncertain. The move would've sent him reeling over the edge.

He forced himself to train his eyes on the red grass in the distance, on the glowing blue man with his hand outstretched.

"Come on!" Favian cried to him.

But he was going as fast as he could on that staticky, narrow strip.

Suddenly, behind him, one of the wraiths let out an ear-blasting scream—that shriek of attack Rick remembered too well. It was so close to him that he couldn't help himself. Instinctively, he twisted in fear to look back over his shoulder.

It was a terrible mistake. He caught one glimpse of the cliff behind him, that shore of reality at the edge of this sea of emptiness. He saw the wraiths gathered there at the edge, straining helplessly in their desire to come after him and feed on his life. The one who had screamed had tried to do it. Rick just had time to see the thing sucked down into the blackness, swiftly down and down, shrieking into that unimaginable nothing, until it was gone.

He saw all this in a single second. Then he lost his balance and fell.

There was a dreadful moment when he tried to stay steady, when he wobbled this way and that, fighting to regain his equilibrium with his outstretched arms. Then there was a moment more horrible still when he realized it wasn't going to happen.

Then the energy bridge slipped out from underneath his sneaker soles and he plummeted down with mind-boggling speed.

"Rick!" Favian cried out, his hollow voice echoing in the darkness.

With a short, high, despairing cry, Rick threw his hand out to the purple line of energy and tried to grab it. He missed—or he thought he missed, because he felt nothing against his palm, because the bridge seemed to have no substance to it at all. And yet the next thing he knew, he was hanging there, dangling there, gripping the bridge with one hand, his feet swinging dangerously above the blackness below. He had done it. He had caught hold of the narrow bridge.

But his hand was slipping—no, it was being pulled off. He was being sucked down. It was only now that he realized: that blackness, that emptiness, that nothingness below him—it was alive somehow! It had a will. It wanted him! It was pulling him into itself.

Strangely—luckily!—that fact—the living pull of nothingness, its hunger to consume him—sent such a burst of terror through Rick's heart that it gave him an instant of unnatural strength. Before he could even think about it, he had pulled himself back up toward the bridge. He got his other hand on it. He chinned himself up until he could get his knee on it, too. Slowly, perilously, he rose to his feet again, balancing once more above the hungry maw of sheer emptiness.

He heard Favian cry out again. No words this time. Just a grunt of effort as he tried to keep the energy bridge flowing. Rick knew that Favian's energy, like Mariel's, was slowly draining out of him. He knew that every time he drew energy from the portals and expended it like this, he grew weaker than he was before. He knew there wasn't much time before his friend's strength gave out and the bridge vanished from beneath his feet.

So, shaken as he was from that near fall, he immediately started moving forward again.

Step-by-step, inch-by-inch, the red grass on the far side of the gap grew brighter, clearer, closer. Step-by-step, Favian's form grew more distinct. Rick could now make out Favian's long, lanky body. He could make out the twisted expression of effort on the boyish, innocent face beneath the close-cropped hair. Soon, he could even see the shifting light particles of which the man was made, the stuff that gave him his weird, sparkling, almost magical aura.

A few more steps. A few more. He was almost there.

"I can't . . . ," said Favian, straining. "I can't hold on . . ."

Rick was close enough now to see his friend's gritted teeth, his eyes narrowed with effort. He was close enough to see that Favian was almost out of strength.

"I . . . ," Favian said.

Rick forgot caution and rushed forward. He crossed the last few yards of the bridge in a quirky, balletic heel-to-toe run. He was one last step from the edge when Favian lost it. The sparkling blue man cried out one more time and tumbled backward onto the red grass.

Rick didn't have to look behind him to know that the energy bridge was snapping and sizzling back across the canyon into Favian's hand with lightning speed. He didn't wait for it to happen. He leapt.

The next second, he was tumbling, falling to the earth, rolling across the red grass, sending a heartfelt *Thank you!* up to heaven as he came to rest right beside the fallen Favian.

He lifted himself up on one elbow. He looked back over the Canyon of Nothingness. On the far side, he saw the army of wraiths beginning to give up on their prey. They were drifting back toward the ruins that rose darkly against the sickly yellow sky.

Exhausted, Rick toppled back down to the grass.

Exhausted, his sparkling blue friend rolled toward him and gazed at him with the worried expression that Rick remembered well.

Favian gave a little gasp, and then a little laugh, and in a voice barely louder than a whisper he said, "Welcome back to the Realm."

12. LORDS OF THE REALM

"SOMETHING IS GOING on in the ruins."

Kurodar paused in his latest act of creation, annoyed at the interruption. "What is it?" he said, speaking English in his thick Russian accent.

The thundering voice came back, echoing all around him. It was the voice of the Octo-Guardian who surrounded his WarCraft and kept watch over the Realm below.

"A possible intrusion," the Guardian told him. "The Energy Wraiths sensed fresh life. They chased . . . something—I'm not sure exactly what. They chased it to the edge of the protective barrier."

Kurodar felt a burst of anxiety. Was it the Dial boy? The Traveler's son? Had he ignored the threats to their hostage and returned to the Realm? Kurodar tasted something coppery and sour inside him. He knew what it was. It was fear.

In RL, the man known as Kurodar, though a brilliant scientist, was ugly. There was no other way to put it. His face, said those who had seen him up close, looked something like a cross between a skull and a toad. His father used to tease him about this. After a few glasses of vodka, his father used to sneer at him from the wing chair in their living room. He used to say, "You are lucky, Ivan (which was Kurodar's name at the time). You will never be disappointed in your children as I am. You will never have children at all because you are so hideous to look at, no woman would ever come near you."

Kurodar knew this must be true because his father said it and, to him, his father seemed nearly godlike in his power and wisdom. A colonel in the Soviet Union's secret police, the KGB, Kurodar's dad was feared by everyone. Kurodar could remember walking with the old man through the streets of Moscow. He could remember how people dropped their eyes and stared at the pavement as they passed, afraid to even look the colonel in the face. They had good reason to be afraid, too. Kurodar's father had only to say the word, and anyone he didn't like would be dragged off to Lubyanka Prison in the middle of the night. And once there, they would vanish forever.

This—his father's power—the fear he caused in others—made young Kurodar very proud. All he wanted in life was to grow up to be like him.

But when Kurodar was still a youth, the Soviet Union collapsed, destroyed by the stratagems of the Americans and the uprisings of the people the Soviets had conquered. What had happened to his father then . . . well, it was too awful for Kurodar to think about. Not just the way his father died, but the humiliation of it. This, Kurodar knew, was the price of failure.

The MindWar, therefore, must not fail. Here, in the MindWar Realm, Kurodar was as powerful as his father had ever been. Here, he was no longer ugly. In fact, he barely had a physical being at all. He was merely a presence, a sort of pink mist that contained his most powerful asset: his intelligence. It was with this intelligence that he was going to have his revenge on the Americans for what they had done. His only fear was that he would fail as his father had failed.

This was why he was so afraid of Rick Dial.

"Track it down," he told the Octo-Guardian now. "Find out what it is. Destroy it if you find it. Whatever you do, don't let it get away."

"As you wish," the Guardian replied, his voice echoing all around the craft.

"Meanwhile, I will communicate with RL," said Kurodar. "We will make sure the Traveler understands we are serious. We will send him another video of the girl."

There was a pause before the Octo-Guardian spoke again. He didn't like to contradict the Lord of the Realm and so he hesitated. But finally he said, "If the Traveler wasn't discouraged by the first video, why should it be any different with a second?"

If Kurodar had still had a face, he would have smiled.

"Because in this video," he said, "the girl will be screaming."

13. ESCAPE PLAN

MOLLY WOKE UP. For a moment, she didn't know where she was. Then, her heart sinking, she remembered.

Her kidnappers had locked her in this room. A bare room. Wooden walls, barred windows. A splintery wooden floor of bare boards. Outside, through the bars on the windows, nothing but forest, naked trees in pale winter light, light already beginning to fade and fail.

It had been hours since she'd seen anyone, days since anyone had spoken to her. It was two days ago, to be exact, when the kidnappers had come in here and forced her to appear on their stupid video. Incredibly humiliating. There had been four thugs in the room, watching her, grinning at her: Smiley McDeath, Thug One, the Nose Guy, and another thug, a giant, a huge muscleman who looked like he could crush her with a single blow. They had forced her to kneel on the floor. They had forced her to say she was scared, forced her to beg Rick and Professor Dial to do whatever they were told. They had hovered over her the whole time and bared their teeth as they laughed at her. It was awful.

There was only one saving grace to the whole experience. She had heard them downstairs talking about the video. They didn't realize. Her ear pressed to the floor, she had heard them making

109

their plans about an hour before they'd come up here. That had given her time to devise her simple code, to try to send a message to Rick and his father. It wasn't much of a code. It wasn't much of a message. She doubted anyone would understand it or that if they did understand it, it would help them find her. But it was something, anyway. It gave her hope. Maybe Rick *would* get it. Maybe he was searching for her even now. Maybe he was coming to rescue her like a white knight in a story . . .

It was a thought to cling to.

After the thugs had shot the video, they left her alone. They had not spoken to her again. Every few hours one of them had unlocked the door, poked his head in, and tossed her a greasy bag full of fast food. Burger and fries, cold and rubbery. Soda, flat and stale. Disgusting. They tossed the bag at her as if she were an animal in a cage. And she ate the food like she was an animal in a cage. She was so hungry all the time, so desperate for any food she could get.

That's the way it had been. Little food. Less sleep. She was exhausted. Weak. Close to despair. She had no bed to lie on. Only a plastic bucket for a toilet. It was cold in the room, but stuffy, so that her whole body had grown sweaty and sticky. Most of the time, she lay on the floor, curled up on her side. She cried a lot. She couldn't help it. She prayed. She slept. There was nothing else for her to do.

She had been sleeping just now when something woke her. What was it? Some noise. There it was again. Coming up through the floor from downstairs. An electric song. A phone ringing.

Molly was still wearing her elastic hairband, but her hair

was slipping out of it, coming loose around her cheeks. She had to tuck it back behind the band so she could hear better. Then she pressed the side of her face to the rough wooden boards and listened.

Downstairs, the phone rang again. Then, a voice:

"Yeah, what do you want?" It was Smiley McDeath. She recognized his weirdly high-pitched gasp of a voice. "All right. Sure. Fine. No problem. It's all the same to me. Whatever he wants. We'll do it now."

A moment later there was another voice, thick, deep, dull. That was the Giant. He sounded like Frankenstein's monster. "What do they want now?"

"Another video."

"Another."

"Yes. Only they want us to torture her this time. Really make her beg for mercy."

"All right," said the Giant. "Whatever."

"Yes. Let me just wash up and get my tools and we'll get started."

That was the way they talked: casually, as if it were nothing to torture her, just another day's work: *Let me get my tools.*

Molly had thought she was afraid before, but now she understood: she had never really known fear, not this kind of fear. Why would she? She was a student, a university professor's daughter. She lived in a pleasant house with parents who loved each other and their children. She had a good-natured brother who wasn't even annoying, as brothers were supposed to be. She had only seen evil people in the movies: the villains in thrillers, the slashers in horror films. She knew such people existed in theory, but she'd never actually come across them in real life, and deep down she didn't believe in them. Even when the thugs came to get her, even when they kidnapped her out of the gym, she hadn't really thought they would do anything as bad as this. Deep down, she believed everyone had a conscience, everyone could be reasoned with.

But the way they spoke. The casual way they talked about hurting her. It shattered all those pretty ideas. Suddenly she knew: evil was real.

And it was coming for her.

What could she do? How could she fight them? There were four of them. Every one of them stronger than she was, and the Giant stronger than all the rest. She was tired. She was hungry. She was weak. She was afraid. What could she do? There was no chance for her. No hope.

She looked up at the ceiling as if she could see heaven through it. *You know my need*, she prayed. *Help me to be strong.*

The moment the prayer left her, she knew: She couldn't just sit there. She couldn't just wait for them to come. Anything was better than that. Anything was better than just letting it happen. She had to fight. Even if she lost. Even if they killed her. She had to try at least, no matter how bad the odds, no matter how completely she was outnumbered and overpowered. She had to do *something*.

Fighting off her weakness, she climbed to her feet. *A weapon*, she thought. It was her only hope. She couldn't do battle against these people hand to hand. She needed a weapon.

Her eyes scanned the bare room desperately. What was there? Nothing. Nothing at all. Not even a piece of furniture. The bars on the windows prevented her from breaking off a piece of glass. The plastic bucket was too light. What was there? What was there?

More voices downstairs.

"Should we bring the camera up like before?"

"No, we'll do it here. We'll bring her down."

Panic wildfired through her. They would be coming any minute. If only she had a weapon . . .

She looked down at the floor. A floorboard? Could she wrench one up? She dropped to her knees. She tried to get a handhold. Impossible. The boards were held solidly in place with heavy . . .

. . . nails!

Molly's desperate eyes went wide as she scanned the floor. Each board was held in place with heavy iron nails. If she could pry up one of those nails, at least she'd have something to strike with. She'd have a chance, anyway. A small chance, but a chance.

She moved her gaze from one end of the room to another, hoping to see one of the nails sticking up, loose, so she could pull it free. There were none. All of them were hammered in close to the wood, only their heads showing, flat against the boards.

Almost crazy with terror now, she tried to pull a nail out with her fingers. She could see at once it would be impossible. She could just barely get the tip of a fingernail under the head. If she pulled up on it, her fingernail would break.

Another voice spoke below. The Giant. He laughed. They were making jokes about what they were going to do to her.

Molly's breath squeaked as it squeezed out of her. If only she had something to use, something that would loosen the nail.

Kneeling there, she ran her hands over her clothes. They had left her nothing. Her pockets were empty. Her keys were gone. Her exercise outfit was all soft cloth, no zippers. The only other solid object she had was . . .

Her hairband! Her hand went up to it and she felt the two bobby pins that held it in place. Quickly, Molly yanked one of the pins out. Looked at it. Not much. Thin, flimsy, weak. But something. Something.

On her hands and knees, she worked the edge of the bobby pin's loop under the head of the floor nail. She wriggled it, trying to loosen the nail. The pin's metal was too soft. It bent. But she tried again. She worked it in deeper, trying to slip the loop around the head of the nail.

And she heard Smiley McDeath speak again, his eerie high-pitched voice coming up clearly through the floor.

"All right. I'm ready. Go get her and bring her down."

And the Giant answered in his thick, heavy voice: "Will do."

Molly's breathing was ragged and hard. She worked the pin's loop under the head of the floorboard nail. Her hair slipped out of the band again, spilled forward over her face, obstructing her view. Sweat poured into her eyes, blurring her vision. Her knees hurt. Her back hurt. The pin itself was digging into her fingers. Its weak metal was starting to shred.

And now she heard another noise below. A door opening. A heavy footstep. The Giant's footstep. He was stepping out into the downstairs hall. Coming for her.

She dug at the nail, sliding the pin back and forth.

Then, with a little jolt, the pin broke in half. Molly let out a tearful gasp. But without a moment's pause, she pulled the second

HOSTAGE RUN

bobby pin out of the hairband. She worked it under the nail as she had the first.

And all at once, the nail gave way! Just like that. It came loose in the wood.

With a little gasp, Molly tossed the bobby pin aside. She grabbed the nail head with her fingers. The iron bit into her skin as she pinched it tight, but she ignored the pain. She pulled and twisted, baring her teeth with the effort. Grunting.

Footsteps. Heavy footsteps in the downstairs hall. The Giant moving toward the stairs. Coming for her.

Molly gave a little cry and pulled harder. The nail wobbled and began to rise. Bit by bit, she worked it up out of the wood. Up it came. And then it came free.

The Giant reached the bottom of the stairs. She heard his heavy footsteps start to climb up toward the second floor, her floor.

Molly held the iron nail up in front of her eyes. It was big. Three inches long. Thick metal. Sharp point. Not exactly a dagger, but something. Something. If the Giant was coming alone . . . if she could take him by surprise . . . if she could deliver a painful blow . . . If, if, if.

But she had to try.

She shifted the nail in her hand so that the long shaft slid between her first two fingers. Slowly, she closed her hand into a fist, a fist with a nail pointing out of it. A weapon. Something she could fight with.

And she would. She would fight. You can't just stand by and let evil happen. She would fight with everything she had.

Thump, thump, thump. She heard the big thug's footsteps reach the top of the stairs. Now they started down the landing.

Wide-eyed with fear, Molly stared at her fist, at the nail, then lifted her gaze to the door. She had no idea whether she would have the courage for this. But she might. They were evil. They were coming for her. She just might.

She climbed to her feet.

Heavenly Father, give me strength. Give me the strength to do what I have to do.

The footsteps stopped just outside her door.

14. HUNTER

VICTOR ONE SAT quietly in the cab of his pickup truck. He was looking through the windshield at the main street of a small town on an ordinary winter's afternoon. Wilford was a quaint and homey little nowhere of a place. Redbrick and clapboard store-fronts. A diner, a clothes boutique, a news agent, a travel agency, and so on. Christmas wreaths decorated the lampposts. Christmas lights lined the windows. The few pedestrians out in the open hurried along the sidewalks with their hands jammed into their jacket pockets, and their chins tucked into their scarves against the cold. The gray sky lowered and the air smelled of snow.

For miles around this town, there was nothing. Empty fields and swamps and forests, cranberry bogs and wet wilderness loud with the cries of birds and frogs. Occasional mobile homes were planted in the middle of weeds and water. The odd gas station rose up here and there. There was not much more than that. It was a good place to hide.

Victor One sat very still and watched and waited. And he thought about Molly.

He didn't know the girl. He'd never met her. Never even seen her before he'd watched that video. But he couldn't get the video out of his mind. The image of her kneeling there on the floor while the thug behind the camera hissed commands at her like some sort of bullying snake . . . The courage she'd shown in the face of his nastiness . . . The defiance in her eyes . . . The presence of mind she had to put together that code, to send the message that had allowed them to trace her app, which had led them in turn to Wilford.

Not to mention the fact that she was extremely cute with those freckles on her soft cheeks and . . . well, never mind that.

The point was, the girl had touched him somehow. The girl, her predicament, her courage—all of it had touched him. Trained warrior though he was, Victor One was a very easygoing guy. It was almost impossible to get him angry. And really, you couldn't insult him badly enough to move him to violence. His fighting skills were something he used only on the battlefield, only to protect his own life or the lives of others. Where there was no serious physical threat, he would never raise his hand against anyone.

But ever since he had seen that video, he had been aware of a fire burning inside him, a fire that felt very much like a steady state of rage. The idea of this Molly girl in the clutches of those thugs . . . Well, it got to him, there was no denying it.

So he sat in the cab of the truck, and he looked out the windshield at the town, and he watched and he waited. He did not know exactly what he was looking for, but he knew he would know it when he saw it. This was the only town anywhere near Molly's last known location. It was the only place her kidnappers could come to get supplies. They would come eventually. And when they did, they would not look like the other people here. Victor One would know them on sight.

He lifted his right hand to the left side of his chest. He touched the bulge of the weapon there in the holster under his arm. A Glock 19. A square, ugly little pistol but his personal favorite nonetheless. Quick to aim and easy to fire, with a magazine that carried a generous fifteen bullets, plus the one in the chamber.

He would recognize the kidnappers when they came into town for supplies, he thought. He would follow them and he would find Molly and then . . .

Like Lawrence Dial, the Traveler, whom he was assigned to protect, Victor One was a Bible guy. He knew the book well. He liked to think of himself as more of a New Testament sort of fellow: loving; quick with compassion; ready to forgive even his enemy seventy times seven times.

But there were situations in which only the Old Testament would do. And right now, the quote that came to his mind was this one:

Woe to the wicked. Disaster is upon them! They will be paid back for what their hands have done.

He sat. He waited. It was a long time, almost nightfall, before his moment came, but when it came, there was no mistaking it. On this quiet street lined with parked pickups, family SUVs, and gas-saving compacts, a black BMW sedan pulled to the curb near the diner and stopped.

Victor One sat up straight in the pickup's cab, his blue eyes alight.

The sedan's door opened quickly. And, as storekeepers and housewives and Realtors and farmers hurried along the Main

Street sidewalk from one place to another, a trained killer emerged from behind the BMW wheel.

Victor One was a trained killer himself, and he knew one when he saw one.

The killer was wearing a heavy green flight jacket and black jeans. He was small and lithe. His face was narrow and pale. His eyes were watchful and cold. He swaggered from his car into the diner and came back out only a few minutes later carrying four white paper bags, greasy with the food inside them.

Because wherever they're holding her, they need to eat, thought Victor One. *And they're not the types to learn how to cook.*

He reached for the pickup's ignition and started the engine.

The killer returned to the black sedan. He opened the front door and leaned in to toss the food bags onto the passenger seat, then he lowered himself behind the wheel.

A moment later, the black sedan drove away.

Woe to the wicked, thought Victor One.

He put his truck in gear and followed.

15. RUN!

MOLLY THOUGHT THAT moment—that long moment before her cell door opened, before the Giant came in to take her downstairs to her agonizing fate—would forever after be the most frightening moment of her life. Even the suffering to come, she thought, could not be more terrifying than this, this suspense, this waiting. She did not think she could feel more fear than she was feeling right now.

But she was wrong about that.

Because the next moment, when the door opened, her fear grew even worse.

The Giant loomed in the doorway. He grinned at her. The terror that had seemed to fill her to overflowing now flared and exploded through her, filling her even more. She thought she was going to faint. She thought she might simply collapse to the floor and die.

But she did neither. She stood there, frozen to the spot. Her legs were quivering now like leaves in a strong wind, but she didn't lose consciousness. She wasn't lucky enough to lose consciousness. Instead, she was painfully, horribly aware of everything that was happening. Every second seemed to last for a year, and each was more dreadful than the one before. And she could not block any of it from her awareness.

The Giant might well have been the single biggest man she had ever seen, bigger even than the guys on the university football squad. Not just tall, but thick around. Not just thick but bulging with muscle. His face was chunky, long, and pale, and the look in his eyes was both stupid and cruel. Molly knew deep down that he would not only hurt her if she tried to resist him, he would be happy to hurt her. He would enjoy it.

The Giant ducked his head to keep from banging it on the lintel as he stepped into the room. His footsteps were so heavy that Molly felt the floor quake underneath her as he came. He approached her, and she couldn't move, couldn't. She just stood there, frozen, staring, watching him rise up in front of her, like a mountain rising out of the sea, until he filled her vision. His huge body. His cruel face. Grinning down at her.

"You're coming with me," he said in that deep, grumbling, thunderous voice. "They want you downstairs. Now."

Molly tried to answer him defiantly, but it was as if her voice had turned to ashes in her mouth. She tried to say, "Stay away from me," but the words came out a whisper, barely audible.

Her fear made the Giant's eyes sparkle. He reached out to grab her arm.

Terror flashed through her like lightning and gave her strength. She made her left hand into a claw and swept it at the thug's face, trying to scratch at his eyes.

The Giant barely moved in response. He batted her hand away as if he were flicking at a fly. Then, with the same motion, he wrapped his thick, powerful fingers around her throat. He gripped her neck and lifted her off the floor. Molly's feet kicked helplessly in the air as her breath was cut off. She was strangling. The Giant lifted her face up to his so that his grin was huge to her.

"I said, 'You're coming with me,'" he repeated.

Molly drove her fist—and the three-inch flooring nail that was sticking out of her fist—up under the Giant's chin.

The Giant's eyes went wide as the nail sank into him. His hand opened and Molly dropped to the floor. On impact, she sank down into a crouch, trying to keep her balance as she fell. Crouching there, she watched as the Giant staggered back, the room quaking underneath his footsteps. He gagged, clutching at the nail buried deep in his flesh. Blood flowed out through his fingers. He stumbled to one side, putting his free hand out for balance.

That left the door unblocked.

Molly sprang out of her crouch and ran.

The next wild moment she was in the hallway, a second-floor landing. Eyes wide, mind racing, she looked right, then left. She saw the stairs. She bolted for them. She heard a tremendous crash behind her and realized the Giant had fallen, dropped to the floor in the room behind her. She didn't look back. She just kept running.

She reached the top of the stairs. She had a brief, confused impression of the place she was in. A worn-out inn or hotel of some sort, with doors all along the landing. The paint was gone from the walls, the wood exposed, the light fixtures either stripped away or empty or carrying naked bulbs.

That was all she had time to notice. Then she was stampeding down the stairs, her hand lightly tracing the splintery banister to her side. A few steps and she saw the foyer beneath her. The front door. She could see trees at the sidelights. The outside. Freedom. She flew down the stairs toward it.

She was halfway to the bottom when Smiley McDeath stepped out in front of her.

He had heard the Giant fall. He came around the corner, stood at the base of the stairs, looked up, and started to call out, "What was that noise up . . . ?"

But he hadn't expected to see Molly barreling toward him.

Startled, he froze where he was for a second, his snaky diamond-shaped face a blank. He was wearing his usual black jeans and T-shirt, but he'd taken off his windbreaker and Molly could see the gun in the holster under his arm. His hand instinctively went for the weapon.

But Molly was now only a few steps above him. She grabbed hold of the banister with both hands so she could lift herself up, lift her leg up high and draw it all the way back.

She snapped her foot out hard and kicked Smiley McDeath in the face.

Smiley McDeath stopped smiling. Dazed by the blow, he fell backward and sat down. Molly, meanwhile, reeling from the force of her own kick, lost her balance. She stumbled helplessly over the last two stairs and fell onto the foyer floor, rolling past her captor.

Smiley McDeath was already climbing onto all fours, trying to stand. Blood was dripping from his mouth where Molly's sneaker had connected. His eyes were nearly white with rage.

Molly used the speed of her roll to jump to her feet. She was standing over Smiley as he tried to rise. She kicked him again, hard as she could, bringing her powerful volleyballer leg straight up off the floor and into the killer's chin.

It was such a powerful blow that Molly hoped the man would go flying backward and land unconscious—the way bad guys did in the movies. But that was in the movies. In real life, men are thick and heavy. They don't go flying anywhere very easily. Molly's kick connected well, but Smiley McDeath only let out a grunt and dropped down onto one knee.

That was enough, though, all Molly needed. She rushed to the door. She grabbed the knob, twisted it, pulled. The door flew open. The winter cold of the outside world flooded over her. Another step and she'd be over the threshold, out of here.

Smiley McDeath reached out and grabbed her ankle.

In her panic, Molly found the strength to pull free at once, but even as her foot slipped out of the man's grasp she felt herself spinning, tripping, falling. She went out the front door and toppled over the threshold. She hit the hard, cold dirt outside, the gray sky and naked branches twirling crazily above her.

The fall jarred her. It was a second before she recovered, before she leapt to her feet again. She was facing the building. It was an inn, in fact, she saw. Four stories, clapboard, once white, now weather-worn. Windows boarded up or black with broken glass.

She saw it for only an instant. Then she saw Smiley McDeath. He was on his feet, too. He was moving into the doorway. He was drawing the pistol from the holster on his belt. That weird, narrow face, pointy at top and bottom, was twisted with deadly determination.

Molly had only two choices: surrender or run. She ran without thinking. She turned her back on the gunman and dashed with all her speed across the dirt cul-de-sac. There was a car in front of her, a black sedan of some kind. She headed for it, expecting the crack of the gunshot every moment, the bullet in her spine.

She reached the car, grabbed the hood, flung herself over it—just as the first deadly blast sounded behind her.

The window of the car cracked and collapsed into fragments as the bullet struck. But Molly was unhurt. She went on flying over the hood. Landed on it, rolling. Rolled off and tumbled to the earth on the far side.

She heard Smiley McDeath let out a curse. The car was blocking his next shot. She heard him shout, "She's making a run!"

But she didn't look back to find out what happened next or how many thugs rushed to come after her. Crouching low to keep the car between herself and Smiley's gun, she raced off the cul-de-sac into the high grass, toward the deep, tangled forest beyond.

Another gunshot sounded behind her. The bullet whistled past her head. Bark exploded off the tree in front of her.

She did not slow down. She did not look back. She ran. Soon the winter woods surrounded her.

And she kept on running.

16. THE FOREST

FAVIAN WAS DYING. Rick took one look at him and knew.

The excitement of the chase was passing now. Rick was recovering from his wild escape from the wraiths, his tightrope walk over the energy bridge across the Canyon of Nothingness. He was catching his breath. His mind was clearing. When he was calm enough to take a good look at his friend's shifting, light-made face, he could see at once that the life was draining out of it.

The last time Rick had seen Favian—the last time he'd been in the MindWar Realm—Favian had seemed like a young man. Now, only two months later, the sparkling creature appeared to have aged bizarrely, even supernaturally. Favian still had the same boyishly worried expression, but his face had dried out and caved in somehow. It was collapsing into its own wrinkles like a balloon that was losing air.

Favian lay propped up on his elbows in the red grass, too weary to move. He stared dully out over the black canyon. Rick, sitting up, rested his arms on his raised knees. He did not know what to say. He knew that Favian was a fearful fellow, that he hated to think about the endless death that was hanging over his head here, over his head and Mariel's, too. Rick figured he already knew how close to that death he was. There was no point in talking about it.

127

So instead, he said, "What were those things?" as he lifted his chin to point at the retreating army of wraiths. "They were like vampire ghosts or something."

"Energy Wraiths," said Favian. Even his voice sounded creaky and old. "Kurodar sent them to clean up the ruins of the fortress after you blew it up. They sense the energy in the forms Kurodar created, and they drain it until the forms are gone. Your energy must be so much more powerful than the energy of broken stones. They sensed you there and came after you to drain you."

"What about this?" said Rick, gesturing toward the canyon.

"Kurodar put that there to keep the wraiths in check," Favian told him. "That's what I think, anyway. He didn't want them to spread out over the whole Realm and devour everything he's made."

Rick remembered dangling off the energy bridge. He remembered that feeling that he was being sucked down into the nothingness beneath his feet.

"It felt . . . ," he began. "It almost felt . . . alive somehow. The darkness. Like it was trying to pull me in."

Favian nodded weakly. "Yes. I've felt that too. This place—the Realm—it can be pretty to look at sometimes. The red grass; the yellow sky; the blue trees. But underneath that, I think it's all darkness. I think darkness is the heart of the place, and the darkness wants to devour everything. It even wants to make you part of itself. I guess pretty soon, I won't be able to fight it anymore. Pretty soon, the darkness will have me."

There it was. Spoken aloud, out in the open. Favian was dying the living death of the Realm. Rick stole a quick glance at him. He could see the fear embedded deep in his eyes—fear and desperate hope because he, both he and Mariel, believed that Rick was some kind of hero who had come to rescue them.

Rick looked away, embarrassed. He tilted his head back and gazed up at the yellow sky just to have something else to look at. "I brought you some energy," he said. It was all he could offer for now. "There's enough for you and for Mariel. It should help keep you going for a while, anyway."

"For a while," Favian repeated in his strangely distant and echoic voice. "But not for long." It was an unspoken accusation: Rick had not turned out to be the hero they had hoped for; not yet at least. "My energy is draining faster now. And once death comes, it'll never end. I'll be part of the darkness here for as long as the Realm exists."

Rick didn't know how to answer. He wanted to say: *My father is working on bringing you out.* And he wanted to say: *I've been trying to find out the truth about you.* He wanted to say: *No matter what happens, I promise I won't forget you.* But everything he wanted to say just sounded lame and empty. Cheap encouragement without any real meaning. If he were really a hero, as Mariel had said, he would have found a way to save them by now.

Rick turned to his friend. Favian's sparkling blue form wavered and shifted like smoke in a swirling breeze. In one sense, the man hardly seemed to be there at all, seemed more like a phantom than a person. But in another sense, Rick felt his presence strongly: he understood his anxiety, his sorrow, his fear.

Rick lifted his left hand—the hand with the energy pod pulsing red and shiny under the skin.

"Well," he said, "let me give you some of this. It'll make you feel better."

But Favian shook his head slowly. "Not here. Not now. The longer we stay out in the open, the more energy we expend, the more likely we are to draw Kurodar's attention. Once he knows we're here, he'll start sending security bots. You remember the Spider-Snake, right?"

"Right, right," said Rick. He did remember, and he shuddered at the thought of the hideous creature who had chased him through the forest and nearly devoured him. And now he had to think about Molly, too. If Kurodar detected his presence here, the kidnappers would kill her. "You're right," he said. "We should hide ourselves first. Where can we go?"

"Help me up," said Favian. "I have a place. I'll take you there."

Rick got to his feet. He reached down and Favian reached up. The touch of Favian's insubstantial hand was like a low electric hum going up Rick's arm and through his body. Rick tugged and Favian rose slowly to his feet.

"This way," Favian said.

And he flashed off—a blue streak—yards away before Rick could even think to be surprised at his speed.

They traveled that way over the red grass, under the yellow sky, Favian streaking away and Rick jogging after him. Up ahead, a misty blue expanse of trees appeared and Rick realized they were heading for a forest, another blue forest like the one in which he and Favian had first met.

It was a relief when they reached the tree line, when they ducked under the aquamarine leaves and the greenish trunks rose up on every side of them. Rick supposed it was silly to think that Kurodar couldn't find them here eventually. The whole MindWar Realm grew out of his imagination, after all. Every place must be accessible to his consciousness. Still, he felt safer in the forest.

They traveled through the woods a long time. Rick felt the pressure of the passing seconds. He was painfully aware of the clock in his palm ticking away. He remembered Miss Ferris's instructions: don't waste time on his friends; just find Kurodar's new outpost before the terrorist could launch his devastating attack. Rick forced her words out of his mind. It was bad enough that he could not rescue Favian. He wouldn't add insult to injury by telling him to hurry up. He followed in silence.

Finally, they came to a cottage. It was strange to see it there. It looked different from everything around it. It was made of sawn logs and thatched branches. The green-brown wood had dried out and turned a wondrous pinkish-gold. The place almost seemed to glow.

"You built this?" Rick asked, catching up to where Favian had flashed ahead. They both paused there outside the cottage's stone gate. Rick leaned forward to catch his breath, his hands on his knees.

Favian nodded in answer. His strangely old-young face had turned wistful at the memory. "I knew I would need a place to hide until . . ." He didn't finish the sentence, but Rick knew: he was going to say *until I died*. "So I built this. It was something I'd seen somewhere. Something I remembered from RL . . . but I don't know what exactly."

Rick gazed at the cottage. It looked like an illustration from a book of fairy tales. Something from Favian's childhood maybe, something from that life in RL that the sparkling man could no longer remember.

Then a darkness came over Rick's heart, like a cloud inside him. And he realized what Favian had said: *I knew I would need a place . . . I built this . . .*

I, not we.

"What about Mariel?" Rick asked him. "Where is she?"

But Favian only shook his head in answer. The expression on his face was so sad that Rick felt his heart grow even darker. But before he could ask another question, Favian flashed away again: to the cottage door and through, out of sight.

Rick hurried after him.

The first thing he saw inside the cottage was a portal: a glowing purple diamond of energy floating just off the floor.

"I built the cottage around this," Favian told him. "In case you came back."

The unspoken accusation again: *In case you came back as you promised you would.*

The rest of the cottage was small and sparsely furnished. Only one room. A heavy wooden bed against one wall, a wooden table and chairs under the window. A stove. A basin.

"Looks . . . comfy," Rick said. In fact, the place was melancholy and lonely-looking.

Favian nodded sadly. "I wish I could remember where I'd seen a cottage like this before. There was a woman who told me about it, I think. I remember her voice."

Probably his mother, Rick thought. *Reading to him from a book of fairy tales.* But all he said out loud was, "Come on, let's get some of this Happy Juice into you. Give you some strength."

He drew the broken sword from his belt. Once more, as his fingers closed around her image on the hilt, he felt Mariel's warmth and energy rise through him. Before he could think too much about it, he pressed the jagged blade against the pulsing red spot in his left palm and plunged it in. There was a flash of pain and then he felt the energy start to flow out of him like blood.

"Quick," he said, "high five."

He raised his glowing hand and Favian raised his and they struck their palms together, red against blue.

The effect was instantaneous and remarkable. Rick could feel the energy pulsing from his hand into Favian's. He could see Favian growing fresher, younger, stronger before his very eyes. With every heartbeat, Favian's sagging face seemed to flush with new youth and vibrancy. In moments, the wrinkles and the heaviness and weariness were gone from him entirely. He straightened and grew strong.

Rick had an internal sense of how much energy there was, like a meter in his brain. When half the supply was gone, he pulled his hand away.

Favian staggered back, gasping. He lifted his chin and spread his arms wide, glorying in the fresh life passing through him.

"Oh! It's like growing young!" he cried.

Rick sheathed his sword and pressed his two palms together to stop the energy flow and preserve what was left. "I have to save some for Mariel."

At the mention of Mariel's name, Favian dropped his arms to

his sides. The joy that had flooded his face for a moment receded, and the sorrow and anxiety came back into his expression.

"What?" said Rick tensely. "What is it?"

"Rick . . . ," said Favian. "Listen . . ."

"What? Tell me."

Favian averted his eyes. "It's Mariel."

"What about her?"

"She's . . . she's gone."

At once the darkness in Rick's heart turned to anger. He was a hot-blooded guy, and he'd never had much control over his temper. He had seen what death was like in the Realm. He had seen the dried-out shell of a creature lying in the Spider-Snake's tunnel, its body shrunken and empty like a snake's shed skin, but the eyes—the horrible eyes—still alive and glowing with the pain of slow decay. He had seen the poor creature's desperate yearning to be freed from Kurodar's mind prison, freed into true death and the life beyond. The thought of Mariel being trapped like that, dead like that, suffering like that, hit him in his core like a blow.

He stepped close to Favian, his eyes flashing, his teeth gritted and bared.

"It's not true!" he said.

"Rick . . ." Favian still wouldn't look at him directly.

"You're lying, Favian."

"You have to understand . . ."

"She's still here. I know she is. I can feel her spirit in the sword."

"You can't help her anymore."

"Tell me where she is."

"She . . . she wants you to forget her. She made me promise . . ."

In his fury, Rick tried to grab his friend by the shirtfront. He felt only the electric buzz of Favian's presence as his hand somehow slipped past him. In an instant, Favian had flashed away across the room so that the portal floated and glowed between them.

"Tell me!" Rick shouted in rage and frustration.

"There's nothing you can do!" the blue man cried out.

"You're lying!" Rick yelled again, taking a step after him. "Tell the truth! She's still here! I've got to find her. I've got to help her!"

Favian's voice grew high and thin with strain. "She doesn't want your help! She doesn't want you to see her!"

"I don't care. Take me to her."

"She . . ."

"I don't care! Take me!"

The two men stared at each other across the portal. Favian was the weaker personality. He turned away first. He looked down at the floor.

"You won't like what you see."

Even Rick was startled by the strangled sound of his own voice. "Take me to her!"

Wearily, sadly, Favian nodded.

"All right," he said. "Come on."

17. POOL

THEY WENT BACK out of the cottage and through the woods, Favian flashing ahead and Rick jogging after. Rick's eyes were now hot and bright with fear and determination: fear of what he was going to see; determination to do something about it. Nothing would stop him from helping Mariel. Not even Mariel herself.

The woods seemed to grow darker around them as they traveled. The leaves above grew thicker, blocking out the buttery light of the sky. The tree trunks became more twisted and the tortuous branches interlocked in a grim weave-work that seemed to press in on them from every side. They were in what appeared to be a haunted forest now, a place more indigo than aquamarine, a tangle of hidden corridors draped in a permanent night full of shadows.

Here Favian finally came to a stop. Standing straight, full of fresh energy, his shifting blue form was bright in the gloom. He watched as Rick approached. He said nothing. He simply lifted his hand; pointed.

Rick, catching up to him where he stood, followed the gesture. He saw a small hollow: a clearing at the center of low, dead, interlacing trees. A strange sickly mist spread over the space.

And through the mist, Rick saw a dark pool of water.

He felt something inside him grow heavy and afraid. Water was Mariel's element. She lived in it, moved in it. It formed her and carried her from place to place. But until now, she had always occupied the Realm's vital, silver, mercurial lakes. She had been silver, flashing and mercurial herself. But this—this pool—the water here—was thick and brackish. There was still a metallic sheen to it, but it was as if the metal had become oily and rusted.

What was worse—much worse—was that as Rick stood there staring at the pool, as he stood trying to work up the courage to go near it, a voice seemed to bubble up out of its depths, a sound that was half a whisper and half a cry. The voice broke through the water's surface and spread through the mist and, like the mist, hung in the air all around him. The hollow was filled with its mournful noise.

Rick could not make out any words. But Favian apparently understood. The blue man flinched and drew back from the edge of the clearing. His anxious eyes grew even more anxious and he called out, "He made me do it! He made me bring him here! He wouldn't stay away."

"Mariel?" said Rick, breathless.

He stepped forward into the hollow. Dead leaves, some blue, some red, some golden, crunched beneath his sneakers.

The sorrowful noise continued to rise from the pool. It continued to spread out through the mist, growing thinner and thinner, dimmer and dimmer. Then, suddenly, like an elastic band pulled to its limits, it snapped back into itself, coming together in a faint echo of Mariel's rich, resonant, musical voice.

"Stay away!" she moaned.

But Rick didn't even pause. He kept moving into the hollow, moving toward the pool. "I'm here to help you, Mariel," he said. "I've brought energy. Like I did before."

The sound boiled out of the water again, spread through the mist again, and again it snapped together so that she answered him like an echo: "Stay away!"

Her melancholy tone made Rick hesitate, but only for a second. Then he told her, "I won't," and he kept walking forward.

Now he was deep in the mist. It surrounded him. He felt its clammy cold clinging to his skin. More than that: He felt her—Mariel—as if she were inside the haze itself, as if she were part of it. He felt dampness clinging to him as if it were her fingers trying to hold him, trying to draw him back from the edge of the pond.

Her voice, like the mist, seemed to be everywhere. "I don't want you here, Rick."

"You helped me," he insisted, still coming forward. "So many times. The sword you gave me. The armor. The things you told me about the Realm. I'd be dead if it weren't for you, Mariel."

"Then do what I tell you. Stay away."

"I won't. You helped me and now I'm going to help you. Let me help you, Mariel."

"No!" cried the mist, and it clung to him but it didn't have the strength to hold him back. He reached the edge of the water. The mist seemed to quiver with Mariel's anguished cry: "Please!"

"Let me help you."

"Please! No! Don't look at me!"

"I will."

And he did. He peered into the brackish depths of the pool and he saw her there.

For two months he had been thinking about her, even dreaming about her. For two months her image had been in his mind. Her high, noble, warrior beauty. The grace of her silver form, her steadying wisdom and the gentleness in her eyes. Lying in his bed at night, he had imagined her floating in the dark above him. He had asked himself: Who was she? What was she? Did he love her? Could he?

Two months. It was only two months since he had seen her last. And this was what she had become.

Her image floated like a corpse in the water, just beneath the murky surface. It dissolved in passing ripples and re-formed as the pond grew still. It was the image of an old woman—no, an ancient hag. Mariel had been drained not only of her youthful beauty, but of every vestige of vitality. She was like a withered plant; a near-dead thing. Her high cheeks had caved in on themselves, and so had her full figure. Her once-flowing hair hung like weeds around the shriveled remnants of her features. Her arms were knotted twigs and her fingers trembled, shimmering. Her eyes—once noble and compassionate—were now full of nothing but death and anguish.

Rick had tried to prepare himself for what he would see. He had known it was going to be bad. But nothing could have readied him for this. One look at her and he caught his breath and had to turn away. He lifted his eyes to the tangled branches that blocked out the yellow sky above him.

Seeing his reaction to her, Mariel cried out in pain. Her wail became the mist and the mist echoed with pain all around him.

Rick's weakness lasted only a moment, though. He recovered quickly. He marshaled his strength—his strength and his courage both—and lowered his eyes to her again and looked at her directly.

"Just let me die!" she cried up to him out of the depths of the pool.

"No," he said quietly. "Never."

"I'm so horrible! I can't live like this. Look—look at what's happened to me! I'm horrible. Look."

He did look. He refused to remove his gaze from her again. "You'll never be horrible," he told her. "Not to me." Only after he had forced himself to say this—for her sake—did he realize it was also true. His first reaction—his dismay—was over, and he was only sad for her now; sad for her and for himself as well; for what he'd lost; for what he might now lose forever. But then, he told himself, this was the way things were, whether here in the Realm or back in RL. Beauty withered. People died. You just had to remember: withered—even dead—they were still who they were—always.

She was still Mariel, even now.

This time, when he put his hand on the hilt of his sword, when her energy ran up into him, it was not the majestic force it had been before. Instead, he felt the full flow of her sorrow. It touched him. In a funny way, it made him feel closer to her. She had been so much like a spirit to him before, so queenly and powerful. Now, in her pain—and in her embarrassment at the way she looked—she was more . . . well, real. More human. More like a girl he might know.

He drew the sword.

"Save your energy," the mist whispered around him. "Save it for Favian. You can't help me anymore."

He didn't even bother to answer her. Rick's hot nature may have given him a quick temper, but it also made him immovable when he set his mind to something: immovably loyal, immovably determined, immovably courageous. He would not turn away from Mariel again.

"Give me your hand," he said gently.

"Let me alone, Rick."

He knelt down by the side of the pool. "Give me your hand."

He took the broken blade and pressed the point against his palm again, against the old wound that had barely healed.

"Don't . . . ," said Mariel through the mist.

But he ignored her. He reopened his palm. The red energy began pulsing out of him.

"Your hand," he said. "Quickly."

And he thrust his own glowing hand into the pool.

The water was cold and not just cold, but deathly chill, as if the chill of Mariel's fading life had poisoned it. The red energy in Rick's palm flashed with his pulse and the water glowed with the flash and grew dark then glowed again. With each new beat, Mariel's aged, tormented face turned bloodred then sank away into the watery shadows.

"Give me your hand," Rick insisted. "Don't let this go to waste."

Slowly, and with an obvious effort, she lifted one dwindled arm. Rick felt her twig-like fingers intertwine with his. Then their hands were together and she gasped as the energy pulsed out of him and into her.

Rick also felt something spreading through him—something good—some warmth and gladness. What he saw as he gazed down into the pool seemed to him almost like a miracle. With each beat of his heart, with each fresh pulse of energy out of his palm and into hers, Mariel's youth and beauty and majesty returned to her. Her hair grew lush, her cheeks grew high and proud again, her figure re-formed into the figure of a young woman. Within moments she was again as he remembered her. And when the last of the energy had flowed out of him, he found a strong hand entwined with his own. Even the pool's color had changed. The murky water had cleared and become silvery so that he could barely make Mariel out through his own reflection.

Then suddenly, with a prismatic splash, she blossomed up out of the depths and hung in the air before him, silver and tall and graceful and powerful once again.

For another moment, she kept his hand in hers. Still kneeling on the ground, he lifted his eyes to look up at her. Everything inside him and all around him seemed suspended, as if time held still. She was so beautiful.

She released him. Her voice did not dissipate in the mist anymore. It was as it had been: resonant and flowing like echoed music.

"You should have left me, Rick," she told him gently. "You should have stayed away as I told you to."

He shook his head. "That's just not happening," he said. "Not now. Not ever. Just not; it's not."

She tried not to smile down at him, but she did. "Well, thank you then."

Her smile made his heart swell. He sheathed the sword in his belt. He rose to his feet.

Mariel drew a breath, a fresh breath. Rising above the pond, she turned her majestic head and looked across the hollow to where Favian stood, watching. The mist all around them was dissipating. The air was clearing. Favian nodded to her. She nodded back.

She forced her smile away. She looked down at Rick, serious.

"You'd better come with us at once," she said. "There's not much time. And there's something you have to see."

18. WARCRAFT

A MOMENT LATER, she was gone. Where Mariel had been, there was only a sparkling silver shower shot through with rainbows. Her form had spilled back down into the pool.

For the first time Rick noticed that there was a small stream trickling away beneath the hollow's fallen leaves. As he watched it, the stream rose and burbled and frothed—and he knew that Mariel was flowing into it. Before Rick could even take a step to follow her, Favian flashed after her. Rick followed him.

They moved through the forest swiftly. The stream grew broader and bigger up ahead. Its silver water rippled and lathered wherever Mariel passed through. Favian was right behind her, a blue glow streaking from place to place. And then came Rick, racing over the forest duff, the leaves crunching under his sneakers as he dodged between the green-brown trunks of trees.

The three soon emerged from the haunted darkness in which Mariel had been hiding herself. They came back into the bluer, brighter woods. Within minutes, the dense forest was thinning out around them. Rick looked ahead and saw the yellow sky appear through the thinning branches.

Another minute and they broke out of the forest completely. Rick jogged over a brief stretch of red grass and then pulled up short as he came to a sudden cliff, a broad ridge made entirely of quartz-like stone that glittered and flashed in the yellow light. The stream, almost a river now, poured over the ledge and tumbled down in a roaring waterfall. The quartz sparkled beneath the swift flow.

Beyond the ridge a broad vista spread to the far horizon: a vast plain of scarlet grass crisscrossed by winding quartz roads twinkling in the light. All the roads led to one place: the soaring skyscrapers, spires, and domes of the Golden City. They rose darkly against the yellow sky, surprisingly close.

At the edge of the cliff, just where the silver water frothed and roared over the ridge, Mariel appeared again. She bubbled up out of the raucous flow. She hovered in the air, her silver substance catching all the colors around her, the blue of the forest at her back, the glitter of the quartz beneath her, the yellow of the sky above, the scarlet of the plain beyond.

As Rick looked up at her, entranced—joyful that he had raised her from near death—she made a graceful gesture with one watery hand, sweeping it out toward the distance.

Rick thought she was pointing at the city skyline.

"Right, I know," he said. "You told me last time. The Golden City—it's the heart of this place and its battery—and it's full of the ghosts and horrors of Kurodar's imagination—and I'm going to have to destroy it if I want to bring the MindWar to an end. See, I was paying attention."

"And it's all true, Rick," said Mariel—and Rick could have sworn he caught a new note in her voice, a thrilling new tone of tenderness. Or maybe that was just wishful thinking on his part.

"But that's not what I want to show you," she went on. "Before you can enter the Golden City, before you can do anything else, you're going to have to destroy Kurodar's new machine. And you're going to have to do it soon, before he uses it to unleash a fresh attack on Real Life."

Rick's eyes followed her gesture again. But what was she pointing at? There was nothing there. Nothing but the red plain, the Golden City, the yellow sky. He glanced up at her again.

"I don't see any new machine," he said.

"Wait," said Mariel, her voice an echoing music. "It crosses this place every two hours to take in fresh energy and supplies. It'll be here any minute now. Watch."

Rick's gaze lingered on her beautiful face another moment—and he could tell she knew he was looking at her, though she didn't glance down at him. Finally, he drew his eyes away and turned in the direction she was pointing.

A quiet second passed, then another. Then it began.

He felt it before he saw it. There was a drop in the temperature. The air turned chill—that sort of chill that eats into you, that makes your very bones go cold. And more than that. The cold air began to snap and shimmer. Rick's hair stiffened on his head, as if electricity were going through him.

Next, the sky began to change. Lavender cloud-like patches grew out of its yellow depths. They billowed and grew and joined together, thickening into the deep murky texture of thunderheads. The color drained out of everything below. Red grass, blue forests, sparkling quartz roads, and mountains and the amber sky all sank into one sickly greenish-purple gloom. A wind rose, stirring the

ANDREW KLAVAN

plain, swirling over the ridge, passing across Rick's skin and making him shiver as the goose bumps came out.

The wind, the cold, the electric shimmer, the gathering dark: Rick tensed as he felt the thing coming. It was almost here. Almost . . .

A moment later it began to rumble up over the edge of the world. Vast—it was unimaginably vast. The whole Realm muttered and shook and purple lightning flashed through the darkness as it kept rising and rising until it seemed it would blot out the sky completely.

It was a thing of nightmares. At its core, there was a black oblong mothership. It spread from one end of the horizon to the other. Orange and blue lights flashed and flickered all across it, like window-glow from a distant city. And surrounding the disk, overtopping it, blending into it, so that they seemed to be one thing, there was . . . he couldn't name it: some enormous beast, its tentacles waving and undulating over half the world below. It was like an octopus, only its face was malevolent and repulsively human: a man's face of enormous proportions that, like the tentacles, seemed inseparable from the black ship itself. Rick wasn't sure why, but the face seemed familiar to him somehow. Its skin had a greenish tinge, blotted with patches of dripping red. And its eyes—that was the worst of it, its eyes . . . they were huge and burning with murderous fury. And he had seen them somewhere before.

Something rose into Rick's throat. He felt nauseous and weak at the sight of this living battleship. He was supposed to get onto that? Destroy that? How, exactly? The thing was as big as the city beneath it; it was bigger! Almost as big as the digital heavens.

The whole ridge shook under Rick's feet as the ship kept rising. Loud, crackling, electric jolts shot up out of the towers and spires of the Golden City, shot past the huge wavering tentacles and connected with the oblong ship's edge. Visible within the flashing lines of light were bulky blimp-shaped crafts moving up from the city, riding the energy to the craft above. As the first of the blimps reached the black battleship and entered it, the ship glowed an even deeper black. The whole vista flashed and sizzled and roared as Rick and Mariel and Favian stood at the edge of the waterfall, openmouthed, staring.

Rick didn't know how long they stood like that. The ship passed overhead with what seemed titanic slowness. At one point the Octo-Guardian's great tentacles were right above them, their undulating forms so huge, their slimy scales so close, Rick was afraid the beast might reach down and grab them all and carry them off. All the while the flashing of energy carried a long caravan of oblong energy ships upward from the city to the craft. The roar of engines and the burr of the electric dark filled the air.

When finally the battleship moved on over the trees—when finally the great lightning-like shocks began to flag and fizzle out—when the purple darkness of the sky began to recede and the yellow light began to shine through again—when the air grew calm and still—Rick let out a long breath. He felt as if he had been holding it in his lungs for over an hour.

Except for the rush of the falls, it was quiet. Rick and Favian stood in silence, Mariel hovering over them. Rick could not think of a thing to say—or at least could think of nothing to say that wouldn't reveal his deep sense of anxiety and helplessness. How on earth was he going to get to that monstrous battleship, get past those tentacles, stop Kurodar from launching his new attack? Impossible. It was impossible.

He lifted his eyes to Mariel, hoping his fears weren't written on his expression. His lips parted as he tried to find some brave or hopeful words for her.

But it was Mariel who spoke. "Your sword," she said. She gestured toward him.

Rick looked down at the hilt of the sword sticking out of his belt, the image on it: her image. He drew it, held it up to her. "What about it?" he said.

Mariel gestured again, lowering her hand to the jagged, shattered blade. As Rick watched—and before he could stop her from expending the energy—a portion of her substance flowed out of her fingers and covered the broken sword in fresh metal. In a moment, as if by magic, the sword was whole again, a long, sleek weapon shining in the light.

Rick raised his eyes from the blade to Mariel. It was a beautiful sword, he wanted to tell her, but still, it was not going to be enough against that monstrous ship.

But before he could say anything, he felt a twinge on his palm. Then another.

The timer! It was sounding an alarm.

A silver sheath had appeared on his belt: another gift from Mariel. He slipped the sword into it and looked down at his palm. The numbers were ticking away the last five minutes. He had to get out of the Realm quickly or his mind would begin to disintegrate.

"You have to go now," Mariel told him gently. "Favian will take you back to the cottage. There's a portal there. Go."

LEVEL THREE:

RL

19. SINS OF THE FATHERS

IN HIS DREAM, those tentacles were wrapped around him. He twisted and turned in their muscular grasp, but he couldn't get free. He pushed desperately against the slimy snake-like skin, but the vile, enormous human face above him laughed at his weakness. Its hate-filled eyes shone blindingly bright.

All around him was the dark—that absolute dark he remembered from the Canyon of Nothingness—that living black that wanted to drag him into its depths, to consume him and make him part of itself.

The tentacles squeezed tighter around his waist. They coiled around his legs so that he couldn't even try to kick free, but was held fast like a fly waiting to be devoured by a spider. And as Rick felt the breath slowly squeezed out of him, he looked down and saw with horror that the thing was . . . *transforming him!* His skin was changing . . . becoming slimy . . . scaly . . . and even as his hands pushed against the tentacle's grip, it became harder and harder for him to tell where his hand ended and the tentacle began . . . The scales were climbing up his arms, covering his chest, rising over his neck . . . He could feel his face beginning to morph into something unimaginably dreadful and reptilian.

That was when he woke up, his breath catching in his throat, his eyes flashing open. Where was he? He sat up quickly.

Through shadows, he saw his black jeans crumpled on the rug. The football poster on the wall. The window with the sunlight gleaming through the break in the curtains. The messy desk with the computer on it. The workout equipment and weights piled in the corner.

His room. He was in his room. It was late. Late afternoon. He'd slept most of the day away.

His breath began to steady. His hands went to his thighs as he became aware of the old familiar pain in his legs. It all came back to him. The MindWar Realm. The wraiths in the ruins. The bridge across the black canyon. Favian's cottage. Mariel in the pond . . .

And that thing! That nightmare thing, half battleship, half beast. His sense of fear and helplessness at the sight of it, its tentacles waving over half the sky. And that face. Those eyes. So horrifying and yet so familiar.

Rick's lips parted. Suddenly he realized where he'd seen the Octo-Guardian's face before.

It was the face of the Troll! The Troll on the video. The ugly little man who had kidnapped Molly!

He had to tell his father. If that Octo-Guardian and the Troll were somehow related, then . . . well, maybe there was some direct connection between where Molly was and the Realm. Maybe if he could get on board that ship, he could help locate her.

It came to him all at once that while he was sleeping, he had somehow begun to formulate a plan. He remembered those blimp-like ships that had risen out of the city, that had traveled upward on lightning bolts to enter the mothership above. If he could get into one of those things somehow. If he could ride it upward. Get inside the WarCraft . . .

Ignoring the dull ache in his legs, he tried to leap out of bed, but he was stopped cold by a fresh pain, a sharp stab in his forehead, right behind his eyes. Oh yeah, he'd forgotten about those headaches. Wow, this was a bad one, too. Going into the Realm definitely was not good for his health.

But too bad. Football players live in pain all the time. You just suck it up, brother, that's all. That's what he had to do now. Suck it up and get going.

He threw the coverlet back and got out of bed, unsteady on his feet, his head throbbing. Leaning against the edge of the bed to keep himself from falling, he hobbled around it to his desk. There was an Advil bottle somewhere in that mess. There it was, under a day-old pair of underwear. He shook a couple of tablets out and shot them to the back of his throat, washing them down with his own saliva.

Bracing himself against the desk, he sighed. At least no one had found out about these attacks yet; no one was trying to keep him from reentering the Realm.

He gathered his strength again. His father. He had to find his dad.

He half hopped, half walked to the window. Drew back the curtains. A groan escaped him as the late light hit his eyes and pain lanced up from his eyebrows to his hairline. He rubbed his temple with one hand. The headache was so distracting, it was a moment before he realized what he was looking at.

Rick's bedroom was on the first floor of the two-story house. The family had arranged it that way so he wouldn't have to climb the stairs with his bum legs. Just outside his window, there was a little orchard of apple trees, all clustered together. They nearly blocked the view of the barbed-wire fence that surrounded the compound.

And Rick saw his father there. He was standing right there, under the trees. He was talking to a woman. She was about his father's age, but whereas Rick's dad, in his absentmindedness, was kind of sloppy and disheveled in a ratty old fleece with a black watch cap pulled down over his bald head, the woman was elegant and even (for a woman her age, Rick thought) kind of beautiful. She had golden-blond hair, worn short and swept back from her thin, sophisticated features. She had a long, lean figure like a model in a magazine, and she wore what even Rick recognized was a fashionably short coat, clipped at the waist, with big buttons running down the center.

He guessed who she was the minute he saw her. Leila Kent. His father's old girlfriend from college. She worked for the State Department now, a liaison with the country's intelligence departments, including the MindWar Project. When his father's work had first caused him to stumble upon the MindWar Realm, when he realized that he could create a system by which the United States could send agents into Kurodar's cyber territory, he had contacted Leila, his old flame. She—and Commander Mars—had been so afraid of Kurodar's capabilities, so fearful that Kurodar would be able to reach into any computer or phone, discover any secret, hack and destroy all of Lawrence Dial's work, they had convinced the scientist to go into hiding. Rick's dad had left his family with only a note—a note suggesting that he had run off with Leila. Lawrence Dial had hoped this secrecy would protect his family from the vengeance of Kurodar and the Axis Assembly.

It hadn't, at least not much. It hadn't prevented the attack that shattered Rick's legs, for instance, or the break-in by a gunman who nearly killed them all . . . And what the Dial family had suffered emotionally, meanwhile, believing the father of the house had abandoned them . . . Rick still didn't like to think about that. Being without his dad when he had lost the use of his legs—when he had lost his promising future as a college quarterback—it had left Rick empty inside. He'd lost his confidence. He'd lost his drive. He'd lost his faith. He'd become bitter, solitary, angry.

He was still angry, even now. Even now after he'd begun to work his way back to some kind of inner stability, after his battles in the MindWar had restored some of his confidence in himself. Even now, seeing his father out there under the apple trees with Leila Kent made a flame of irritation rise and dance in his belly.

What's more, as he looked out the window, it was painfully clear to him (as it was clear to almost everyone who saw them together) that Leila Kent was still in love with his father. He could see it in the way she gazed up at him, the way her hand kept reaching for him as she spoke, the way she touched her hair when he answered her. And what was his father feeling, Rick wondered. What would any man feel—even an absentminded professor like his dad—to have such a beautiful woman crushing all over him like that?

Rick took a long breath to ease his anger. He wasn't going out there in the middle of that. He would have to wait to tell his father about the Octo-Troll.

There was a knock on the door behind him. As he turned, the door swung in and there stood his kid brother, Raider. The nine-year-old was still wearing the sweatpants and Dark Knight T-shirt he had used for pajamas. His round freckled face was as bright and eager as always. What was with the kid? Did he never have a dark thought—ever? He should leave his joy to science so they could bottle it!

"Hey, Rick! You're finally awake! Cool! You wanna have breakfast! Mom said she'd make another breakfast 'cause you slept through the last one! She said she'd make french toast! Cool, right?"

Rick couldn't even pretend to match his enthusiasm—it just wasn't in him—but he managed a smile, even through his headache.

"Cool," he said. "I'll be right there."

All the while Rick was eating his french toast, he watched his mom. It was she who had told him the story of Leila, the story of his father's college romance. Leila was a smart, ambitious woman who had always wanted a big career. Over time, she had come to realize that being married to an absentminded genius like Lawrence Dial would be a full-time job in itself, especially once there were a couple of kids to take care of. That wasn't the future she pictured for herself. So she and Lawrence had parted ways and eventually Rick's mom had become . . . well, Rick's mom.

When Rick's dad left home, leaving that note, Rick had thought his mom was devastated. She lost her energy. She stopped taking care of herself. She pretty much stopped smiling altogether. But as it turned out, she had understood the situation a lot better than Rick. She had trusted the man she loved. She knew him well enough to figure out what he was up to—or at least part of it—and she had held on to her faith, even in her distress.

But what did it do to her inside? Rick wondered angrily. How did it feel now to have her husband out there under the apple trees, chatting away with the beautiful Leila? What was she thinking? Feeling? As far as Rick could tell, she seemed fine with it. She seemed perfectly calm, relaxed. She was going about her business, moving from the table to the counter and the sink, cleaning up the breakfast dishes, putting away the food, murmuring "Mm-hm," whenever there was a break in Raider's near-constant chatter. In general, she seemed her usual peaceful and contented self.

Well, maybe she was good with the whole thing, but it still annoyed Rick.

Now Raider's fork clattered down onto his empty plate. The boy had consumed what must've been an entire loaf of french toast and was now looking around as if he might start eating the furniture next. Which would not have surprised Rick all that much.

"Go upstairs and put some clothes on," their mother said. She was at the sink, with her back to them, but she glanced over her shoulder at Raider. "It's almost night already. Just because it's Christmas break doesn't mean you can turn into a hobo."

Raider was polishing off another glass of milk when she said this and, for some reason, the remark made him laugh so hard he snorted milk up through his nose. "A hobo!" He giggled, practically choking to death.

Rick shook his head. The kid's eternal jolliness was one of nature's mysteries.

Raider now leapt off his chair and rushed off down the hall, shouting, "Here I come to save you!" Save who? Who was he shouting to? Some imaginary damsel in distress probably. And then Rick heard his footsteps thundering up the stairs, a decent imitation of a herd of elephants in stampede.

Chewing the last of his own french toast, licking the syrup off the fork, Rick went on considering his mother.

"Whatever they pay you for this job, it's not enough," he told her.

She laughed—and turned back to the sink to continue scouring the bottom of the french toast pan.

Rick went on watching her back, thinking about his dad outside with Leila.

"You might as well go on and ask," his mother said, her voice coming to him over the sound of running water. "I can already hear you thinking it. Go on and ask me how I feel about Leila being here."

Rick shook his head. He had a bizarre family. Raider the Constant Jolliness Machine, and Mom the Mind Reader. "So you're gonna tell me you're all good with it, right? Dad hanging out there with his old girlfriend? No problem."

"They've got business to talk about. You know that. There are bigger things going on here than me being jealous over your dad's college flame."

"I know. I'm just saying . . ." His voice trailed away.

His mother shut off the water and laid the pan in the drainer. Drying her hands on a dish towel, she turned to face him. She leaned back against the edge of the sink. "What *are* you saying?"

Rick hesitated. What *was* he saying? He wasn't sure. He

wasn't even sure what was getting him so aggravated—except for everything. Molly was in danger and he couldn't help her. Mariel and Favian were dying and he couldn't rescue them. He knew he had to be in the Realm, but he felt guilty for being with Mariel and not with Molly . . . "Stuff gets so complicated, you know," he said out loud. "All these choices. It's hard to know what you're supposed to do. It's even hard to know what you think or what you feel about things."

"Yes, it is sometimes."

"But *you* always seem to know."

"No, no," his mother said. "That's silly. I don't always know. We're all just trying to do our best."

"But it's, like, you never doubt Dad. You never lose your faith in him."

"Well, I know him, that's all. You know him. Don't you trust him?"

"Sure," said Rick, unsurely. "I mean, I always used to, anyway, but . . . Well . . . when he left—and I got hit by that truck . . ."

"It made you unsure."

"Yeah. It shook my faith."

"In Dad?"

"Yeah. And in, you know, all the stuff he taught us."

"In God, you mean."

Rick nodded. "Yeah, that too."

"That's tough," his mom said. "When you lose your faith in God, it's like you lose your faith in everything."

"Yeah, yeah. It is. It's, like, how do you know what's right or wrong? Why should anything be more right or wrong than anything else? And then you can't make up your mind about anything and it's like . . ." He didn't finish.

"It's like what?" his mother asked.

But he still didn't answer her. He was thinking about that canyon in the Realm, the Canyon of Nothingness. He was thinking about how the darkness wanted to draw him in and make him part of itself. Losing your faith was like that, he thought.

But he wasn't supposed to tell his mom about the Realm, so he tried to put it another way.

"Before Dad left? Things were sort of simple, you know? I thought that you and Dad would always do the right thing. I thought, if I was good and I prayed hard, God would make everything go well for me."

"And now?" his mother asked.

"I don't know," said Rick. He tried to think it through. "Now . . . I guess . . . I realize Dad's just a person. Like me. He's a good person, I get that. He's a really good person. But he makes mistakes. He has hard choices. He has to feel his way. Just like me."

His mom nodded. "What about God?"

"Well . . ." Again, Rick worked it out in his mind while he was talking. "Obviously, sometimes things go wrong no matter what, no matter how good you are, no matter how hard you pray."

"Yes, they do."

"And I guess maybe from God's point of view, it's not so important how things go, it's more about the right and wrong of it: what you do, who you are . . . that you try to follow the good way no matter what's happening. Something like that, anyway."

"Uh-huh," his mom said. "It sounds to me like you lost your boy faith, and now you're starting to find your man faith."

Rick's lips parted but no words came out. He hadn't thought about it like that, but now that she said it . . .

But before any words came to him, he heard the front door open. He heard his father's footsteps in the hall. The next moment, the small man was standing in the doorway. His cheeks were white with cold and his watch cap was in his hand.

Rick watched his mother carefully as she looked up at her husband. Her face lit up with a warm smile. Because she believed in him, Rick thought. She believed in him and she wasn't afraid of Leila Kent. She believed, and she wasn't afraid of anything.

"You look like you're frozen solid," she said with a laugh, just as if there had been no blond beauty fawning over him out there under the trees.

"It's cold, all right," said the Traveler. "If you hadn't reminded me to take my hat . . ."

"And your coat," his wife added. "And your shoes."

Even Rick laughed at that.

"Well, sit down now," his mom told his dad. "Have some coffee and warm yourself up."

Lawrence Dial returned his wife's smile, and Rick realized it was as easy to see that he was in love with her as it was to see that Leila Kent was in love with him.

But he said, "I wish I could, but I don't have time right now." Then he turned to Rick and said: "You and I—we have to talk."

20. FOREST SURVIVAL

MOLLY RAN THROUGH the winter forest. She ran and ran and ran, but she seemed to get nowhere. It was as if the woods went on forever. The dead trees on every side of her grew denser. The ground beneath her feet grew wetter, swampier. The branches scratched and tore at her face and arms. The earth turned soft and muddy beneath her sneakers. She stumbled and fell, and when she rose again, the knees of her jogging pants were soaked through. She felt as if the forest were pressing down on her from above and trying to swallow her from below.

And every time she stopped—to catch her breath, to find her footing, to look for a way out—she heard them. The killers. Their voices called to one another through the woods. Their footsteps tromped through the brush. All around her. Everywhere. Hunting her. Getting closer. No matter how fast she ran, she could not escape them.

She ran and ran until, finally, she was exhausted. She tumbled into a thick patch of weeds. She lay on her back, breathing hard. For a moment, she thought maybe—maybe—she had lost her pursuers. She held her breath and listened . . . listened . . . No, there they were. She could see them. They were still far enough away to be hidden by the dense jumble of tree branches—as she was hidden from them. But she could hear their voices through the trees.

"Spread out this way . . ."

"Keep moving together. She can't get past us."

"Stay in line. We'll get her."

"Keep looking left and right."

Lying there, staring up through the branches at the sky, Molly began to weep with weariness and frustration. Her body trembled as tears spilled over her temples into her hair. She prayed wildly, *Please, please . . .*

But the voices of the killers kept getting louder. The footsteps kept getting closer, crunching on the forest duff. Soon, very soon, they would be able to see her through the forest. She knew what they would do if they caught her. But how could she lose them? How could she escape?

She rose to her knees. She choked down her tears. Dragged a sleeve across her face to dry her eyes and wipe her nose.

Crying time was over.

She looked around her. She had no idea where she was. No idea how far she'd come from her prison or in what direction. She'd dashed out in such a panic that she hadn't paid any attention. All she knew at first was that the gunmen were behind her, the bullets whizzing past her through the branches: she had to keep moving.

She scanned the distant trees. They were blurry with her tears. Still, she saw pale winter light cutting in through the low branches. Something soured inside her as she realized: the sun was getting low. Night was falling. Soon the forest would be dark.

It would be cold, too. It was already cold and it was getting colder. She hadn't noticed it so much when she was on the move. But now that she had paused here, the damp chill closed over her skin, rose through her damp pants, ate into her. Her breath misted and vanished in the thickening air.

And the voices were getting very close. Any minute now, the hunters would be within sight.

"Keep together. Don't give her a chance to slip past." That was Smiley McDeath. She knew his raspy high-pitched voice well by now. "Count 'em out," he shouted.

"Here," came the answer.

"Walking here."

"Here."

"Over here."

She understood what they were doing. They were steadily marching toward her in a disciplined line. Five of them it sounded like. Spaced far enough apart to cut off her escape, but close enough together to spot her if she tried to sneak back between them. They sounded very confident, she thought. They sounded as if they didn't care which direction she went, how fast she ran, how cleverly she tried to evade them. Their confidence made her feel so hopeless she wanted to start weeping again.

But she didn't. She gulped down a deep breath. She climbed painfully to her feet. She started moving.

"I heard her!" one of the men shouted. "I heard her footsteps."

"There she is!"

"That way!"
"Keep together."
"Don't let her get away."
Molly ran.

21. HISTORY

"WE DON'T HAVE much time," Rick's father said. "They're going to want you to go back into the Realm soon."

"I'm ready to go back in now," Rick told him.

"No, you're not," his father said. "You're having headaches. Bad ones. And bad dreams, too, I'll bet."

Startled, Rick turned to his father. Was *he* a mind reader, too, like his mom? "How do you know that?"

They were walking by the compound's barbed-wire perimeter fence, strolling shoulder to shoulder, both wearing woolen watch caps, both with their hands pressed into the pockets of their fleeces to keep warm in the fading day. Rick couldn't help but notice the way his father's eyes kept moving. He kept glancing back over his shoulder, looking all around him. Making sure no one was near them, no one was listening in. Who was he afraid of? Rick wondered. Weren't they in a guarded, secret compound surrounded by good guys? Weren't the bad guys being kept out? Wasn't that why they were here in the first place?

"How'd you know about the headaches and the bad dreams?" he asked again.

His father's narrow shoulders lifted in a brief shrug. "I've been studying the MindWar Realm a long time. I don't understand all of it yet. But I'm beginning to think that the barrier between the mind and reality, between the Realm and Real Life, is porous."

"Porous?"

"Things can pass through from one side to the other. The way we think about the world in our minds changes the world in fact."

"I've seen that in the Realm," Rick said. "You can change reality there if you focus your spirit."

His father nodded. "That's true here, too, to some extent. If you let your spirit get poisoned and dark, the world gets poisoned and dark with it. Keep your spirit bright, the world gets brighter."

"No matter what happens," Rick murmured, thinking about his conversation with his mother.

"So as for your headaches and bad dreams . . . Well, when you go into the Realm, in effect you're entering Kurodar's imagination. I'd guess that's a pretty dark place. And like all darkness, it wants to turn you into itself."

Rick's lips parted in surprise. He hadn't even told his father about the Canyon of Nothingness yet. "You mean you think the darkness is getting inside me. You think that's where the nightmares are coming from."

"Well, that's not a very scientific way of putting it, but . . . Yes. Something like that. It's as if you were becoming part of the Realm yourself. As if Kurodar's imagination were somehow connecting to yours."

The idea gave Rick a little twinge of nausea. If there was one thing in this world he didn't want living in his imagination, it was the blackness of the Realm.

"I saw something in there," he said. "While I was immersed,

I saw something that makes me think you're right: there is a connection between the Realm and RL. There was this monster. Like a giant octopus. Only it had a person's face. And I'm pretty sure the face was the face of the guy from the video. That troll guy on the video about Molly."

His father was still looking around him, his eyes moving this way and that as if to make sure no one was trying to listen in on their conversation. But when he heard this, he stopped and fixed his gaze on Rick.

"Really? That's interesting," he said softly. It was typical of him: he sounded like he was considering some sort of mathematical equation in his absentminded-professor way. "With these drones disappearing the way they have, I've been worried that Kurodar may have found a way to bridge the Realm-RL divide directly, a way to reach into Real Life even without the Internet. It would give him a lot of power. An amazing amount of power."

"I was thinking if I could get to this monster, maybe I could make him tell us where Molly is."

His father went on gazing at him, but Rick could tell his mind had gone off on some other tangent somewhere. Then he blinked as if he were waking up. And he said, "Hmm? Oh. Yes, maybe."

"Have you heard anything about her?" Rick asked. "Has Victor One found her? Is she all right?"

His father shook his head. He started looking around again as they walked together by the barbed wire. "Victor One has purposely severed all communications with me. With anyone. We don't want Kurodar tracking him. We don't want Mars tracking him either, if it comes to that."

Rick was struck by the steadiness in his dad's eyes as he spoke about all this. Whatever he was feeling, whatever was worrying him, he didn't show it. He wasn't unemotional like Miss Ferris. He was just . . . well, weirdly calm. But then he'd always been like that, even when Rick was little. No matter what happened, no matter what nonsense Rick got up to (and Rick had pulled off one or two historic feats of mischief in his time), his father never lost his temper, never raised his voice. Even when he had punished Rick (like after that time Rick had stuck a potato in the exhaust pipe of his chemistry teacher's car and nearly gassed the man to death), he had delivered the sentence with the quiet objectivity of a judge and with no apparent anger at all. Rick had always admired that about his dad. He had always wished he could be that calm, that cool, instead of being the hothead he often was.

"You don't like Commander Mars much, do you?" Rick asked him now.

"It's not that I don't like him," his father said. "It's not really a question of whether I like him or not. Mars is a powerful man, that's all. And people who have power may start out thinking they're going to help other people, but far too often they end up trying to control them, trying to tell them what's best for them, trying to keep secrets from them in order to protect them . . . It's hard to find a powerful man who's a friend to freedom. And I think God made us to be free. That's why I'm fighting Kurodar. But I'll fight Mars, too, if I have to, if he becomes a danger."

Rick remembered now why he admired his dad, why he was so disappointed when he thought his dad had betrayed the family. Because his dad was like this.

They continued strolling around the fence together, as if they were just a pop and his son out for a walk. But as Rick watched, his dad did that thing again: looking back over his shoulder, moving his eyes around to make sure no one was near.

"Why do you keep doing that?" Rick asked. "Looking around like that? Aren't we supposed to be among friends here?"

His father took a deep breath. "I got a visit this afternoon."

"From Leila Kent," said Rick. The name came out of him in a curt, sarcastic drawl. He couldn't help it.

One corner of his father's mouth lifted. He heard the tone all right, but he didn't respond to it. He simply said, "When she was helping to transfer me here from my hiding place, we were attacked on the road by a couple of gunmen. I hadn't used the Internet in months. There was no way Kurodar could have tracked me to that cabin in the woods. Leila thinks someone told the Axis where we were."

"A traitor? Like who?"

"There weren't that many people who knew where I was. Mars. Miss Ferris. Victor One. Leila herself. That's exactly why I did what I did. Why I left you all like that. So no one would know my location—and no one would think you knew it."

Just the mention of this made Rick's old anger flare. He turned away, trying not to let it show. When he turned back, he found his father had stopped walking, was simply standing there a few feet behind him. Rick stopped too. He turned and faced him.

"I'm sorry, son," his dad said quietly. "It wasn't supposed to turn out the way it did. Mars was supposed to protect you. He was supposed to keep you out of it. He brought you into the project without telling me."

Rick nodded and looked away. He wanted to tell his father he forgave him, but he couldn't make the words come out. "I guess we all have to make tough decisions in an emergency."

"That's it," his father said. "There was an emergency. Something went very wrong with the MindWar Project. That's why they brought you into it on such short notice. That's what I wanted to talk to you about."

"What do you mean?"

"I don't know the whole story. All I know is this: you're not the first MindWarrior."

Rick's lips parted, but all that came out was a frosty puff of breath. He had known this. Somewhere inside. Things Miss Ferris had said, and his own intuitions, had planted the suspicion beneath the surface of his brain. There had been MindWarriors before him. Other human beings who had gone into the MindWar Realm . . .

"The others didn't make it out," he said aloud.

His father shook his head. "I don't know what happened. No one will tell me."

"It was Mariel, wasn't it? Mariel and Favian and . . . that other guy. The guy in the Spider-Snake tunnel. The guy who died. They all got stuck in there, and now they're all dying, and no one's doing anything about it."

"I don't know . . . ," his father began.

"What do you mean you don't know?"

"Calm down. Listen to me."

Rick tried. He tried to calm down. He'd never been very good at it.

His father went on. "I stumbled upon the Realm by accident. I was doing experiments with Professor Jameson."

"Molly's dad?"

"That's right. We were working together on computer-brain interfaces, trying to develop methods of downloading portions of the human mind into computers and vice versa."

"Yeah," said Rick. "I remember that. You did some of that with me and Molly. You had us wear those helmets on our heads and we played video games just by thinking about them. It was cool."

"That's right. We did that with a lot of different subjects. And while you were playing the games, we translated portions of your minds into computer code: an experiment in transporting the human spirit into cyberspace, as Kurodar has done in the Realm. It's while I was studying that, that I discovered Kurodar's interface: the MindWar. I realized the danger at once. I thought it unwise to tell anyone, even Jameson. Instead, I contacted Leila, the one person in the government I knew I could trust because of our . . . old association. Leila passed my work on to Mars and . . . well, I'm not sure, but I think he may have used it without telling me. He may have enlisted some of my subjects and sent them into the Realm."

Rick had managed to keep his temper until now. But when he thought this might be the key, the secret that would help him rescue Mariel and Favian, he blurted out, "Well, where are they? How can we get them out?"

"That's what I'm trying to tell you," his father said. "We had so many subjects. Students, soldiers, volunteers. I don't know which ones they used or if they used my methods on others or . . . any of it. Neither Mars nor Miss Ferris will tell me. And Leila doesn't know. They're all so obsessed with their blessed secrecy around here . . . If I knew who was in there, if I had their mind scans—and of course their bodies—it's possible I could create programs that could extract them, bring them back."

Rick was no science guy. He could not begin to understand the details of what his father was trying to tell him. But he did get the general idea.

"So we've got to find out who they are," he said. "And find where Mars is keeping their bodies. We've got to. Mariel's dying, Dad. And Favian too. They're dying. Even the energy you sent them isn't enough to . . ."

"Give me your hand," his father said. His voice was low, but sharp and urgent.

Rick hesitated only a second, then he lifted his hand out of his fleece pocket, held it in the air in front of him. At once, his father clasped the hand in his own. He put his other hand on Rick's shoulder and gave him what would look to anyone like a fatherly embrace. As they were close together, he murmured in Rick's ear: "This will help you find the answers."

When his father stepped back, there was a flash drive in Rick's hand.

"What's on it?" he asked.

But before his father could answer, there was a call:

"You! Dial!"

At the sound of that unmistakable voice, Rick closed his hand into a fist and shoved the fist back into his fleece pocket, hiding the flash drive away. For another long second, he and his father locked eyes.

Then he turned and saw Miss Ferris striding toward him. Even in this winter weather, she was wearing her usual uniform of dark slacks and a dark jacket.

Of course, Rick thought, *you can't freeze if you have no blood in your veins.*

"Where have you been?" she said—her eyes were angry, but her voice was its usual monotone. "We've got to get you back into the Realm. Right now."

22. THE DARKNESS

THE GROUND BROKE beneath her like thin ice, and Molly's foot plunged into cold swamp water. She tried to keep her balance, but she was already reeling. Tired, stumbling. When her foot sank, she went over like an axed tree, hitting the earth hard with her shoulder. A thin layer of freezing mud splashed up over the side of her. She lay where she fell.

She was finished. She knew it. Out of breath, out of strength, out of hope. She started crying again, but there were no tears anymore. She was all out of those, too. She merely lay there, sobbing, trembling, praying fitfully—for her parents again, for Rick, her friends. Not for herself—not for her safety, anyway. She no longer believed she had any chance of getting through this ordeal alive.

All the same, after a few moments of praying, she found she was calmer. She caught her breath. She lifted her head off the frozen ground and looked around her. The forest was nearly dark now. The shadows were gathering beneath the trees and blending together and deepening every second. The rays of the setting sun were nowhere visible. She could barely see more than a few yards in any direction. Wherever she looked, there was nothing but wood and water and mist.

She had lost the killers for a while. They had fallen behind as she raced ahead. But they were closing in again. Once more, she could hear their voices. Calling to one another. Coming steadily closer. They still sounded confident. They still sounded unstoppable. Tireless. Merciless.

"You see her trail?"

"Oh yeah. See how the leaves are turned over. She went this way."

"It's all swamp up there."

"It's all swamp everywhere in these woods."

"That's the whole point. The swamp hems her into this narrow corridor of dry land. She can't get away. She's got nowhere to go. All we have to do is follow."

"There's her trail. This way."

At first, the voices were distant, soft. But the killers came on, steady and relentless. Very quickly their voices grew louder, and more distinct. Very soon, she could hear their footsteps again.

Turning her head, Molly saw a fallen tree a few yards away from her. Using what little strength she had left, she got up on her hands and knees, feeling the damp cold earth on her palms and through her pants. Breathing hard from the exertion, she crawled to the big trunk and lay down close to it. Maybe it would hide her from the killers. Maybe they would march right past her.

Maybe. But she doubted it.

The footsteps grew louder. The voices grew nearer.

"Don't rush. We don't want to step on her traces."

"I can barely see."

"Use the flashlight. Move it back and forth slowly."

"We could lose her in the dark."

"Believe me, we won't lose her. She hasn't got a light. She's not going anywhere."

Molly lay as still as she could, breathing as softly as she could. The dark grew even darker. The cold air grew colder still. She hugged her own shoulders, but the chill ate into her and she began to shiver. Her lips grew stiff and raw. Her jaw trembled. She struggled to keep her teeth from chattering.

The footsteps and voices were very close now. Molly thought that if she lifted her head above the log and peeked, she would see the five killers looming above her just a few feet away. She didn't try. She didn't dare. They might spot her. So she lay still, shivering, more and more miserable with every passing second.

"This is no good," said one man. "It's too dark to track her."

"I can't see anything."

"We're gonna have to—Ah!" The man cried out.

"What's the matter?"

"Stepped in water. It's all swamp here."

"I'm freezing."

"Me too."

Molly was now so cold and was trembling so hard, she had to bite her lip to keep from groaning aloud. The cold was taking her over, filling her inner world. The world around her seemed to be sinking away into unreality. The voices of the killers—so close to her, in fact—were beginning to seem like something from a distant dream.

The next voice she heard was Smiley McDeath's: his high-pitched whisper. "All right. All right. Quit complaining. We'll go back to that clearing we just passed. Set up camp for the night. Two men on patrol in shifts. I don't want her slipping back past us. I'll call in and tell the head office what's up. They won't be happy."

"They've got nothing to worry about. I've tracked plenty of people. She's not going anywhere in this dark."

"Yeah. Well, neither are we."

Molly lay shivering, listening. The footsteps receded, the voices grew softer. The killers were moving away from her. Was there some chance she might escape them now?

Slowly, she reached up with a quivering hand. She gripped the rough log and drew herself up until she could peek over the top.

The forest dark was very deep now. The woods were no more than a tangle of black shapes. The only light came from the men's flashlights. Molly could see their beams crisscrossing as they moved here and there. In the outglow, the silhouettes of the men themselves were just barely visible.

The killers went on calling to one another. Their flashlights darted and crossed. Their footsteps crackled in the brush, and sometimes Molly could see an illuminated hand clutching branches. She understood. They were gathering wood. They were going to build a fire.

Soon, Molly saw the first spark. Then there was a blue flame. Then the flame grew orange. It grew bigger. The flashlights went out. The fire snickered and rose.

For Molly, it was a kind of torture. She could see the flames, but she couldn't feel the heat, and her body was racked with shivering as the cold invaded every inch of her.

She kept an unsteady grip on the log, holding herself up as she watched the black shapes of the men arrange themselves around the flames. Their faces leaned in to the orange glow. Their eyes gleamed brightly. Their voices murmured to one another. One of them laughed.

Molly's strength ran out. Too weak to keep holding on to the log, she lowered herself back down to the ground. She rolled over and lay on her side, hugging herself, shivering. She listened to the warm sound of the fire. She heard other sounds. Paper crinkling. Voices becoming thick and muffled. The men were eating. The thought made hunger come on her, sudden and severe. Her mouth watered so that the saliva ran over her chapped lips and chilled her chin. She listened to the men talking with their mouths full. Laughing with their mouths full.

After a while, she heard more crunching footsteps. A couple of the killers were moving away from the fire, moving off into the woods. She saw their flashlight beams sweeping through the darkness over her head. She understood: They were patrolling the area. Watching for her. Making sure she wasn't on the move, trying to escape. If she budged from her hiding place, if she tried to make a run for it, they would catch her in seconds. But even if they didn't, even if she somehow got past them, where could she go? She was exhausted. She had no strength left at all. She had no idea where she was. And the night was black as black. Swamp everywhere. There was no chance of escape.

Molly trembled uncontrollably. Her head was swimming. Her thoughts were becoming unclear. She tried to think of warm things, good things. Her room at home. Her family around the dinner table. Her friends hanging in the student lounge, talking, laughing. Those moments after a game, when all the girls were cheering, slapping hands, triumphant. That time Rick kissed her . . .

Funny, she thought. She had spent so much of her life worrying over things. Did she love Rick? Did he love her? Was she training hard enough? Would her team win? Where was her life going? What was she going to do? All those questions that were in her mind constantly. But now . . . now that she was here—now that she was nowhere with nowhere to go, with little chance of living through the night—all those questions were gone. There were no worries in her memories. There was only light and warmth and people together talking and laughing. What had they been saying? What had been so funny? What had been so important that she had to send a text right now . . . ? She couldn't remember. It didn't matter. It had been the fact that they were there—her parents, her friends, Rick, all of them—just the fact that they were together meant more than all the words in the world.

And now, here she was, alone. No company. No phone. No Internet. Just dark. Just cold.

Molly blinked slowly. The voices of the men had blended into a single murmur. She was getting sleepy now. Reality was slipping away.

Molly was not an outdoorswoman, but she thought she remembered seeing in a movie that you shouldn't fall asleep in the cold. It made your body temperature drop or something and you died. Was that true? She didn't know. She just knew she couldn't fight it. She was getting sleepier and sleepier. If she could just stand up.

If she could just move around, jump around, warm herself up. But the flashlights kept crossing above her. The men kept patrolling, watching for her.

She closed her eyes . . .

23. GEARS OF WAR

"WE'RE OUT OF time," said Commander Mars.

They were now in the big steel-walled elevator, descending into the underground MindWar facility. Mars was standing by Rick's right shoulder. Miss Ferris was by his left. Mars wore a dark suit, sharply creased. So did Miss Ferris. Mars's silver-haired, craggy countenance seemed carved out of rock. Miss Ferris's expressionless expression seemed set in stone.

"We've been through the data from your immersion," Miss Ferris told him. "That flying outpost you saw—that WarCraft: It seems almost complete. We detect only a few last unfinished places in it, anyway. That means it could be operational in hours, if it isn't operational already."

"That means Kurodar could launch his attack at any time," said Mars.

"Unless you stop him," Miss Ferris said.

"You have to stop him," said Mars.

Rick stood between them, silent with confusion. His mind was still reeling with what his father had told him.

You're not the first MindWarrior.

The others didn't make it out.

I need to know who they were in order to extract them.

189

This flash drive will help you find the answers . . .

It was all about Mariel and Favian. His father hadn't said exactly that, but Rick knew it was so in his heart of hearts. Mariel and Favian had been the first MindWarriors—they and the other man who had died in the Spider-Snake's tunnel—before the project enlisted Rick. Somehow they had gotten trapped inside the Realm and could no longer remember who they were. Without that information, Rick's father couldn't extract them. They would simply remain in there and continue to bleed out energy until they entered the living agony of decay that was death in the Realm.

Unless Rick could find them. Find their names. Find their bodies. Find their identities.

But first . . .

"You have to get on board that WarCraft," said Commander Mars brusquely.

"You have to find out what Kurodar is planning," said Miss Ferris.

"You have to find a way to put an end to it," said Commander Mars.

"Our guess is you'll have about two hours," Miss Ferris said.

Rick turned to her, his eyes widening. *Two hours?* he wanted to say.

It was too much time and it wasn't enough.

It was too much time because immersion in the MindWar Realm was hard on the brain. An hour and a half in there was just about all a person could tolerate before his mind began to come apart at the seams. Rick had felt the disintegration start when he'd stayed too long. It was a horrible sensation: disorientation, nausea, reality pixilating around you. When he finally had come back to RL—just in time—he was so far gone, he couldn't even remember who he was for a while. And even now, the headaches and bad dreams continued to plague him.

It's as if you were becoming part of the Realm yourself. As if Kurodar's imagination were somehow connecting to yours.

So how could he last for two hours this time? he wanted to ask.

But he didn't ask. When he turned to Miss Ferris, her blank expression didn't change—it never changed—but she turned away from him, averting her eyes. And Rick understood. He could go in for two hours because they just didn't care what happened to him. Mars didn't care, at least. Who knew what Miss Ferris was thinking? Mars didn't care whether Rick's mind fell apart or his face fell off or his head exploded. He didn't care if he had killing headaches for months or for the rest of his life or even if he died. All Mars cared about was that Kurodar was planning to unleash a massive attack on his country. He was about to wipe out thousands of people, maybe millions. They had to stop him, and if they lost another MindWarrior in the process—and if Molly was kidnapped and killed—that just didn't count for much.

"Two hours," Rick finally said aloud as the elevator continued its long descent.

Miss Ferris didn't face him—wouldn't face him—and didn't answer.

"Two hours," Mars barked back without apology.

Too much time; not enough.

It wasn't enough because the battleship was immense, so huge it darkened the Realm's yellow sky, and the giant octopus-like humanoid that was grafted onto it was ready to fight off all invaders with its vast tentacles. Two hours to get on that thing and dismantle it? Make it five hours, make it ten. No matter how long he had, the chances were slim.

The elevator touched bottom. The heavy doors slid open with a grinding whirr. Mars broke out of the box without a backward glance. Miss Ferris hurried after him. And Rick, flinching a little at the pain in his legs, followed last, limping awkwardly. They hurried past two armed guards into a faceless hallway, then down the hall toward the Portal Room. They were moving so quickly, Rick could hardly think. As the door to the Portal Room loomed in front of him, one idea after another, one anxiety after another, crowded through his brain. He thought of Mariel and Favian, stuck in the Realm. Of Molly, lost and alone somewhere with men who were threatening to kill her. Of Kurodar, on that monster ship planning an atrocity. And of himself, his head already throbbing, his dreams already twisted and terrifying, preparing to let Mars and Miss Ferris project him back into the nightmare world of MindWar.

And could he trust them? Mars and Miss Ferris? Were they even on the right side of the war? Rick remembered how his father had kept looking around, this way and that, over his shoulder. Fearful there was a traitor in the ranks. Maybe Mars. Maybe Miss Ferris. Maybe Leila Kent. Or maybe Victor One, who was supposed to be rescuing Molly . . . Which one had gone over to the other side?

Thoughts within thoughts, fears within fears, each connected to the other, each moving the other, like the gears of a great machine churning inside Rick's brain, a machine so complex he couldn't understand it, couldn't control it or figure it out. How did life get so complicated so quickly? How could he know how to do the right thing when the situation was beyond his understanding?

The door to the Portal Room stood open. Mars charged through. Miss Ferris went after. Rick came to the threshold and looked through the entranceway.

Some darkness of foreboding spread over him, like storm clouds spreading over the sky. He stared down the length of that narrow room, over the flashing machinery, over the faces of the technicians who had turned from their monitors at his entry. They had all turned in their seats to watch him, their faces harsh with the reflected glow of their machines. Rick could see the expressions in their eyes. Was that compassion they felt for him? Admiration? Pity? All of the above? The MindWar technicians knew—probably better than Rick knew himself—the risks he was taking going into this place again so soon and for so long. And yet, like Mars and Miss Ferris—like his own father—even like himself—they were willing to let him take the risk, on the chance he could stop the horror that was coming.

Rick swallowed hard. His gaze came to rest on the glass box set in the far wall, the stairs leading up to it, the great hulk of a bodyguard—Juliet Seven—standing by it with his rectangular arms crossed over the massive square of his chest. That glass box— the portal: it had always reminded him of a coffin. Ironic, right? Because it was probably going to *be* his coffin for real this time. Just another MindWarrior sacrificed to the battle with Kurodar.

Like Mariel. Like Favian. Like that unknown other in the tunnels beneath the Realm.

Rick hesitated there at the threshold another moment. And what came to him then—what broke through the gears of fear grinding together in his mind—was the 3-D image they had shown him of that Arkansas factory, the one that had gone up in a ball of fire and smoke after being attacked by a renegade drone.

What if New York City went up in smoke like that? he thought. Or St. Louis or Chicago, Philadelphia or Los Angeles? What if hundreds of thousands of people were consumed in such a fire, merely because Kurodar in his madness imagined the disaster into being?

Maybe Mars was right, Rick thought. Maybe the life of one washed-up high school football star wasn't too big a sacrifice to make to prevent such a mass murder.

He stepped across the Portal Room threshold.

The glass box in the wall—the coffin—slowly opened to receive him.

LEVEL FOUR:
TIME RUNS OUT

24. BATTLE BEAST

OF ALL THE many strange aspects of Rick's adventures in the MindWar Realm, the strangest by far was this: when he was in Real Life, the Realm seemed to him like a dream; but when he was in the Realm, it seemed more real than Real Life itself. In his home, in the compound, in his bed at night, the bizarre colors of this cyberworld, the deadly monsters that roamed its fields and forests and flew across its skies, the flashing blue form of Favian and the majestic silver beauty of Mariel—all seemed like some fantasy he'd had in a fever, impossible to believe. Even as he ached from the wounds he suffered there, even as he worried about Kurodar's threats and plans, even as he yearned to look into Mariel's eyes again, the truth of their existence faded away from him until he felt as if he was aching, worrying, yearning for what lived only in his imagination. Half the time, he was unsure whether any of what he remembered had ever really happened at all.

Then he returned. He came back through the portal and was here again in Kurodar's constructed universe. And then—then the solidity of it, the danger of its threats, the power of Mariel's silver spirit filled and surrounded him. Just like that, he knew that what he did and felt here—whatever fights he fought, whatever good he accomplished—was more important to him than anything that had ever happened to him before. Here, where the bizarre was commonplace, it was Real Life that seemed unreal.

So now, once again, suddenly, everything changed for him. One moment, he was in the Portal Room, lying in the glass box, the transparent coffin lid closed over him, the metallic lining gripping him tight, a thousand pinpricks making his head swim and a thousand anxieties churning in his mind. He was trying to figure out how to rescue Mariel and Favian . . . whether to trust Miss Ferris and Mars . . . whether he'd ever see Molly again . . . and how he felt about her when all was said and done . . . and even bigger questions about his father, about his future, about his faith . . .

And the next moment, that world, the so-called real world, was gone, and he was slipping like water through a straw into another.

When Rick stepped from the purple diamond floating in space he was in Favian's forest cottage again. For one final instant, he experienced the strangeness of the place. He felt as if he had become a figure in an illustration in a book of fairy tales. Then the reality of the Realm overwhelmed him, and the Portal Room and the compound and the pain in his legs faded away.

The first thing he saw here was his sword. Full-bladed now, it stood upright, powerful and gleaming, its point thrust into the packed earth of the cottage floor, its sheath lying beside it. He wrapped his hand around the hilt and felt at once the warm surge of Mariel's presence, traveling up his arm and flooding all through him. Once again he was reassured: she was still here, still in the Realm, still able to inspire him and give him strength. He fastened the sheath onto his belt and slid the sword into it again.

Then he looked around him. The cottage was just as he'd left it. The yellow light, laced with the shadows of branches, fell through the windows and shone into the wood-walled room. Rick's eyes traveled over the sparse furnishings: the rude table, the chairs, the stove, the bed . . .

And in the bed lay Favian.

Or, that is, Favian lay *above* the bed. His sparkling blue form was stretched out horizontally and floating in the air about two inches above the bed's surface. He was fast asleep.

Rick gave a small smile to see him like that. Why have a bed at all if you were going to float above it when you slept? You could float above the floor just as easily, couldn't you? But then everything in the Realm was like that. It had its own illogical logic. You just got used to it after a while.

Rick moved to stand over his friend. His smile slowly faded. Looking down at the sleeping blue man, he could see how much, how rapidly, he'd aged, even in the few hours Rick had been gone. His face, which had become youthful again with the fresh supply of energy Rick had brought him, was already growing lined and starting to sag. It was only half a day since Rick had last been here—so short a time he hadn't even thought to bring more energy with him. But it was clear to him now that Favian was losing the ability to retain even what energy he had.

This thought made Rick think of Mariel, of the way she'd been when he'd seen her in the pond. It hurt to think about her that way, haggy and decrepit before her time, dying and close to despair. Where was she now? he wondered. And how was she? How much energy had drained from her? How much life did she have left? She and Favian were dwindling away and he—Rick—the only one who could help them—could not help them until he'd completed his mission—a mission that might well kill him before he could help them at all.

Lost in those meditations, he was startled when Favian's hand closed around his wrist. He blinked and looked down and saw that his friend had awakened. Favian's eyes were open. Open and—as always—full of anxiety.

"You're back already?" he said in his hollow, echoing voice. "I didn't think they could send you back so soon."

Rick nodded and sighed. "They're not supposed to."

"They had to then."

"They did. We have to hurry, Favian. I've only got two hours, and I need to get on that battleship."

In a blue flash, Favian was upright. He shook his head to clear the sleep from it, his face going into full-worry mode. "Get on the battleship . . . ?"

Rick explained his plan: "I thought if we could somehow get to the Golden City before the WarCraft passes overhead again . . . if I could somehow get on one of those cargo blimps that carry energy and supplies up on the lightning bolts . . . then if I could somehow slip from the blimp onto the ship . . ."

"That's a lot of 'somehows,'" Favian said, but he was nodding thoughtfully, staring into the middle distance. "Still, it's possible, I guess. The Boars load the blimps at the launch docks in the city walls . . ."

"The boars . . . ?"

"I've seen them."

"The boars?" Rick said again.

But Favian wasn't listening. He went on, thinking aloud: "The problem is: How can we get there fast enough? To the Golden City, I mean. It's a trek across the field—it would take us ninety minutes at least just to reach the walls. And that's assuming we don't run into any thresher bots."

Thresher bots?! Rick was about to say—but he decided he didn't want to know.

"Ninety minutes is too long," said Favian. "You'd be out of time before you could reach the ship. And the battlecraft is due to pass over again in only twenty minutes. But maybe . . ."

Rick waited while Favian considered. He could feel the seconds ticking away on his palm. Finally, he prompted, "Maybe . . . ?"

Favian's only answer was to shoot out the cottage door in a blue flash.

"Hey . . . ," said Rick—but Favian was already gone.

So, once again, Rick found himself racing through the woods after the darting blue figure. He had a dozen questions he wanted to call out to him: *Where are we going? Where's Mariel? Boars?* And those were just for starters. But each time he approached the glowing man, Favian streaked away again, his shimmering blue shape nearly vanishing into the surrounding blue canopy of the forest leaves. There was no time to ask questions. There was no time to do anything but run.

Fortunately, the trip was brief. After only a few minutes, they were standing together in a bright clearing, surrounded by a half ring of blue trees. On the open side of the ring was a steep orange wall of dirt and rock, the side of a hill.

"He sleeps in there," said Favian.

"Who does? Where?" said Rick.

"Rollie. In there." Favian lifted a glowing hand and pointed. Rick followed the gesture and saw there was an opening in the rock, a cave entrance. It was a rough, rounded hole about four feet high. It led into deep darkness.

Oh man! he thought. *What now? And who's Rollie? And what did he mean by boars?*

"Rollie can get you there fast. Really fast. If you ride him to the eastern wall of the city—the wall to your right as you approach—there's a field of high grass there. You might be able to sneak up pretty close to the wall, get to one of the launch docks without being seen. After that . . . I don't know."

"Who's Rollie?" Rick asked.

Favian shrugged. "I'm not sure. I'm not sure what he is. I think Kurodar built him to patrol these woods. But he's not really much good at it. Most of the time he just sleeps in his cave. When he wakes up, he comes out and eats a few twigs and some grass. Then he goes back into the cave and sleeps some more."

"So what use is he to me?" asked Rick.

"Like I said, you have to ride him."

"He doesn't sound like he'd be very fast."

"Not usually, no. But when you get him angry, he flies like the wind."

"All right. Good. We'll get him angry, then."

"But just watch out, okay? When he gets angry, he tries to roll over you."

"What?"

"That's why we call him Rollie."

"Cute. What do you mean, roll over me?"

"It's kind of hard to describe, but you'll see what I mean. Just wait till he stops rolling, then jump on top of him. Then he really flies."

"Uh-huh," Rick said doubtfully.

"No, no, it's not that hard. It's easy, really. You'll see. Just wait here."

With that, Favian streaked off and disappeared into the cave entrance.

Rick watched him go in, then stood alone in the clearing, waiting.

It's easy, he thought. *Right.*

A moment later, from the depths of the cave's darkness, there came a noise. It was high-pitched and melodious, as if a singer were warming up her voice in preparation for a performance. But it was not a singer. It was Favian. And he was not singing. He was screaming at the top of his lungs.

"Aaaaaaaah!"—and then there he was, streaking out of the cave so quickly he was invisible but for the line of blue light trailing behind him.

Startled—stunned—Rick gaped at Favian as he flashed past across the clearing to the tree line. There, the glowing man stopped and re-formed into his usual shape. He was gesturing frantically toward the cave.

And he shouted, "Watch out! Here he comes!"

Rick turned just in time to see Rollie come bursting from the low, rounded opening in the earth.

This was one of those moments that occurred from time to time here in the Realm when the months Rick had spent hiding in his room obsessively playing video games suddenly came in very handy. If he had not been a gamer, he probably would have stood there in shock and disbelief while "Rollie" rolled right over him.

But because he played games, he'd seen creatures like this before. Rollie, it turned out, was one of those beasts like the ones in the game *Onimusha* that can curl themselves up into a spiky ball and roll at you at high speed until they skewer you and plant your bleeding body in the earth, where they proceed to jab you full of holes just before smashing you to pieces. Which was exactly what this beast was planning to do to Rick right this very moment.

The giant spiky ball came tumbling toward him as if he were a pin at the end of some fantastical bowling alley. Rick dove to the side. He flew through the air, landed hard on the earth—and the beast powered past him. The ground shook beneath his outstretched body as Rollie skittered across the clearing and went crashing blindly into the thick trunk of a tree.

Lying flat on the forest floor, Rick looked over his shoulder. As the beast smashed into the tree trunk, it snapped out of its ball and back into its normal shape. And what a shape: it would have looked something like a bull if bulls were the size of pickup trucks and had flaming red eyes and black steam coming out of their nostrils and three horns the size of spears on their heads and hides that looked something like concrete with lots of stones sticking out.

It's easy? Rick thought—and he leapt to his feet, his heart hammering with terror.

"Now jump on its back!" Favian instructed.

"Jump on its back?!" Rick screamed. "Are you crazy?"

But before Favian could answer that question, Rollie swung round and spotted Rick with its fiery eyes. In a mind-stunning instant, it rolled its enormous body into a ball again and thundered across the clearing at Rick full speed.

"Flash out of the way and then flash on top of him!" shouted Favian.

At least that's what Rick thought he said—it was difficult to hear while he was hurling himself wildly through the air to get out of the monster's way. Again, Rick hit the dirt, letting out a loud "Oof" as the air was knocked from his lungs. And again, the earth shook as Rollie careened blindly into the side of the hill. On impact, he became the enormous bull-like beast once more.

And Favian shouted, "Now! Now! Flash! Flash on top of him! Hurry!"

"What are you talking about? I can't flash around like you can!" Rick screamed back.

He looked Favian's way just in time to see the glowing blue man blink once in realization. Then Favian said, "Oh yeah, I forgot."

"You forgot?" Rick shrieked.

But then the ground started trembling under him and, sure enough, here came Rollie, rolled up into a ball again and bounding across the clearing at Rick's outstretched form.

Rick had no idea how he got to his feet so fast, but he was running before he knew it, the Rollie-ball right behind him. The next second, Rick broke through the tree line. On instinct, he dodged to the left behind a tree.

Rolled up into a ball like that, Rollie was fast all right, but it was tough for the creature to turn. When Rick ducked left, Rollie thundered past him again, and went *crunch* into yet another tree up ahead. Then, with a squealing grunt, it popped out of its ball and back into its enormous bull-like shape.

Rollie swung around and Rick swung around, the tree at his back now. Man and mega-bull faced each other, only yards apart. Rollie's eyes flamed—literally, there were flames leaking out of his eye sockets around the edges of his bright eyes. His nostrils smoked. He lowered his three horns at Rick, about to curl up again, about to charge.

Rick tried to think. He couldn't just keep playing dodgeball with the beast. Eventually he'd slip—jump left when he should jump right or vice versa—and next thing he knew, he'd be a human pancake bleeding out onto the forest floor. He had to come up with a better plan. But what? He couldn't just flash around like Favian . . .

Or wait . . . Wait, maybe he could.

Mariel had taught him about the power of his spirit, hadn't she? How he could transform the Realm's reality with enough spiritual focus, transform even his own body into another shape. But what if he could transform his own body into no shape—or into a streak of light like Favian? He'd only have to do it for a moment. That's all it would take.

Could he pull it off? Did he have that power?

There was no time to be sure. There wasn't even enough time to finish asking himself the questions. Already, Favian was screaming and Rollie was rolling into a spiked ball and the earth was shaking and the spiked ball was tumbling toward him.

Not easy to focus with that thing hurling toward him. Not easy to think about anything but the spiky death bearing down on him. But hey, he was Rick Dial, right? He was Number 12—the quarterback who'd had to focus on the play at hand even with linemen almost as big as Rollie charging at him almost as hard.

He used that power now. As sure destruction rumbled down on top of him, he dropped his consciousness down deep into the very self of himself. He thought of Favian. He thought of light. He thought of streaking away.

And now the daggered Rollie-ball rose up above him like a crashing wave and . . .

Whoa! Rick thought.

He had never felt anything like it. It was as if his body had exploded into a million million pieces and yet at the same time it was as if he had been transformed into one great lightning-like piece of motion.

"Yeah, yeah, yeah!" he heard Favian cheering.

And before he fully realized what had happened, he found he had reassembled himself and was standing about six feet to the right of where he'd been. Stunned, he could only stand there watching as the enormous Rollie-ball rolled right past him. It smashed into the trunk of the tree that had been behind him. It struck so hard that the trunk crunched and splintered. Branches and blue leaves showered down to the ground, and Rick felt the earth jump underneath him. The next moment Rollie once again snapped into the shape of an enormous, snorting, smoking, flaming, concrete-skinned, three-horned mega-bull.

And Favian shouted, *"Now! Now! Do it now!"*

Rick did not even have time to think—only to drop into that rich wholeness of focus that seemed to bring some inner truth about his being up to the surface, spreading through his physical form.

And then it happened again. That sense that he was bursting apart and yet still a single amazingly swift and thoughtless oneness of movement.

And the next thing he knew, he was sitting smack on the mega-bull's back!

"That's it!" Favian shouted triumphantly. "Now steer him with the horns!"

More great advice from Mr. Oh-Yeah-I-Forgot! Still, Rick didn't have much choice in the matter. His perch on Rollie's back was precarious, to say the least. The beast was so wide that Rick could just barely straddle him. He had to grab hold of something to keep himself in place. The horns were the only something around.

Rick grabbed two of the three horns on the enormous head. Rollie reacted at once, throwing his head this way and that, trying to dislodge the rider, hurl Rick off. Rick held on tight. The beast shook his head more and more furiously, sending up gouts of black smoke, flashes of bright flame. Rick felt like a rider in a rodeo in hell.

Then Rollie stopped. He stood still. For a moment, nothing else happened. It was as if the immense creature were giving the situation some careful consideration before deciding what he should do.

Then, apparently, he decided.

Rollie let out a roar so loud it seemed to fill the forest. More flames spat out of the corners of his eyes. More smoke poured out of his nostrils. His huge beastly body gave a violent shudder that nearly flung Rick into the air. Rick pressed his legs tight against Rollie's rough flanks. He kept his fists closed tight around the scraping surface of the horns. Somewhere off in the distance, he heard Favian shouting something—some fresh instructions probably—but what they were he would never know.

Because just then, the mega-bull bolted—and suddenly Rick was flying through the blue forest as quickly—and as wildly out of control—as if he were riding on the back of a rocket.

25. COLD FEAR

AT THAT MOMENT Molly woke up and let out a shuddering moan of agony.

The cold had not killed her in her sleep, but it had quietly, steadily, deeply, relentlessly eaten its way into the very heart of her. She was now shaking so violently, she could not control herself. Her hands were cramped like claws and clutched in front of her. Her legs were pulled up nearly to her chest. Her chest felt as if it were clamped in a vise of ice, and filled with ice. She could barely pull air into her lungs, could barely let it out except in stuttering half gasps. She was frozen to her core. It was the shivering and the pain that had brought her awake.

She bit back another moan, trying to keep quiet. Had the killers heard her? They must have. Their camp was so close and their guards were patrolling only yards away, and she couldn't stop the shuddery sounds from coming out of her.

Lying on the earth, trembling hard, she tried to listen. The woods seemed silent all around her. She tried to turn her head. It wasn't easy, it felt frozen in place. She tried to look up to see if she could spot the flashlight beams passing back and forth above her. But she saw nothing. Darkness. Thick black branches against a starry sky. That was all.

She coughed thickly. More noise. She went on trembling. She knew she couldn't lie here like this anymore. She had to start moving. She had to get warm. Yes, they would catch her. Yes, they would torture her. When they were done, they would probably kill her. But she didn't care. She was just too cold. She had to move. She had to.

It cost her a high price in pain to uncoil her shaking body, to get the frozen limbs in motion. All the strength seemed to have bled out of her arms and legs. Her hands were quivering so violently they seemed to vibrate. It was hard—really hard—to control them, to get them to do what she wanted them to do.

Still, somehow, by force of will, she managed to reach up. To clutch the top of the log behind which she lay hidden. Gasping with pain, with cold, she dragged herself up over the fallen tree. Immediately, she spotted the fire in the clearing a few yards away. It had dwindled down to almost nothing, just a snickering red glow beneath a pile of charred branches. But that was enough for her. The very sight of it made her moan again. Heat. She had to get to it. Had to. She needed heat.

Suddenly, a beam of white light smacked into her. A gruff voice shouted, "There she is! I've got her!"

Gripping the log, she turned and saw the killer in the darkness. It was Nosey, the guy whose beezer she had crushed. Lit by the outglow of his own flashlight, his face now looked monstrous. He looked like he had a red hole between his eyes. The eyes themselves seemed huge and white.

"She's over here!" he shouted. "Wake up! Come on! I've got her!"

When he stopped shouting, there was quiet again. No answer

from the surrounding woods. The killer and Molly were frozen like that a moment, staring at each other, linked together by the beam of light between them. Under his damaged nose, Nosey's teeth were bared in a ghoulish grin. Molly could barely keep her grip on the log. She was trembling, weak with cold; helpless.

Slowly, Nosey smiled. "O-o-h," he said, drawing out the syllable. Cruelty and anticipation warmed his strange voice. "Oh, little girl, you have given us a tough time—a tough time—but you are about to find out—"

Then two things happened very fast, one right after the other. Under the hole in the center of his face, Nosey's mouth opened in a great round "O"—and then the flashlight beam that had been shining in Molly's eyes flew up and pointed into the sky.

The next thing Molly knew, the light went out. Confused, freezing, she stared into the dark. The bright flash had blinded her, and now that it was gone she could see nothing. She listened. She could hear nothing. The woods seemed supernaturally quiet.

Had Nosey been a vision—the frightened hallucination of a dying girl? Had he been a dream? Was she still dreaming now?

What little strength there was in her arms gave out. She sank, trembling, against the log. She looked through the trees toward the red embers of the fire in the clearing. She knew she had to get to it, but she couldn't, she couldn't move.

Then the woods, the night, the pain, reality itself, began to reel away from her into a spinning distance. She was losing consciousness. Her whole body spasmed violently and she began to slide off the log, tumbling back down toward the earth.

But before she hit, something grabbed her. Hard, powerful

hands gripping her shoulders. Fingers pressing painfully into her flesh. Holding her up. Her eyelids fluttered as she tried to fight the blackness closing in on her mind. She tried to keep her eyes open, to stare through the swimming obscurity.

She saw a new face. A man. He loomed over her, pressed close to her. A man she had never seen before. A killer, by the look of him. Hard, tough, weather-beaten. Yet, strangely—as Molly thought in her fainting confusion—he did not seem unkind.

"I've got you," he said to her. "You're gonna be all right now."

The next thing she knew, she was being lifted up. Lifted into the air. The man was holding her against his chest, carrying her through the darkness. She shuddered uncontrollably in his arms. She leaned her head against him.

"Who . . . who are you?" she only just managed to whisper.

"Victor One," he said. "Your knight in shining armor."

"Love those," said Molly—and she passed out.

26. VELOCITY

RICK HEARD SOMEONE screaming in wild, uncontrollable panic. Slowly, he realized it was himself. That fact frightened him almost as much as the speed of the great mega-bull. Almost. But Rollie was shooting through the trees like a bullet—racing so fast, the blue forest had become one big blue blur on either side of them—and it was full-on terrifying. Up ahead, tree trunks were flashing straight toward Rick's face. Only at the last minute did the bull manage to swerve past them, before Rick could even think to duck or dodge. Boulders, streams, tangles of vines—one after another, they sprang up in front of him as if out of nowhere—barreled toward him like a runaway train—then vanished as the huge mega-bull somehow adjusted his trajectory without slowing down and managed to avoid a collision by inches.

Rick gripped Rollie's horns with all his might. He clutched his flanks with his aching legs. He tried to hold on, but the mega-bull's muscular back rippled and bucked as he ran and, to Rick, it felt almost impossible to stay in the saddle. The speed made Rick's body feel light, insubstantial. Any minute now, he thought, he would fly off into the air like a dandelion seed and blow away through the branches, never to be seen again.

But that scream of his—that high, crazy, panicking scream

that just kept coming out of his mouth—no matter how scared he was, he had to stop that! Guys aren't allowed to scream like that. It's in the Guy Rule Book. He clamped his lips shut, gritted his teeth. He fought to keep the noise inside him.

I have to turn . . . , he started to think—but just then, a thick branch came whipping toward his face. He ducked, pressed his cheek against the top of Rollie's head. He felt the wind in his hair as the branch whipped over him. When he next dared to peek up, the mega-bull had lifted off the ground in a tremendous onrushing leap and was flying over a stream. When the thundering hoofs hit the far bank, the impact nearly jolted Rick into oblivion. He bounced hard against the rough surface of the bull's hide. But he hung on, and Rollie kept running.

He finally managed to finish his thought: *I have to turn him.*

He drew a deep breath, fighting off the urge to let out another scream as yet another branch whipped past his forehead, just missing. He dared to take a quick look left and right to determine where he was. He saw the red grass through the trees to his right. Gripping the mega-bull's huge horns as hard as he could, he wrenched them rightward.

To his absolute astonishment, it worked. Rollie's head turned to the right and then his body turned—as smoothly as a car turns when you spin the wheel—and the mega-bull went on running in the new direction, the direction of the Golden City.

Rick didn't try to steer much after that. Rollie was racing through the forest faster than a human could think. The mega-bull seemed better able to direct himself past the onrushing obstacles. Rick knew if he tried to do it, he'd crash them into a tree and probably kill them both. Forcing down his urge to take control, Rick lay low on the mega-bull's back and let him run.

Seconds later they broke out of the woods and were shooting like a flash of light across the Scarlet Plain. Rick breathed a sigh of relief to be out of the forest, away from the oncoming trees and streams and stones. Now there was nothing but open red field and yellow sky in front of him—and the rising skyline of the Golden City in the distance, but coming closer at a speed Rick could never have believed unless he'd seen it for himself.

Rick's hands hurt from gripping the horns so tightly, but he didn't loosen his hold on that account, not at all. He hung on, pressed as close to the concrete skin of the mega-bull as he could, and prayed wordlessly that they would not hit a bump that would break his grip and send him flying.

The journey to the Golden City—the journey that Favian had said would take them ninety minutes at least—was finished in three minutes flat. Rollie the Mega-Bull's speed never slackened, not once. His hooves barely seemed to touch the ground as the red grass whipped at his flanks and the foggy yellow of the sky sailed over him.

Soon, the gleaming golden walls of the city were rising up above them, flashing in the light of day. Tall spired guard towers shot up out of the walls at intervals. In each tower, Rick could see the dark shape of some security bot, watching the horizon for attacks. Behind them, beyond the battlements, the domes and spires and towers of the great city thrust themselves up to the sky.

As he and the mega-bull came closer to the city—and they

came closer fast—Rick began to see creatures and vehicles moving in and out of the tall, arched city gates: beasts of Kurodar's imagination, created to supply his central city with the building materials and energy it needed to fuel the rest of the Realm. There were guards watching them go by. He couldn't make them out clearly yet, but they were big and had strange shapes and long weapons of some kind strapped to their backs.

Rollie kept running, and Rick was nervous about shifting too much on his back lest he lose his grip. But he did manage to peek up again over the mega-bull's head. Through the smoke and flames still shooting out of the creature's eyes and nostrils, he spotted the acres of high red grass that Favian had told him about. A small tug at Rollie's horns and the creature shifted and headed in that direction.

What now? Rick wondered. How was he going to dismount this thing? If he just jumped off the mega-bull at this speed, he'd be killed. The high grass was coming at him with unfathomable rapidity. Another fifteen seconds or so, and they'd be in the midst of it. Another five seconds after that, and they would shoot out the other side, visible to the guards.

Could he stop Rollie's headlong rush? He didn't know, but he was going to have to try. He hated the idea of sitting up, of unbalancing himself and making his perch on the creature even more unstable than it was. But what else could he do?

The high grass came racing toward them. Rick shifted his backside under him and straightened on the back of the mega-bull. Pulling back on the horns with his powerful arms, he murmured in a low steady voice, "Whoa, Rollie! Whoa!"

No one could have been more startled than Rick when the beast beneath him began to slow down. Like a once-wild horse that had accepted the guidance of a rider. The scenery that had been flashing by in smears of bright colors now steadied and cleared and the world around them became real again. A moment later, the high red grass was all around them, brushing at Rick's arms and face with a strange living warmth that was not like the cool, damp feel of grass at all.

The mega-bull's rush grew slower—and then slower—as Rick pulled back on his horns. The walls and towers and rising skyline of the Golden City, visible through the grass, grew tremendous. The edge of the field and the sparkling quartz road that wound into the city gates became visible. Another moment and they would break out of the grass onto the road. Then they'd be out in the open, exposed.

Luckily, before that happened, Rollie the Mega-Bull came to a full stop. It was as if he knew what Rick wanted and was willing to obey. He snuffled out some smoke and blinked out a bit of fire and bowed his head and began to nibble peacefully at the roots of the grass. As suddenly as the journey had begun, it ended.

Breathless, Rick tumbled off the creature's back. Still clutching one horn in one hand, he slid down and down the mega-bull's flank until his feet touched ground and the grass surrounded him. Finally, he let go of the horn and dropped to his knees. He was exhausted from the wild ride.

"Whew!" he said aloud.

He knelt in the earth, dazed and openmouthed. He turned to look at Rollie. Rollie turned to look at him. They blinked at each other. Then Rollie went back to grazing and Rick just knelt there, shaking his head in wonder at the fact that he was still alive.

At last, when he could, he climbed to his feet. He checked the timer in his palm. One hour and forty-three minutes left. Not a lot, but it would have to be enough. In fact, Rick wasn't even sure he'd be able to last in here that long.

Standing there like that, he could see very little besides the scarlet grass rising above his head on every side and the yellow sky floating above that. Before him, he could just barely make out the presence of the city walls. He moved toward them, the high grass whispering as he passed through.

Just before he came to the edge of the grass, there was a loud snort behind him. Rick's heart seized in his chest. He thought Rollie was about to roll himself up into a ball and charge again. But when he looked over his shoulder, the bull only nodded at him, a big heavy bull nod. Then he turned and galloped off amiably through the grass, heading back in the direction of the Blue Wood.

Thanks for the lift, Rollie, Rick thought.

Strange creature. Strange place.

Another moment and the beast was gone. Rick was alone. He continued moving through the grass.

When he reached the spot where the high grass ended, he peeked out. The quartz road ran past him, nearly at his feet. Beyond, maybe fifty yards away, was the city wall and its watchtowers. From here, Rick had to crane his neck to see the massively huge buildings that made the city's skyline. What a place this was close-up! Who *was* this Kurodar, anyway? What sort of man imagines something as magnificent as this into being—and then uses it as a way to bring destruction down on the real world?

Well, there was no time to think about it now. The next moment, Rick caught a movement out of the corner of his eye. He turned and saw a small cadre of five soldiers marching along the base of the walls. Well, they weren't soldiers exactly. They were Kurodar's security bots: the monsters that sprang out of that sick but fertile imagination of his. These were . . . what were they? Long slimy bodies that sometimes slithered along the ground and sometimes waddled on stump-like legs. Whip-like arms and flat, wicked faces with small, emotionless black eyes and huge fangs.

Cobras! They were walking cobras, with spear-like weapons strapped to their backs. And the weapons squirmed—and had eyes—and could watch out behind the Cobra Guards while the Cobras looked ahead.

The sight of these slithery monsters made something thick and sour rise in Rick's throat. He remembered the Alligator Guards who had patrolled the Sky Dome Fortress. He remembered how he had morphed himself into their alligator shape. It was hard to do. He could hold his concentration at that intensity for only a minute or so. But the thought of reshaping himself into one of these snake men—even for a second—disgusted him. Even with the intensity of mind focus he had used to flash out of Rollie's way, he didn't think he would be able to overcome his repulsion and pull it off.

As Rick watched, the wavering, slithering, stump-legged Cobras came to a halt in front of the city wall. Looking more closely, Rick saw there was a panel set in the base of the golden stone there. As the guards took up posts on either side of it, the panel slid open.

Out stepped a large creature, walking upright on two legs. It was something like a man but it was not a man. It was ovoid and its skin was covered in rough brown fur. Its face consisted of beady eyes and an extended snout with sharp tusks coming up on either side. It was dressed in blue overalls, opened in the back to let out its small scraggly tail.

The Boars! Rick realized. These were the Boars that Favian had told him about, the ones who loaded the blimps at the launch docks in the city walls.

Sure enough, as Rick crouched squinting from behind the screen of grass, a pair of smaller piggy men came trundling up the quartz road from the city gate, drawing a cart behind them. There were heavy metal canisters loaded on the cart. As the cart approached the Cobra Guards, a motion at the open panel caught Rick's attention. He saw a gray blimp-shaped rocket being drawn nose-first through the launch gate.

As Rick turned, he saw other carts being drawn to other launch doors where there were other Boars and more Cobra Guards with their living spears. The blimps were being prepared for the coming of the great WarCraft.

Maybe if I can change myself into a Boar . . . , Rick thought.

Just then—just as he thought that—a shadow fell across the sky. The temperature dropped and the air began to snap and shimmer as if charged with electricity.

Rick turned his eyes from the commotion and lifted them to the sky, where cloud-like splashes of lavender were beginning to spread over the yellow surface.

Rick's hair bristled on his head.

The WarCraft, he thought. *It's coming back.*

27. RESCUE

FIRE FILLED MOLLY'S vision. She sat up fast, afraid. Where was she? The woods. Yes, she remembered. The night. The cold. Her whole body shuddered. Her very bones felt frozen.

But she was warmer than she'd been. The bonfire was blazing high and the heat was moving through her. Plus she was wearing a fleece she hadn't been wearing before. She leaned toward the flames hungrily, letting the warmth wash over her, into her. It was wonderful, but . . .

But as her mind started to clear, a dark thought came to her: If she was sitting by the killers' fire, then the killers must have found her, must have captured her. She tried to remember.

Now, though, a series of sounds made her stiffen. Crackling branches, crunching leaves. Footsteps. Coming closer. She stared in the direction of the noise, but the light of the flames blinded her and all she could see was darkness on the far side.

Then the man stepped into view, his weather-beaten features lit like a demon's by the flames. Molly remembered: He was the one who had found her. Carried her from her hiding place. Her "knight in shining armor," he'd said. A cruel, sneering joke from one of the men who were planning to torture and kill her . . .

The man—Victor One, he had called himself—was carrying

a fresh load of sticks in his arms. He dumped them on top of the fire. The flames were already so high they swallowed the fresh wood easily, rising and snickering and smoking up into the black reaches of the forest sky.

The man looked across the fire at Molly. "You're up. Good. How you feeling?"

She didn't answer, wouldn't answer, wouldn't give the thug the satisfaction. She pulled her knees up high and hugged her legs to herself. She was beginning to feel warm. She was beginning to feel as if she might still be alive.

"Pretty old-fashioned stunt—fainting in my arms like that," the man went on with a half smile. Molly tensed as he began to move around the fire toward her. "Like one of those ladies in the long dresses in old movies. I kind of enjoyed it, to tell the truth. I wish more women would faint in my arms like that. Practically never happens."

He was standing over her now. She could feel the threat of his presence above her, the insinuating threat of his words. She did not know how she was going to get through this ordeal, but she didn't suppose it mattered much in the long run, seeing as he was almost certainly going to kill her in the end.

"I mean, you know, I try to be a modern guy and all that," said Victor One—and now he crouched down beside her, his elbows on his knees. He was playing with a small twig in his fingers. Molly cringed away from him, frowning with distaste. "But there's something about an old-fashioned girl . . . ," he went on.

"Get away from me, you pig," Molly snapped. "You disgust me, all of you."

The crags on Victor One's face deepened as his eyebrows drew together. "I'm gonna try not to take that remark personally," he said. "But I think you may be mistaking me for some other pig."

Molly looked away from him. She stared into the fire bitterly. "You're all the same to me. You're just another killer, like the rest."

Crouched beside her, Victor One smiled into the flames. "Well, I am a killer, sure enough. A good one, too, trained by the United States government for the job. But I'm not like the rest, Molly. I'm your killer . . . Wait, that didn't sound right. What I mean is: I'm a killer who's on your side."

It took a moment before the meaning of these words sank into Molly's mind. Slowly, she raised her eyes from the fire. She glanced quickly at Victor One. His relaxed attitude. His half smile. Then, just as quickly, she looked around herself, all around, searching for the men who had hunted her here.

"The others," she said, trying to think. "Where are all the other ones?"

"In all honesty, Mol, you probably don't want to know the answer to that. Not in any detail, anyway."

Molly felt her lips part as she began to understand. This time when she turned to Victor One, she was staring at him, gaping at him.

"You . . . ? What did you . . . ? You mean . . . ? But . . . You couldn't . . . There were five of them!"

Victor One shrugged modestly. "Actually, there were six, if you count the one I followed out of town. I took care of him back by the house. But really, it wasn't as spectacular as all that. Oh, all right, it was pretty spectacular. But it was mostly a matter of waiting for them to leave the pack one by one. The first went off into the woods to go to the bathroom. The second went off to find him when the first didn't come back. The next one wandered away from the group looking for you. The last one—well, you saw me take him just after he found you."

As Molly remembered, as the picture of what had happened became clear, her mind was crowded with questions.

"That's only four," she said.

"Yeah, one of them got away—the pale snaky-looking one with the weird smile. He's the leader, I'm betting."

Molly nodded, dazed. "He is. Smiley McDeath, I call him."

Victor One laughed. "That's good. Smiley McDeath. He's the smartest of the lot. He figured out what was happening pretty quick. I was hoping he'd come looking for me, you know. But he was too smart for that. I guess he figured he wasn't sure what he was up against: one man or twenty. So he just ran for it."

"Then he'll get others. He'll come back for us," said Molly.

Victor One nodded. "He will, for sure. And we won't be too hard to find with this fire going. Soon as you can walk, we better get out of here. Meanwhile, you're going to need this."

He reached into a pack that lay on the ground beside him— one of the packs abandoned by the killers, she thought. He brought out a couple of energy bars and a bottle of water.

As Molly's fear receded, her hunger came back to her with a vengeance. Without a word, she snatched one of the bars from Victor One's hand. She tore the wrapper off and bit the bar in half. Food. Bliss. Almost as good as the heat from the fire.

"Hungry a little?" said Victor One with another smile.

Molly tried to speak around the great gob of gunk that filled her mouth. It came out something like "Humpharumphayumph."

"I couldn't agree more," said Victor One.

Molly swallowed. "Who are you?" she said.

"I told you. I'm called Victor One. That's how they name us, a designating letter and a training rank: Alpha Nine, Bravo Four, Charlie Ten. Juliet Seven got the short end of the stick, if you ask me, but I never tease him about it since the guy's built like a refrigerator and he's big enough to drive me into the earth with a single blow. But the point is, I work security for a secret government agency."

Molly's mind was still moving slowly, but she thought she was beginning to understand. "Rick sent you. It was Rick, wasn't it?" Even as she said it, the idea pleased her. However Rick might feel about her, he hadn't abandoned her entirely.

Something flickered behind Victor One's eyes. Molly wasn't sure what it was. But he said slowly, almost reluctantly, "Rick, yes. Rick and his dad. I'm assigned to protect Rick's dad, and he was worried no one else would come looking for you. It's a long story."

"You came alone," she said. "No . . . police, no FBI."

Victor One looked down at the ground. "Like I said, a long story. When you're warm enough, and you've had some water, we better go."

"Shouldn't we call for help?"

"We can't. The people we're up against—the bad guys—they're using new technology, state-of-the-art stuff—all very hush-hush. Even I don't really know what they're up to. But I ditched all my comms before I started after them. Otherwise, they might have tracked me, seen me coming a mile off."

Molly went on tearing at her energy bar, washing the stuff down with long draughts of water. She was done with the first bar in a minute and moved on to the second. She could not believe how good it felt to eat. She remembered all the times she had said—to her mother, to her friend—*Let's eat. I'm starving.* She realized now that not only had she never been starving, she'd never even been hungry, not really, not like this.

She had a million questions she wanted to ask this Victor One guy. For instance: Where was Rick? And what did Rick say when he found out she had been kidnapped? And where were the police, too? Why hadn't *they* come looking for her with helicopters and rifles and all that stuff? And who were these men who had kidnapped her, anyway. What did they want?

As she ate, she stole glances at Victor One where he crouched beside her, his craggy face lit by the flames. Now that she knew he wasn't one of *them*, she had begun to kind of like him. He was so relaxed and easygoing with all this danger around them. It made her feel safe just to have him there.

"What are we going to do now?" she asked him.

"Well, soon as you can, we better start moving before your pal Smiley McDeath comes back with reinforcements. The question is: Where do we go?"

"Out of these woods, for a start," said Molly.

"Right. But here's the thing: there's swamp all through here. There's really only a narrow corridor of dry land—that's one of the reasons they could track you so easily. Assuming the smiley guy *has* called in the troops, we can't go back the way you came without being spotted."

"So what do we do?"

"Well, there's a road about two miles in the opposite direction. If you can make it that far, we might be able to get a lift back to my car."

"I can make it," said Molly.

Victor One gave her a full-fledged smile—and when he did that, Molly noticed, he was actually kind of cute. For a killer and all. "I kind of thought you'd say that. Ready?"

He stood up quickly and offered her his hand. She took it and he drew her up to her feet. She swallowed the last of her energy bar.

"I'm sorry I called you a pig," she said.

He smiled again, his eyes crinkling at the edges. "I've been called worse—and usually by guys with machine guns. Let's go."

He picked up a pack and slung it over his shoulder. He brought out a small flashlight and trained its beam on the ground before them. With a final glance back at her, he headed off into the darkness. Molly followed.

It felt good to be moving. It felt good not to be so hungry. It felt good to be warm and have a fleece on. And it felt good to have her own personal killer out here in case Smiley McDeath returned with reinforcements. It made her feel safe—or safer, at least.

The two traveled in silence for a while. Victor One moved smoothly and steadily. He followed his flashlight beam and Molly followed him. Victor One said nothing and that was okay for a while. Soon, though, the questions rose up in Molly's mind again.

"Why did these people kidnap me?" she asked.

Victor One glanced back at her but didn't answer. He kept heading through the night, through the woods.

She pressed him: "Was it to get at Rick? It was, wasn't it?"

"Yeah," he said after a moment. "It was, pretty much."

"Because he's fighting them somehow," said Molly. "Whoever they are."

"That's right."

"And they thought they could make him stop by threatening me."

"You got it all figured out, haven't you?"

"But he couldn't stop, could he? Because people's lives are in danger."

"That's right."

"And he knew I wouldn't want him to stop."

This time when he looked at her, she could see the look of admiration in the glow of the flashlight. "Maybe so. Probably."

"So he sent you instead."

"Right."

"And how did you find me?"

"Your code. The JogHard app. Rick's kid brother figured it out."

"Little Raider?"

"I think he can name every app in the app store."

Molly's mind kept returning to Rick, though. "What about Rick?" she asked. "What did he say about it all? Did he send me a message or anything?"

Victor One gave her a searching look. She wasn't sure what he was thinking. What he said was, "He wanted to come himself. He really did. I had to talk him down. We need him somewhere else and . . . well, like I said, I have the training for this kind of thing."

"But he wanted to come?" Molly couldn't stop herself from asking.

"He did."

She nodded, satisfied. Victor One gave a wry smile. Again, she couldn't read what was on his mind, but she sensed her questions irked him. Which pleased Molly somehow. She didn't put it into words exactly, but instinct told her Victor One was irked because she was asking about Rick, because he was jealous of Rick.

"Why don't you have a gun?" she asked.

"What makes you think I don't have a gun?"

"I didn't hear any shots before when you were . . . dealing with those men."

"Gunshots would have alerted them. And we might need the bullets later on."

"Well, then why—"

"Let me ask you a question," he interrupted her.

"All right," said Molly. He was clearly getting even more irked, and she found herself smiling at this as they moved together through the darkness.

"How'd you get away from them?" he asked. "How'd you escape from that room?"

"I dug a nail up out of the floorboard and I hit one of the men in the neck with it."

She was startled by the sound of Victor One's deep booming laughter. "You did not!"

"I did so!"

He laughed again. "And here I thought you were just an old-fashioned—"

Suddenly his voice stopped. He stopped moving. The flash-light went off.

"What was that?" said Molly.

"Get low," he said.

He crouched down and so did Molly.

They had broken out of the thicker trees now, she noticed. The sky above them was broad and strewn with stars. In the star-light, Molly could see that they had come into what must've been a swamp area. All around her there were open stretches of lowland. There were zigzagging ridges of thick foliage with the jagged trunk of a dead tree sticking up here and there.

Molly listened. In the winter cold there were none of the usual wetland sounds. No crickets or frogs. The silence seemed wide and deep. At first she couldn't imagine what Victor One had heard, what had made him stop the way he did.

But then she heard it, too.

There was a low, steady thrumming whisper in the air above them. It was getting louder by the second. It wasn't a woodland sound, not a natural sound. It was man-made, Molly was sure of it. In fact, after a moment, she thought it sounded familiar, even though she couldn't quite figure out what it was.

Then she knew: it was a propeller.

She turned to Victor One in the darkness.

"Is that a plane?" she whispered.

"Ssh," Victor One hissed at her.

The sound grew steadily louder, closer. Not a plane. Too small. Too low. She stared into the gleam of Victor One's eyes. She thought: *What? What is it?*

He answered aloud as if he'd heard her. "It's a drone," he said quietly. "I'd know that sound anywhere."

"A drone? You mean, like a little airplane? Like in wars?"

"Yeah, just like in—"

But before he could finish, a spotlight shot down out of the sky and pinned them where they crouched. Molly could just make out the miniature white aircraft behind the light.

Victor One grabbed Molly's arm and stood up, pulling her to her feet.

"Run!" he shouted.

They were already moving when the drone opened fire.

28. BAD PIGGIES

THE GROUND JOLTED and trembled beneath Rick's feet. The lavender clouds continued to spread above him, darkening the Realm's yellow sky. The air crackled with electricity. And above the growing roar of the approaching WarCraft, Rick heard the Boars calling to one another in deep, ragged snorting voices.

"Come on!"

"This way!"

"Hurry! Load 'em up!"

Peering through the high scarlet grass, Rick saw that the blimp-shaped supply rockets had rolled farther out of the launch doors. Their cargo bays were open and the Worker Boars were lifting metal canisters off their carts and pushing them inside. He knew the enormous WarCraft would appear on the horizon any minute. He had to work fast.

With the ground quaking beneath him, with the sky growing darker above him, with a sound like thunder filling the air, it took all of Rick's will to turn his mind away from what was happening around him and focus his spirit entirely on himself, his own form. He reached down into that deep essential part of himself. He funneled his attention into a narrow corridor of focus. He held it on the shape of his hand, his arm, his torso. He willed his outline to change.

Slowly, in a weird dream-like shift, his body began to morph.

Only a few seconds later, the sky went night-black as the vast WarCraft of Kurodar rumbled up over the horizon. The tentacles of the octopus-like beast that surrounded the ship whipped out over the roiling sky. The beast's huge head came into view, its repulsive and malevolent eyes scanning the scene below it. All around the walls of the Golden City, lightning began to flicker and flash. The blimps in their launch stations shuddered and lifted as the electric bolts shot over them. The Pilot Boars shouted at the Worker Boars to hurry, and the Worker Boars rushed to throw more canisters into the blimps' bays.

And one of those Worker Boars was Rick himself.

Using all the power of his spirit, he had reshaped his avatar, ballooning his belly, covering his flesh with rough fur, forcing his face to stretch into a tusked snout. It was kind of nauseating when it happened, but he swallowed his sickness and kept at it. Once he was in Boar shape, he had slipped out of the high grass into the busy and chaotic scene.

Above him, the slimy tentacles of the WarCraft monster wafted across the sky, close enough, it seemed, to reach down and grab him as they had in his nightmare. The giant WarCraft continued its long rise, the vast saucer shape blotting out the sky. The Cobra Guards kept watch and their living spears acted as eyes in the backs of their heads. All the same, the scene was so confusing that as a Boar Rick was able to move through the little crowd with a show of confidence and join the other Worker Boars around their cart. In the flashing darkness, he grabbed a canister off the cart and carried it to the blimp-like supply ship. He tossed it into the open bay and immediately climbed up into the bay after it.

"Come on," he shouted back at the others in a snorting pig-voice as he balanced himself atop the stack of canisters. "There's room for a few more, hand them up!"

Outside the air grew even darker as the lightning flashes grew brighter and steadier. The supply ship bucked and lifted under his cloven feet as if it were coming to life. One of the Boars outside handed him another canister. Rick grabbed it and helped shift it up into the bay. The moment it was onboard, he moved his clumsy piggy form across the top of the canister stack. He reached the end of the pile and slid down onto the bay floor. Now he was inside the belly of the ship. And there, a few steps away from him, was the door to the cockpit. He went to it quickly and pushed through.

He stood on the threshold of the cockpit as the thunderous rumble outside grew louder and the flashes of lightning continued and the ship juddered and wobbled all around him. The cockpit, he saw, was cartoonishly simple. There was a swivel seat and a steering wheel like the wheel of a car. There was a broad wind-shield, and a flight deck with a monitor, and a few switches and knobs. Over the crashing noise of the rising WarCraft, Rick heard voices raised behind him.

"It's lifting off! Shut the cargo bay! Hurry!"

Looking back over his shoulder, Rick saw two Boars grab hold of the bay doors and swing them shut. At the same moment, the door to the cockpit opened. Rick faced front and saw a Pilot Boar step in.

The Pilot Boar was large and mean-looking. He had dead black eyes and a long curling snout with two sharp tusks showing. His hide was covered in thick, stiff, bristling hairs. At his waist he wore a belt. In the belt, he had some kind of pistol holstered.

With all the noise outside, and with the ship beginning to roll and quake and rise, Rick was beginning to lose his concentration. He could feel his morphed shape about to slip. He tried to hold on, but his focus was collapsing.

Rick sank back a little into the cargo bay and the Pilot Boar didn't see him right away. The Pilot was working quickly to close the door before the lightning lifted the supply ship into the air and sent it soaring up to the WarCraft.

Rick fought for another second to hold his shape, but how could he with the noise and the flashing darkness outside and the gigantic tentacles waving across the windshield?

The Pilot Boar shut the door hard and pressed a large iron bolt through two metal loops, locking the door in place. He turned to approach the ship's controls.

And as he turned, he spotted Rick standing in the bay doorway.

And as he spotted Rick, Rick's Boar shape began to slip.

"What . . . what are you doing here?" said the Pilot Boar, confused by the sight of the blurred and shifting figure.

Outside, the lightning flashed again—and now became a steady electric blast all around them, turning the windows white. The supply ship lifted unsteadily into the air.

Rick made one last desperate attempt to hold on to his shape, to answer the Pilot in a gruff Boar voice. But it was no use. The next moment his morph slipped away and he turned back into himself.

The Pilot Boar's black eyes went wide. His hand went to the weapon at his side.

"Intruder!" he whispered, startled.

Caught, Rick had no choice. He drew his sword and rushed at him.

29. DUEL

THE FOREST ERUPTED with light and gunfire as the drone dove out of the night at Victor and Molly. Molly heard herself scream as the bullets whispered by her legs. The slugs peppered the ground all around her, throwing up clods of earth to her left and right. The near presence of death erased everything from her mind but fear.

She ran blindly through the darkness. She heard the propeller of the small, deadly plane right behind her. She clutched Victor One's hand as he ran ahead, as he pulled her along over the invisible path. They were moving so fast and it was so dark, she quickly lost any notion of where she was or where she was going. All she knew was that the drone's spotlight was searching her out, and every time it touched her, every time it even came near her, there was a fresh barrage of hot lead.

"This way!" Victor One shouted.

He swerved suddenly, heading for the black shape of a large tree trunk rising to their left. Molly wasn't ready for the quick movement. She tried to follow him, but she stepped on something—a rock she thought—and her ankle twisted. She lost her balance. The next thing she knew she was falling, unable to see, unable to recover. She hit the earth hard, her breath coughing out of her.

"Molly!" she heard Victor One shout.

The next moment, the drone shot out of the sky and its spotlight caught her where she lay. She looked up just in time to see the single white eye of the flying machine bearing down on her. She knew that in the next second, it would open fire again. In the second after that, she would be dead.

A blast sounded right above her. She felt her heart seize in her chest. Was that it? Was she hit, was she wounded? Was she going to die? She saw a hot spark flash up out of the spotlight's glare, as if something had struck the fuselage of the drone and ricocheted off it. A second later, the drone swerved. The spotlight tilted to the side and Molly was lying in darkness again as the machine flew past her.

"Come on!" shouted Victor One.

She looked up. The bodyguard was standing above her, a pistol gripped in his hand. He had fired on the drone, sent it reeling away before it could rake her with bullets. Now he was clutching her arm, hauling her to her feet.

She leapt up. She looked around. She saw the drone soaring away above the swamp hedges in the near distance. It was already banking to the right, already turning, preparing to circle around and come back at them.

"The tree!" shouted Victor One.

He didn't have to say it twice. She was clutching his hand again, flying through the dark again, her head filled with the sound of her own gasping breaths and the deadly whisper of the drone's propeller.

They reached the tree trunk, a looming black ruin of what

had once been an ancient oak. Victor One stopped short beside it. Molly, following blindly, ran right into him. He caught her, held her shoulders in his two hands, pressed her against his chest as if to shield her from the drone with his body.

Held in his grip, Molly turned her head and saw the drone giving chase. It had turned full around now, was heading back toward them. Its spotlight cut a swath through the darkness, searching them out.

"It's going to find us," she said, her voice trembling.

"I know," said Victor One.

And sure enough, the next moment, the spotlight swept over them. The drone steadied and headed their way.

And still Victor One held Molly against him, as if he were just going to stand there, wait for the thing. As if he thought he was so tough the bullets would just bounce off him.

"It's going to shoot!" she cried out, terrified.

"Hold still," said Victor One, his voice firm. "Hold still until I tell you."

The spitting whisper of the drone's propeller became a low, grinding hum. Molly saw the winged craft adjust its path and rocket toward them through the air. It was almost within range again, almost ready to open fire and cut them to pieces.

"Now!" shouted Victor One—and in the same instant, he swung Molly around in a dizzying arc, putting the oak's trunk between them and the drone.

The drone let off a short burst of gunfire. Molly heard the bullets thud into the dead tree. But then the hunting machine must have realized its prey had ducked out of sight: it stopped shooting.

Molly heard the aircraft let out a whine. She understood: Victor One had dodged so quickly it hadn't had time to readjust its flight path. It was heading straight for the trunk.

Molly said a quick prayer that the machine would crash. But no deal. The drone banked and swung to the right just in time. She saw the plane's white belly as it swerved away from the tree trunk and cut off again through the darkness.

"Stay here, stay covered," Victor One told her.

He let her go and stepped out from behind the tree.

"What are you doing?" Molly shouted.

But Victor One did not look back.

Having passed the tree trunk, the drone was now retreating from them. Victor One lifted his pistol, gripping it in one hand while he held his arm steady with the other. He took careful aim at the retreating aircraft.

And then he stood there like that, his legs spread, his body planted, the gun trained on the aircraft.

"Shoot it," said Molly. The words broke from her before she even thought to speak.

"Too far," said Victor One in an undertone. "I've only got fourteen shots left. They have to count."

"But it's going to turn. It's going to come back."

"I know. Just stay behind the tree, Molly."

She did. She hugged the trunk and pressed her cheek against the rough bark. She watched as the drone flew out over the swamp, began to bank, began to turn. Once again, its spotlight shot through the night, searching them out. Once again, the light grew brighter as the drone approached.

Victor One stood where he was, out in the open, his gun leveled at the oncoming plane. It made Molly breathless to watch him. It was a kind of courage she had never seen before: a soldier's courage. It was as if he was challenging the thing to a duel, face-to-face, his pistol against its machine gun. For her. To protect her.

She watched as the drone swept toward him through the night. She held her breath. The light from the drone's spotlight crept across the ground, closer to Victor One and closer. It found him. The glow touched his feet. It traveled up his legs.

"Shoot it," Molly said, but her voice was squeezed out between her gritted teeth, barely audible.

The drone came closer. Victor One stayed still, his pistol trained on the oncoming spotlight.

Shoot it! This time, Molly wasn't sure whether she had spoken aloud or not. She was just willing Victor One to blow the thing out of the air.

Then, at the very same instant, Victor One pulled the trigger, and the drone let loose a deadly barrage.

The blast of the bodyguard's Glock filled the forest. The patter of the drone's answering fire made the earth shiver. There was an explosion of glass and the drone's spotlight went out, drenching the forest in darkness. The drone coughed and wavered in the air.

Molly was about to let out a cheer of triumph—but now, by starlight, she saw Victor One stagger backward in her direction.

The drone—dark now with its spotlight gone—veered unsteadily to the right and missed the tree trunk by inches, flying past and out over the swamp again.

And at the same time, Victor One was falling. He toppled

down heavily at Molly's feet. She stared through the night and saw the blood pouring from his forehead. The gore had already splashed down over the side of his face.

She screamed in terror. "Victor!"

But he didn't answer. He didn't move.

Molly heard the drone retreating. Then the noise of the propeller changed. She turned in the direction of the sound. Now that its spotlight was gone, she could only just make out the pale shadow of the thing.

But she could see that it was turning, circling around.

Victor One lay motionless on the earth as the drone came back for Molly.

30. WHEN PIGS FLY

THERE IS A lot of praying in football. At least there was when Rick played. As the team's quarterback, he had frequently led the other players in a prayer before a game. Some people— even some of the other players on the team—made fun of Rick's prayers. They thought he was praying for victory, and they said that God didn't care who won a football game; God had more important things to worry about. But Rick ignored the jokes. He never prayed for victory. He prayed for excellence. He prayed for a strong spirit in adversity and courage under attack. He prayed for help with sportsmanship in the midst of ferocious competition and for the health of both his team and the opposing players. In those days, when he still trusted God without question, he understood that God could use either victory or defeat to his good purposes.

But once the prayers were over, once he was out on the field, once the kickoff happened and play began, the thought of winning—the desire to win—frequently overwhelmed him. Well, of course it did. He was playing a game, after all. Games are played to win, and he knew that the desire to win can bring out the best in you. You don't strive for excellence with your whole heart if you don't want to win with your whole heart. You don't need a strong spirit in adversity if you don't want victory so badly you're willing to endure adversity. You don't even need sportsmanship really if you don't want to win—sportsmanship, after all, is about rising above the passions of the conflict to treat your opponent with fairness and respect; you can't rise above the passions of the conflict if you don't feel them. In the end, it is the desire to win that lifts you to better things than victory.

But sometimes, too, the desire to win could become all-consuming. There were moments in the thick of a game when Rick felt as if he would rather die than let the "W" slip away from him, moments when the good intentions of his earlier prayers vanished and all that was left in his heart was the hunger to score. In moments like that, the ideas of excellence, of spirit and courage and sportsmanship, slipped from his mind. In moments like that, he wanted nothing more spiritual than the next touchdown.

This was a moment like that.

He had come back into the MindWar Realm for the best of reasons. He was risking his life and his mind to protect his country, to protect the lives of innocent people, to try to save his friends Mariel and Favian. As the lid of the glass portal box had been closing over him, he had prayed, just as he used to pray before a game, prayed that whether he lived or died, he would be able to stop the coming terrorist attack and rescue his friends.

But Rick was a passionate guy. His heart could be overwhelmed with emotion quickly. Right now, all his prayers were forgotten. Right now, his only thought was: *victory*.

With Mariel's sword gripped in his white-knuckled hand, he raced across the cockpit at the huge Pilot Boar. The sporadic lightning outside had become a steady blast, and the supply craft was rising on it, flashing with it, rolling this way and that.

As Rick attacked, the Pilot Boar reached for his pistol. But before he could draw it, the ship's turbulent motion flung the pig back against the cockpit wall. The impact jolted his arm away from his holster. And now Rick was too close for him to draw. Instead, the Boar crouched and lifted his arms to fight off the intruder's assault. His arms were huge, massively muscled, and bristly with stiff brown needles of fur. His snout was curled at the lips, making his tusks seem enormous. His beady eyes flashed black.

Rick and the Pilot Boar came crashing together. Rick brought Mariel's blade sweeping down at the creature's head, but one of those big Boar arms came up and blocked Rick's swing. The bristling forearm smacked into Rick's wrist. Rick's hand snapped open and the sword went flying, clanging against the wall before it dropped down and wedged itself behind the control panel.

In the next instant Boar and Man were locked together, struggling for supremacy. The Boar was incredibly strong, a wild beast, full of power. But Rick's rage for victory surged through him and gave him power to match power. For long seconds, the two combatants were frozen in their wrestling pose, neither able to gain the upper hand.

Then, outside, with a deafening electric crackle, the lightning bridge that linked the Golden City on the ground to the huge WarCraft darkening the sky above was amped up to full wattage. The supply ship shot up into the sky. The floor beneath the fighters dipped and slid and the Pilot Boar and Rick were thrown tumbling across the cockpit. They smashed into the wall and broke apart.

Both fell to the floor and both tried to scramble to their feet immediately as the supply ship tipped and rollicked and flew. The heavy Pilot Boar crashed shoulder-first into the flight controls. Rick was thrown against the Pilot's chair. Both fighters grabbed anything they could—the panel's edge, the chair's back—and dragged themselves upright.

Now the Pilot Boar reached for his gun. He moved fast for such a big creature, his hand a blur. He drew the pistol. He pointed it at Rick's chest. He pulled the trigger.

But by then Rick had pushed himself off the chair. He had a moment—an instant—to focus his spirit. His body dissolved into moving atoms. Like Favian, he flashed across the cockpit. In an instant—less than an instant—he was in front of the startled Boar. He swung his arm at the Boar's arm. He knocked the Boar's hand aside. The pistol shot out a lancing purple flash of energy. Rick felt the heat of it as it sizzled past his side. Then he had the Pilot Boar's wrist in his powerful grip. He twisted until the Boar grunted in pain. The gun dropped. But then, with his free hand, the Boar slugged Rick in the side of the head. It was a powerful blow that might have knocked a lesser man unconscious. But Rick was so wild to win, so full of competitive passion, that he barely felt the punch. He grabbed the Pilot Boar by his thick and furry throat and the two went spinning across the cockpit again, locked together in their death struggle.

The supply ship was now sailing up off the surface of the Realm and shooting toward the WarCraft. The ship's wraparound windshield was filled with lightning and sky—a sky now gone dark beneath the blossoming indigo clouds. As Rick and the Pilot

Boar wrestled in the cockpit, the clouds surrounded the rocketing ship. The windshield was blotted with murky blue. The lightning bridge turned a muted gray. The craft wobbled and shuddered as if it might stall at any moment and plummet to the ground.

And, in fact, the supply ship took a sickening dip. Rick lost his footing. His grip on the Pilot Boar's throat loosened. The beast seized the opportunity, seized Rick by his arm and by the front of his shirt, and used his mighty muscles to hurl the human intruder across the cockpit. Rick's back crashed into the cockpit door. The large iron bolt jutted into his spine, shocking the breath out of him.

Now, carried on the lightning, the supply ship sailed into the central vortex of the purple clouds. The glass of the windshield went starkly black, a blackness riven by the steady bright white flash. In the instant Rick stood stunned against the door, he saw that black sky outside and remembered the living blackness of the Canyon of Nothingness, its power to draw a person into itself forever.

On the other side of the cockpit, the Pilot Boar spotted his pistol where it had fallen. The ship dipped and swung. The gun slid toward the storage bay. The Boar moved unsteadily away from the wall to go after it.

Rick, meanwhile, saw his sword leaning where it had fallen, its silver blade wedged between the control panel and the wall, its carved hilt sticking free. Holding with one hand to the iron bolt in the metal loops of the door and frame, he reached for the sword with his other hand. His fingers scraped the hilt. He felt the power of Mariel's presence. He stretched farther. He got hold of Mariel's image. He grabbed the sword. He pulled it free.

A second later, the Pilot Boar caught up with his pistol. Bending over, he swept the gun up in one hand. The ship swung unsteadily on the lightning and the Pilot Boar stumbled against the far wall, waving his arms wildly as he tried to regain his balance. He tried to bring the pistol to bear on Rick.

Rick held the sword with one hand. With the other, he pulled the door's iron bolt out of its loops. He hurled it at the Pilot Boar.

The heavy bolt spun through the air, end over end. It was a good throw. The bolt went straight for the Pilot Boar's head. The Boar had to duck—and the wild movement of the ship made him stagger. For yet another second, he could not get off a shot with his pistol.

As the Pilot Boar fought to steady himself and take aim, Rick grabbed hold of the unbolted door's latch and tried to pull the door open. It wouldn't budge. He lifted his sword and jammed its point into the doorframe. It stuck. He pressed against the hilt for leverage—used all his strength, pulling at the door.

The door came open.

Rick had seen the blackness outside, and he knew its power. It was the living nothingness of Kurodar's evil, hungry to pull everything into itself. The lightning flashed and sizzled just below the ship's belly, but it was the blackness that filled the doorway and the blackness was hungry. The minute the door opened, the powerful draw of the dark began to seize at everything inside the cockpit and suck it out. The pistol flew from the Pilot Boar's hand and spun out of the cockpit into the dark. The Boar himself, massive as he was, began to slide across the floor toward the opening, fighting as he stumbled toward blackness and death.

Rick too. Holding on to the door's loop, he felt his feet trying to fly out from under him, being pulled out into the darkness. With one hand, he pressed hard against his sword. He held it in place in the doorframe so that the blade lay across the door's opening. With his other hand, he fought to hold the door open. He dug his heels into the floor to keep from flying out.

The Pilot Boar had nothing to hold on to. Fighting the draw of the blackness, he fell on his piggy butt. He fought and struggled and kicked, but the blackness drew him steadily across the floor. At the last moment, his enormous form was lifted into the air. He let out a deep, ragged, snorting scream. And then the darkness sucked him out of the cockpit. As he sailed out the door, he struck Mariel's blade. The Boar was cut in half. With a flash of purple energy, his two pieces vanished and he was gone, back into the digital nothingness from which he'd sprung.

Rick shifted his weight behind the door and, giving a grunt, shouldered it shut. He wrangled Mariel's sword from the frame and drove the blade through the loops to hold the door in place.

The supply ship continued its flight through the black sky, buoyed by the jagged lightning. Fighting its motion, Rick staggered across the cockpit to the pilot's seat. He reached the chair in front of the wheel and dropped into it, breathless, grateful.

It was only then, with the battle over, that the passionate warrior grew calm enough to remember his prayers.

Thank you, he thought, wiping the sweat off his forehead with the back of his hand.

He took control of the supply ship and steered it toward the WarCraft.

31. ALONE

MOLLY'S HEART POUNDED, her mind rushed. Victor One lay motionless on the ground at her feet, his face bathed in blood. Was he alive? She couldn't tell. She couldn't see whether or not he was breathing.

The drone was at the far edge of the swamp now. She could hear the hunter machine's propellers working as it banked in the dark, turning to come back toward her. Victor had shot out the machine's spotlight, but Molly knew it must have tracking machines inside it, too. It wouldn't need the light to find her, or to gun her down.

Her first feeling when she saw Victor fall had been a sense of utter helplessness. In the brief time she had been with him, she had gotten used to having a trained fighter on her side. She had quickly gotten used to following him, letting him protect her. Now she was alone, and she didn't think she was strong enough to survive.

But she remembered how she had felt in her cell with the Giant coming to get her. She remembered her despair, and how she had risen above her despair and decided to fight. She was not going to stop fighting now.

The drone finished its circle. It started to head back toward her across the open ground.

Molly looked around her, panting with fear, her eyes wide and white. She had to get away. She had to hide. What should she do?

Before she could come up with an answer, a sound came to her, just audible under the sound of the oncoming aircraft.

A groan.

She looked down at Victor One. His bloody head moved slightly. He was still alive!

She couldn't just leave him lying out there exposed. If she abandoned him and ran, the drone would riddle the fallen soldier with bullets.

The sound of the drone's propellers grew louder as it flew swiftly toward her. For another second, Molly stood where she was, too frightened to do what she knew she had to do. Openmouthed, she looked down. Victor One stirred. He groaned again. His bloody head shook back and forth as if he were trying to awaken himself.

That did it. Molly started to move. She stooped to the fallen Victor One. The movement brought her out of the shelter of the tree. She glanced up. The drone was bearing down on her. She had only a few seconds. She bent over and grabbed Victor One's wrists, one in each hand. She tried to drag him toward the trunk.

"Oof," she said.

The man was as heavy as cement. Athletic as she was, Molly had to use all her strength to get him moving. Victor One groaned again—and Molly groaned as she dragged him over the rough forest earth and behind the tree trunk. She looked toward the drone again and felt her heart turn dark as she saw how close it was. If its spotlight had still been working, the beam might have already touched her, the gunfire might have already begun.

She let out a final cry of effort. Straining hard, she pulled Victor One's body across the ground. She got his head behind the tree trunk. Quickly, she dropped his arms and rushed around to his feet to turn him lengthwise so his whole body would be covered.

The moment she ran out from behind the tree, the drone opened fire.

Molly screamed as the bullets flashed through the dark. She threw herself on top of Victor One, shielding him with her body just as he had shielded her. The drone swept over them both, firing all the way. She could hear the slugs thudding into the earth all around her. She expected to feel them tear into her flesh at any moment. It seemed almost a miracle to her when the drone passed over and she was still unhurt.

She rolled off Victor and lay on the cold ground, trembling. Shakily, she rose to her knees. She looked down at Victor One. He was stirring more steadily now. He seemed to be trying to wake up, fighting to wake up. His head rocked back and forth. His eyelids fluttered. It seemed he couldn't quite break through.

And the drone was circling around yet again, coming back yet again. Molly understood the truth: she could dodge the machine herself, but she couldn't keep pulling Victor out of the way. He was too heavy. Her strength would give out. There had to be something else she could do.

The drone continued arcing around. In the next few seconds, it would come back toward them.

She had only one option. The thought of it was awful, but she could see no other way.

She waited. She watched the drone turn. She stood still, letting it come at her.

Then she ran straight across its path.

It was the only thing she could think of. Act as a decoy. Draw the drone away from Victor One. If she could outrace it for just a few seconds, if she could take the thing away from him, then . . . well, maybe it would run out of bullets. Maybe it would get lost in the woods. Maybe it would think that Victor One was dead and leave him alone. Maybe he would regain consciousness and escape. Something good might happen, anyway—even if she wouldn't be around to see it.

She darted across the drone's path. It worked. Glancing at the drone, she saw it adjust its course to follow her. She sprinted through the dark, her powerful legs taking long strides. She heard the drone right behind her, its propeller noise growing louder. She barreled past trees, branches scratching at her face. She kept her eyes down, trying to negotiate a path over the forest floor.

But the noise of the drone grew louder and louder and finally Molly couldn't help herself: she looked over her shoulder. She cried out in fear. It was so close! It was right on top of her . . .

And now it started firing, the red death spitting in streams from its guns.

Molly tried to face forward, but it was too late. Looking back like that, even for that second, she had lost her way. She stepped off the edge of the hard earth into a swampy patch of wet ground. She was thrown off balance. Her knees buckled. She went down hard.

The fall probably saved her life: just as she was toppling over, she felt a hot flame of agony streak across her shoulder. She'd been hit. A bullet had found her. The drone had her in its sights and very well might have torn her apart right then and there if she hadn't gone splashing down into the freezing water.

Panicked, she rolled onto her back. She looked up, terrified. She saw the drone bearing down on her, adjusting its guns to find her where she lay helpless on the wet earth.

The red stream of bullets shifted. It ate up the ground in front of her, heading straight toward her. There was no time to roll away, no time to avoid the line of flaming slugs about to cut her in half.

Later she had the image of that moment frozen in her mind. Forever after she could see the last bullet splashing into the wet earth inches from her feet, the stream of gunfire about to pass over her, through her.

Then, with a powerful blast that bathed Molly's face in heat, the drone exploded.

For a second the forest night was bright with flame. Molly stared in amazement at the spectacle as the fireball that had been the drone continued hurtling toward her, then hurtled over her and dropped hissing into the swamp beyond. She raised her arm to protect herself as bits of fiery debris rained down on top of her.

A second later, it was over. Silence descended over the forest again.

Gasping for breath, Molly slowly lowered her arm and looked around the dark forest. What had just happened?

Then she saw.

There stood Victor One. He was on his feet again, gripping

the pistol again, still pointing it at the place where the drone had been. His face was a mask of blood. His eyes were white in the red mess, but blinking hard as if he could barely keep them open, barely keep himself conscious. Yet, somehow, injured as he was, he had managed to blast the machine out of the air. He had managed to save her life.

As Molly watched, stunned, Victor One's hands fell as if he were too weak to keep holding the pistol up. His eyes moved slowly to her. His voice was thick and heavy, his words slurred.

"You all right . . . ?"

She began to nod, but a fiery whiplash of pain went across her shoulder. She stopped nodding. She gripped her arm.

"I think . . . I think it shot me."

Victor One came toward her. He moved stiffly, unsteadily, lumbering step by clumsy step. He looked as if he might fall over at any moment.

He didn't though. He stood above her. He holstered his weapon—it took him three tries to get it in the slot. Then he knelt beside her. Molly flinched and gave a little gasp as he touched her wounded arm, turned it so he could examine the damage. Her running shirt was sliced open as by a knife and an angry red line was slashed across her flesh.

"Just a scratch," Victor One said thickly. "It'll burn a while, but we'll get it cleaned up and you'll be all right. You were lucky."

"What about you?" she said. "I thought you were dead."

"I was lucky too," he told her. "The bullet went straight through my head and blew my brains out. I'm completely unhurt."

She gaped at him for a moment. Then, bloody as he was, dull-eyed as he was, he gave her a lopsided smile, and she understood he was joking.

"Very funny," she said.

"It's nothing. A flesh wound. It just knocked me silly, that's all. Come on," he told her. "Let's get you fixed up and get out of here."

32. SNAKE WARRIORS

UP CLOSE LIKE this, the WarCraft was a horror. As big as the sky itself, it seemed half monster, half machine. The Octo-Guardian wrapped around the central black disk seemed at one with the craft. The former Troll's malevolent yellow eyes seemed the WarCraft's eyes, his slimy slithering tentacles seemed to be the WarCraft's arms, stretching out into the vast blackness all around it.

As Rick's supply ship drew near, the WarCraft filled his windshield. The great yellow eyes stared in at him. Rick was at the supply ship's controls now, guiding the small vehicle up the river of lightning toward the immense mothership. To his left and his right he saw other ships, ships just like his, riding up their own flashing white passages toward the WarCraft's open bays. Above all of them, the Octo-Guardian's tentacles waved and threatened.

And now Rick saw something else as well. As his ship sailed closer to the WarCraft, as the tentacles stretched out directly above him, he saw that each tentacle was equipped with a single yellow eye of its own embedded in its tip: a sort of miniature version of the two vicious and malicious eyes staring their hate-filled stare from the Octo-Guardian's head. The tentacles undulated through the darkness, bringing their eyes close first to this ship, then to another, then another. Rick realized the Octo-Guardian was inspecting the incoming supply wagons. It was making sure that nothing dangerous or threatening was inside them, nothing that might make its way into Kurodar's WarCraft. Rick had once snuck his way into the fortress down below, and clearly Kurodar was determined never to let that happen again. Rick did not want to think about what would happen if a tentacle eye looked through his windshield and saw not a Pilot Boar but Rick himself at the helm.

Rick was weary now—almost dazed with weariness. His fight with the Pilot Boar had sapped his strength, left him exhausted. He felt as if he no longer had the power of will he needed to take control of the Realm's reality, to change his shape back into that of a Boar.

But even now, even as he thought that, one of the enormous tentacles began to snake through space in his direction. Rick's hand moved to the sword in his belt. He was hoping he could draw some strength—at least some inspiration—from Mariel's presence in the metal. He touched the sword's hilt and, sure enough, she was still there, still with him . . .

When the tentacle passed by his windshield, the yellow eye hovering just outside the glass inspected him and saw the very image of the Pilot Boar whom Rick had cut in half just moments ago.

Then the tentacle and its eye passed over. The moment it was gone, Rick breathed a sigh of relief and relaxed his will—and immediately snapped back into his normal shape.

The ship continued sailing over the river of lightning. The head of the Octo-Guardian grew enormous above him, its eyes staring down with a sort of madness of hatred in them. The portal of the WarCraft yawned blackly up ahead.

Just before Rick docked with the great WarCraft, he glanced down at his palm. The timer in his hand had blinked down to 1:05 now. He had over an hour, he told himself. But he knew that was deceptive. The time he had spent in the MindWar Realm had already messed with his brain in some ways. Those headaches. Those horrible nightmares. The longer he stayed here, the worse the effects would be. And this time, the damage might be deep and permanent.

He drew a worried breath and looked away from the blinking numbers. Words his father had taught him once came back to him now: *Let not your heart be troubled. Neither let it be afraid.* Good advice. He had to finish this, no matter what happened, no matter how long it took, no matter what happened to him in the process. It had to be done—so there was no sense worrying about it.

The WarCraft came closer. Its sleek black side and gaping portal filled the windshield completely. The supply ship broke away from the river of lightning and glided free toward the open portal. Rick felt a little spasm of fear as the lightning-striped blackness of space was replaced by the silver walls of the landing tube. The supply ship had now entered the WarCraft.

Here we go, he thought.

The ship grumbled and rocked as its base scraped over the base of the landing tube. Rick gripped the wheel tightly, his breath coming fast and sharp. Bright light appeared up ahead. Grew brighter. And then the ship broke out of the tube and slipped into a landing mechanism. The mechanism snapped shut around the ship's base, holding it in place. The supply ship had landed. Rick was inside the WarCraft.

Through the windshield, he could see that he was in a vast circular unloading bay. Other ships were emerging from their tubes, slipping into their mechanisms, being locked in place. Automatic doors were sliding open at intervals along the curving wall of the bay. Worker Boars were pouring in through the doors. The moment each ship came to rest, the Worker Boars surrounded it, pried open its rear door, and began to bring out the energy pods stacked up inside.

Rick looked beyond the clusters of Boars and saw that Cobra Guards were following them in through the doors: those same walking snakes he had seen outside the Golden City below, giant squirmy snakes with squirmy snake-like spears strapped across their backs, spears that, like the Octo-Guardian's tentacles, had eyes. It seemed the Cobras were on every side of him, lining up all along the wall. They—and their squirming spears—were keeping close watch on the unloading process.

So many eyes. So many eyes everywhere.

Rick knew he couldn't hesitate. Once again, he let his hand rest on the hilt of Mariel's sword. Once again, he felt the warmth of her strength surging through him and, once again, he marshaled his will. He felt his Realm body changing back into the shape of the Pilot Boar. He knew he was too tired to hold the shape for long, but if he could just hold it until he was out of this bay . . .

He threw open the cockpit door and stepped outside.

All around him the Worker Boars were unloading the ships,

pulling out the energy pods. None of them stopped working when he stepped out. None of them looked at him.

But the Cobra Guards—they noticed him at once. The other Pilot Boars had remained inside their cockpits. They were waiting till the ships were emptied, waiting until they could begin their rides back to the Realm below. The moment Rick stepped out of his ship, several of the Cobra Guards around the large bay's perimeter tensed. Their eyes widened in their flat snake-like heads. Their forked tongues slid nervously out of their thin mouths and slipped back in again. The spears on their backs writhed around, trying to turn the eyes on their points in Rick's direction.

Rick pretended not to notice. He moved quickly, looking straight ahead, his face set with purpose as if he had important business to attend to, as if he couldn't be bothered with minor details like some curious Cobra Guards. He headed for one of the open doors, ignoring the two Cobras there, one on each side of the opening. The snakes stiffened at his approach, but he pretended to pay no mind, determined to bluff his way through the door and into the main body of the WarCraft.

It almost worked. Almost.

He reached the Cobras. Working hard to hold his Boar shape in place, he stepped between the snakes to the door. He didn't even glance at the guards. He just kept going—or he tried to. Just as he was about to cross the threshold, two spears suddenly blocked his path. One whiplashed down from his right, one from his left. Both spears stiffened and solidified in front of him, their weird eyes going metallic and dead.

Rick turned to the snake on his left, trying to make his tusked, piggy face look stern and angry. The Cobra spoke—and his voice was weird and frightening, a breathy hiss, just like the voice of a snake trying to imitate human speech.

"Where do you think you're going, you?" the Cobra said. It came out sounding like *"Ha-waaare d'yoooo think yer goyng-yooooou?"*

Rick was aware of the fear pumping through him. He was also aware that if he focused on the fear, if he let his focus slip from his own shape for even a second, he would lose his porky form and the Cobras would be all over him. He pushed the fear to the corner of his mind and held the shape in place with all the power of his spirit.

And he said: "Get those spears out of my way! I have orders from Kurodar!"

Created only to obey, the Cobra became uncertain at the sound of authority in Rick's voice. He seemed about to answer, but he hesitated. Rick's hopes rose when he saw that hesitation. But, at the same time, he felt his Boar shape starting to slip. He was losing it.

Quickly, Rick reached out and grabbed hold of the Cobra's wrist. The feel of the cold scaly skin against his pink palm made him shudder. Taking advantage of the snake's uncertainty, he wrenched the guard's arm upward.

"Out of my way!" he commanded.

Then, charging forward, he pushed past the other spear and went out the door.

He found himself in a long, brightly lit hallway. Its walls were flickering with electronic maps of RL, earthly cities represented by clusters of lights. Groups of glaring bulbs hung from the ceiling with air vents between them. The hall went straight forward for about fifteen steps before it intersected with another corridor. If Rick could just get to that intersection before he lost his Boar shape, if he could just turn the corner and get out of the Cobra Guards' view, he might make a run for it.

He hurried forward—one step, two, three, four, five . . .

And then a harsh, bone-chilling whisper came from behind him as the Cobra Guard recovered from his surprise and uncertainty.

"Ssssstop riiiight therrrrre . . ."

Rick didn't stop. He didn't turn back. He kept on walking. Six steps, seven, eight, nine, ten . . .

"I ssssaid ssssstop!"

As his breath grew short, as his fear and excitement mounted, his concentration slipped. He was no longer focusing on himself. He couldn't. His mind was on the situation. His Boar disguise began to contract back into his normal shape. The bristling fur vanished from his arms. The large piggy arms slipped back into being human. He took another step, another. He was almost to the corner.

"Ssssstop hiiiiim!" hissed the Cobra Guard.

Rick's Boar shape melted off him. He was himself again as, with another step, he reached the intersection. He dodged left— why not? He had no idea where he was headed anyway. He entered another well-lit metallic corridor, running past more maps with more flashing clusters of lights. The bulbs and vents went by in a blur above him. There was another intersection up ahead, another chance to escape his pursuers. Maybe he could reach it, maybe he could get away. How fast could a Cobra run, anyway? They weren't even supposed to have legs!

Rick dashed wildly down the corridor toward the next corner. He glanced back over his shoulder, and to his great relief he saw there was no one behind him, no one giving chase. He was going to make it. He turned the corner at the next intersection. Turning right this time, traveling on pure instinct. Another corridor. More maps, more lamps, more vents. The WarCraft was so huge, this could go on forever. Another corner, another turn . . .

Hope surged through him. This corridor was longer—and at the end of it, there was a doorway.

He glanced back again. Still no one there. He put on an extra burst of speed, heading for the door.

He was halfway there when the Cobras got him.

They seemed, at first, to materialize out of nowhere. Then he realized: they were sliding in through the vents in the ceilings above him. They had been chasing him, invisible in the walls, all this time.

Now they squeezed into the corridor all together. It was one of the most disgusting things Rick had ever experienced. Snake after giant snake slithering through the vents above and showering into the corridor like rain—a reptilian downpour. Soon, the hallway was full of them and every one was coming toward him, half walking, half slithering over the floor, slithering over one another, reaching for him with scaly hands. Snakes everywhere, ahead of him, behind him. There was no place to run.

Feeling panic rise up inside him, Rick drew his sword. Mariel's steel flashed in the corridor's bright lights as the enormous snakes closed in on him. But before he could strike, a powerful Cobra had wound itself around his arm. Another coiled around one leg and another coiled around the other. Their cold scales covered him. Their black eyes closed in over him. Their spitting forked tongues licked at his face. Their bared fangs dripped and gleamed.

The lights of the corridor grew dim as the snakes smothered him and forced him down to the floor. He couldn't breathe. The sword was yanked from his hand. The snakes started to drag and push him forward, their writhing, muscular bodies moving him helplessly along. He was carried down the hallway on a veritable river of snakes.

Terror, disgust, and the lack of air overwhelmed him. His consciousness dimmed, flickered out.

Then there was nothing.

33. KISS

MOLLY HELD ON to Victor One's hand as he led her through the dark for what seemed a long time. She was tired and hungry and scared, and the wound on her arm was burning. She could barely think anymore, and when she did think all she thought was: She wished she were back at school. She wished she were safe at home. She wished Rick was with her . . .

"We should rest and clean up our wounds," said Victor One.

Molly sighed loudly with relief as she slid down to sit propped against a tree. Victor One pulled an energy bar from his backpack and handed it to her. She devoured it with mindless passion, staring into space. She was exhausted. She didn't even have the strength to speak. She never knew she could endure so much, survive so much for so long.

Now Victor One went into his backpack and came out with a box of first-aid supplies. He used a damp cloth to clean the blood off his face. Then, when he was done, he knelt next to Molly. She flinched with pain as he rolled up her sleeve. She looked away as he trained his flashlight on the wound.

"Is it really just a scratch?" she asked him, staring into the trees. She was afraid to look for herself.

"By the look of it, I'd say you've only got about seventy or eighty more years to live," said Victor One.

"Ha-ha."

"You'll be fine," he told her. "Hold this." He handed her the flashlight. "Point it at your arm." Molly did, but she still didn't look at the wound herself. "Say, 'Ow, that really hurts,'" he instructed.

Molly snorted. "What do you mean? Why should I . . . ? Ow! That really hurts," she said as he swabbed the line of pain with disinfectant and the sting went through her.

"Okay," said Victor One. "Hold still while I stitch you up with a sharpened stick and a skein of wool."

"*What?*"

"I'm kidding. Just let me put a bandage on it and you'll be done."

Molly finally turned her head and looked—not at her arm, not at the wound, but at Victor One himself. He was tearing open a bandage wrapper with that ultraserious single-minded concentration that men seem to bring to simple tasks. She thought it was cute the way guys did that: tearing open a wrapper as if it were as complex an operation as defusing an atom bomb. She watched Victor One work. In the glow of the flashlight, he was a lot more handsome than she'd thought at first. Or maybe it was just the fact that he'd saved her life and that he was brave and kind and funny. He didn't have (as she couldn't help thinking) that passion inside him that Rick had, that hot spirit that made Rick seem so fiery and alive, as if he had the life force of two men or three or four. But someone like Victor One would be an easier sort of man to know, she thought. An easier sort of man to love.

As he pressed the bandage gently against her wound, he glanced up and caught her watching him.

"What are you looking at?" he growled.

"Nothing." She smiled. "But thank you."

"It's just a bandage."

"I meant thank you for saving my life."

He rolled her sleeve down over the bandage, but he remained as he was, crouching beside her. Looking at her with that humorous expression on his craggy face.

"You saved my life, too," he said. "You drew the drone away from me, didn't you? That's why you were running like that."

"I couldn't think of anything else to do."

"Pretty brave stuff, Molly," said Victor One. "I've seen some brave people in my time, men and women both, but you're right up there."

Molly didn't know what to say to that, so she didn't say anything. She just sat there against the tree, holding the flashlight and looking at Victor One and looking at him some more. And he just crouched there next to her, looking right back at her.

Then he leaned over and kissed her.

It was a brief kiss and gentle, but it sent a shock of realization through Molly that took her completely by surprise. Before this she had thought about her kiss with Rick a million times, she had asked herself a million times whether or not she was in love with him. And here she was, looking at another man, thinking about another man, attracted to another man—and yet the moment his lips touched hers, she realized: It was Rick. It had always been

Rick. Since they were kids. Maybe longer than that. Maybe since forever. Maybe she was made for him. All she knew was . . .

"What?" said Victor One. He had just drawn back from her. He was studying her face, his eyes narrowed. "Did I do the wrong thing?"

"No, no . . . ," said Molly, confused. "It was nice, just . . ."

"What? What are you thinking?"

Molly shook her head quickly. "I'm . . . nothing, I'm sorry, I . . ."

Victor One's weather-beaten face brightened with a lopsided grin. "Oh, I get it. Wrong guy, huh?"

"I'm sorry, Victor. I should have . . . I wasn't sure, I . . ."

He laughed. "Well, I'm glad I could straighten that out for you."

She reached out and touched the side of his face. "It was a nice kiss," she said.

"It was," he told her. Then, with a look of resignation, he sighed. "Hey, Rick's a good guy. He'll be a great guy if . . ."

He stopped himself before he finished the sentence. And Molly said, "If what?"

Victor One shook his head. He stood up out of his crouch. "We better get moving."

Molly watched him as he began to pack up his backpack again.

"You were going to say 'If he lives,' weren't you?" she said. Victor One didn't answer. And Molly felt her heart take a dip inside her. "Is he really in that much danger?"

Victor One nodded. "I understand it's pretty bad where he is, pretty rugged."

"Do you think he'll be killed?"

"You want an honest answer?"

"Yes, I do."

"I don't know. He might be killed, sure. He's a pretty reckless character, pretty wild. But . . ."

"But what?"

"He's got . . . something. Something inside him."

"Yes," said Molly. "I've seen that. Something bigger than he knows. Better."

"That's right," said Victor One. "If he can find that . . . if he can take hold of that . . ."

"Then you think he'll survive," said Molly.

"Then," said Victor One, pulling the pack's strap over his arm, "then I think he'll almost deserve you."

He reached down, offering her his hand. She took it. He drew her to her feet. They stood face-to-face, very close to each other. The light of the flashlight surrounded them, the darkness spread out beyond. Molly saw Victor One's blue eyes gleaming. She saw his teeth as he smiled again.

"I'm glad I got the kiss in before you figured things out," he told her.

She laughed.

He said, "Let's go."

34. BEHIND ENEMY LINES

AWARENESS RETURNED TO Rick slowly at first—and then very fast. The Cobra Guards were releasing him. Vaguely, as in the last trailing wisp of a dream, he sensed their cold forms withdrawing, slithering away. As the smothering pressure of their bodies receded, cool air washed over his face and made him stir.

Then he sat up quickly, wide awake.

He saw—impossibly—an entire city standing in front of him. No. He shook his head, clearing the fog from his mind. It was a model of a city. Of course. He recognized the place at once: the white monuments, the monumental buildings, the spire and the temple facing each other across a long pool, the sweep of the big river around it. It was Washington, D.C., all in miniature, a room-sized model beneath a digital reproduction of a clear blue sky. The city's quiet majesty was offset only by the strangeness of its silence. Nothing moved here. No sound came from it, other than the whispering babble of water. The Potomac River, shimmering silver, was fashioned out of real Realm water being piped in from somewhere to Rick's right and flowing away through some unseen outlet to his left.

As Rick stared, he saw something move across the shining river's surface. It was a reflection of something, something pink, hanging in the air above him.

Slowly, Rick's gaze lifted—over the mock buildings, past the mock sky. He saw that the sky trailed away to nothing in the room's upper reaches. There was only blackness up there.

Blackness—and Kurodar.

Rick felt his heart go cold. He recognized the madman's Realm form on sight. He had caught a glimpse of it once before. Here in MindWar, Kurodar was nothing like the holographic images Commander Mars had shown him. Those images were of the RL Kurodar: a small, slouched, ugly little man with bulging eyes and sagging jowls. A great scientific genius maybe, but no movie star, that was for sure.

Here, though, in this vast cyberworld born out of his own imagination, Kurodar had cast that unpleasant physical being away. You would think—or Rick would have thought, anyway—that given the chance to take any form he wanted, Kurodar would have chosen to become some handsome superhero type or something, or maybe some great graceful fantastical creature like a centaur or a unicorn. But no. Kurodar chose to be nothing but a sort of pink cloud of pure mind. It was, Rick thought, as if Kurodar was so disgusted with his bodily self that he wanted to be free of a body altogether. Or maybe he was just so proud of his brainpower that he wanted to be nothing but brain . . .

Whatever. The point was: Kurodar floated in the black space above the model city. And even though he didn't have a head exactly or eyes that Rick could see, Rick knew he was looking down at him.

And then the presence spoke. His voice echoed through the room, seeming to come from everywhere at once, like some cheap cartoon version of God.

"Rick Dial," he said.

At the sound of his name, Rick leapt to his feet. As he did, he sensed motion in the unseen outer reaches of the room beyond the lighted city: the Cobras. He could just make them out standing there in the shadows. They tensed at his sudden movement. They were watching him closely, ready to grab him again if he tried to escape.

The pink cloud of Kurodar shifted, and a sort of flickering darkness appeared and vanished within it.

"You are Rick Dial," he repeated, his voice doing that echoing fake-god-thing. A fake god with a Russian accent. "You are the son of the Traveler."

Rick answered boldly. He knew full well that Kurodar could have him snuffed out with a single command, but, weirdly, he wasn't afraid. He felt more angry than anything. He didn't like feeling threatened, or getting pushed around.

"That's right," he said up at the darkness. "I'm Rick Dial. And I guess you're Kurodar, huh."

Laughter. Kurodar's laughter made the city beneath him shake. It filled the enormous room.

"As far as you're concerned, I am life and death," he said. "I am the foundation of the world around you. As far as you're concerned, I am God."

Eh. Not so much, Rick thought. But, for once, he managed to keep his sarcastic mouth shut. No sense antagonizing a guy who could vaporize you at will.

"You are the one who destroyed my fortress," Kurodar went on.

"Yeah," said Rick. "And it blew up real nice, too." *So much for keeping my mouth shut. I really have to work on that!* Rick thought.

The sound that came out of the pink presence above him was like a distant rumble of thunder. Rick knew it was the sound of Kurodar's rage.

"Look down," Kurodar said angrily. "Look at the city in front of you. Do you recognize it?"

Rick glanced at the model. "Sure. It's D.C."

"Of course," said Kurodar, his voice thick with hollow humor. "A good patriotic American boy like yourself would know the capital when he sees it."

"That's right."

"After all, you were willing to come here and risk your life to protect your country, yes?"

"Yeah, I was."

"You were even willing to risk your girlfriend's life."

His girlfriend . . . ? *Molly!* Rick thought. He almost said her name aloud but managed to stop himself just in time. He didn't want to show this monster anything that looked like weakness. But the thought of Molly in this hairball's clutches made his heart turn cold.

Kurodar knew he had touched a nerve. His cloudy presence laughed again, the darkness expanding and retracting inside him. "It was all for nothing, Rick. The girl will die now. And the city . . . Within an hour, it will be in flames."

Rick's anger intensified. He wished he could reach up and grab that pink cloud by the throat—wherever its throat was—and squeeze the breath out of it.

Kurodar laughed again. "If you're very nice, I'll let you watch the city burn before I kill you," he said.

Rick told himself to keep quiet. He told himself not to make Kurodar any angrier than he already was. He told himself to play it cool and meanwhile look around for some chance to escape, even though he was surrounded on every side by Cobra Guards and had exactly zero chance of getting past them.

He told himself all that, and then he said, "So that's it, huh? That's your big idea. All this Realm and MindWar stuff—and it turns out you're just some squirrelly lunatic who likes to kill people." He saw the black rage flash inside Kurodar's cloudy presence, but he couldn't stop himself. "You're brilliant enough to build this whole amazing cyberworld, and all you can do with it is burn stuff down and commit murder. What, you think that makes you special or something? Hey, guess what, fathead? Anyone can kill people. An idiot with a hammer can kill people. An idiot with a match can burn stuff down." He gestured toward the model of the city. "Building a city like that—doing a good job there—even sweeping the streets—that's tough. People who do stuff like that—they're more important in the big scheme of things than wigged-out murderers like you will ever be. How do you like that, Cloud Boy?"

Rick was so wound up he could've kept going for half an hour, but Kurodar's thunderclap of rage cut him off.

"This is nothing!" the presence boomed. Rick could hear his fury. "This is only the beginning. I do this only to show the council what MindWar can do, what it's capable of. Once they know, once they give me the funding I need, it's not just Washington that will burn. I will set the entire continent on fire. I will turn your country to dust and ashes. It would have happened by now, I would have shown them already, only—"

Again Rick couldn't stop his smart mouth. He said, "Oh, right. Only I blew up your fortress. So sad about that, really. But look at it this way, Kurodar. I messed you up pretty good and I'm just one guy. What do you think is gonna happen when my dad sends an army of MindWarriors in here? You're gonna be one unhappy vague pink mass of whatever you are then, my friend."

Kurodar's voice flashed back at him like lightning. "You are a joker, eh? You make fun of me? Me? Well, make fun of death then. Make fun of this!"

Suddenly, the pink cloud of madness expanded. As Rick watched, the blackness of the upper room seemed to open inward into a world of strange green light. Three-dimensional images began to take shape in the depths of that light. Rick realized he was looking up into a kind of movie screen—but what he saw there wasn't a movie, not at all. What he saw up there was Real Life, the life that was going on right now while he was here in the Realm!

At first Rick could not understand what he was seeing. The images clarified only slowly. He was looking into some sort of large building. An airplane hangar, he thought. There seemed to be some thirty or forty airplanes arrayed in rows on the floor of the structure. Or wait, were they planes or were they . . . ?

Drones! Rick thought. *The missing drones.*

He was looking at the rows of missing drones, each armed with both guns and very deadly looking missiles. And beyond the drones, there was an open door, a tall rectangle looking out on what seemed to be a forest on a starry night.

"They are coming," said Kurodar.

As Rick watched, and as the images continued coming into focus, and as his eyes adjusted, Rick saw a light coming forward through the darkness of the woods. A flashlight. In its glow, he saw two people advancing toward the hangar.

"Molly," he whispered. Molly and Victor One.

Kurodar instantly rumbled back: "Yes. Molly. Molly and your friend Victor One. They are coming to the barn. And my people are ready for them."

It was only then that Rick noticed the killers, standing in the shadows of the barn, waiting.

And he understood that Victor and Molly were walking into a trap.

35. FIREFIGHT

THE BARN MATERIALIZED before Molly and Victor One like a vision. It rose up just beyond the reach of Victor's flashlight beam: a hulking blackness in the brighter starlit darkness all around them.

"What is that?" Molly asked, instinctively dropping her voice to a whisper.

Victor One only shook his head in answer. He didn't know.

They approached the place cautiously and soon understood what it was—or, that is, what it appeared to be: an abandoned barn in a place now reclaimed by wetland and overgrown with trees. In the flashlight beam they saw its unpainted wooden boards and its weak, lopsided structure . . . and also its door standing open, as if it were waiting for them, beckoning them to come in.

Molly glanced at Victor One and saw his expression had gone blank, and his blue eyes were practically gleaming with intensity. He was on the alert. But he kept moving forward slowly and Molly kept following.

The barn looked awfully good to both of them. A place of shelter; a place to rest. It was late now, deep in the night. They had traveled a long way and had faced terrible danger. Their energy was nearly gone. And in the darkness, they were not sure of the way.

Victor One had left behind any electronic devices that might be tracked or hacked. He had no phone, no GPS, no Internet. He was relying on his memories of maps and his instincts to find the way. He knew—and Molly knew—if they could find a place to hide out and sleep until daylight, they would have a much better chance of getting out of this forest alive.

Walking slowly, carefully, quietly, almost on tiptoe, they reached the open door of the barn. Victor One shone his light inside. Molly expected to see nothing more than a dirt floor, maybe some old rusted farming equipment.

Instead, the sight that greeted her was so unlikely that she couldn't make sense of it at first. And even as her mind was trying to grasp what she saw, a voice spoke to them out of the surrounding shadows. It was a voice that made her whole body tighten with fear. A voice she knew well, strangely high-pitched and hissing like a snake's.

"Welcome," said Smiley McDeath. "Come in."

As he spoke, the lights inside the barn came flickering on. Molly let out a quick, sharp breath as she saw the lines of drones arrayed on the smooth stone floor, their deadly missiles bristling. She saw the steel walls that had been hidden by the wood facade. And she saw Smiley McDeath himself standing on a balcony set high on the wall. Beside him stood another man, his face masked with a balaclava. The masked man was holding a machine gun, training it on Victor One.

Victor One and Molly stood still in the doorway for a moment. And Smiley McDeath said, "Actually, that wasn't an invitation. That was an order. Come in."

At that moment, another masked man stepped out of the darkness behind them and put a pistol against Molly's head.

"Oh and, you know, hands up and all that," said Smiley McDeath.

Victor One lifted his hands to show they were empty. The pistol man gave Molly a shove.

Victor and Molly stepped into the barn. They came forward under the bright lights until they were standing at the edge of the drone array.

"Quite a collection," Victor said, scanning the miniature planes.

"It is, isn't it? That one I sent after you was the least of them," said Smiley McDeath. He leaned on the balcony, relaxed, his diamond-shaped face grinning down at them over the rail. He surveyed the drones with admiration. "It had a nice tracking device in it, but pretty minor guns. I didn't want to waste the missiles on you. We're saving them for the strike on the city."

Victor One nodded, as if thinking along with him. "Washington?" he asked.

Smiley McDeath only shrugged. "Who can say?"

Victor One went on surveying the field of drones. "It's a lot of firepower. I'm sure they'll do plenty of damage wherever you send them. Use those missiles right and you could kill a lot of people— tens of thousands—not to mention the damage you'd do to the government."

"Well, thanks for your vote of confidence," said Smiley McDeath casually. "Coming from you, it's quite a compliment, seeing as you've done a fair amount of damage yourself."

"Aw shucks," said Victor One, stone-faced.

"Speaking of which . . . ," said Smiley McDeath. "Your gun. Would you mind giving it over to my friend there? The backpack, too, while you're at it."

Before Victor One could answer, the pistol man jammed his weapon against Molly's head so hard, she felt the ache behind her brow. She grunted and stumbled forward a step.

Victor One turned and showed the pistol man a big, friendly grin. "No need for that, friend," he said pleasantly.

It was at that moment Molly knew there was going to be a gunfight. Victor One was smiling broadly, but there was pure, simple murder in his eyes. She felt her body tense. Her heart sped up. She got ready to hit the floor when the moment came.

Still smiling, Victor One drew his gun and handed it to the pistol man at Molly's back.

"Be careful with that. It's loaded," he said. "I wouldn't want you to hurt yourself." Molly saw Victor One's eyes scan the barn as he spoke. He was searching for any other gunmen, figuring his odds. Meanwhile, he stripped off his backpack and dropped it to the floor. The pistol man kicked it away.

When Victor One turned back to look up at Smiley McDeath on the balcony, he said, "You guys must be feeling pretty confident. All this expensive weaponry lying around, and you only have two guards in the place."

"Well, we had four originally," said Smiley McDeath. "Two have gone to meet the reinforcements and lead them here. They should be back any minute. They're bringing a veritable army to assist us."

Molly's eyes flicked from Smiley McDeath's face to the

masked man with the machine gun beside him to Victor One, relaxed and grinning. She could feel the violence coming any second. She could feel it building inside Victor One. Her breath was short and her heart was pounding so hard she was afraid the noise of it would give her away.

But Victor One only nodded pleasantly. "A whole army, huh? Just to defend yourself against little old me? Why don't you just let your pal here shoot me?"

When Smiley McDeath laughed he sounded like a rattler in the grass. "Oh, we'll get around to shooting you, don't worry about that. But first, our employer would like to meet you. Ask you some questions. Cause you some excruciating pain. The army will escort you to him."

Victor One laughed out loud—and Molly had to grit her teeth to keep from gasping with suspense. It was coming, she knew.

"Well, I'm flattered," said Victor One. "Flattered you feel you need an army to deal with one guy."

"Oh, it's not flattery," said Smiley McDeath, still smiling. "After all, you've already killed four of my men."

Victor One gave another pleasant laugh. "Actually, it's eight. There were four in the woods, then one back at the inn." He paused, and Molly could see Smiley McDeath trying to figure out what he meant. Then Victor One added: "And then, of course, there's you three."

And with that, it began.

Victor One started moving, moving so fast that it was only afterward that Molly could slow it down in her mind and reconstruct what happened.

He pushed her, driving his elbow into her shoulder, hard. She stumbled to one side—and, tense and ready as she was, she understood the signal and dove for the floor. She hit concrete and rolled, turning onto her back so that she saw the rest.

Without a break in his motion, Victor One kept turning. The pistol man had instinctively tried to move his weapon to follow the falling Molly. That was a mistake. In a split second, Victor One had grabbed his arm and snapped the pistol from his hand.

The machine gunner on the balcony was in the process of tightening his finger on the trigger when Victor One swung the pistol around and shot him. The noise of the shot filled the barn, deafening. A dark circle appeared just above the bridge of the machine gunner's nose. He threw his hands in the air and collapsed forward. His midsection hit the balcony railing and he bent forward hard and pitched over and tumbled through the air.

Before the machine gunner's body even thudded to the floor, Victor One was turning back to the pistol man. The pistol man had stumbled away and was fumbling to get a grip on the Glock he had taken from Victor One.

No chance. Victor One was too fast. There was another deafening blast and the pistol man dropped to the floor, dead.

"Victor!" Molly screamed.

She saw Smiley McDeath on the balcony. She saw his hand flashing into his jacket, coming out with a black weapon, a pistol. She saw him pointing the pistol down at Victor One.

Victor spun and the two pistols went off at once—his and Smiley McDeath's—a single, unified explosion.

Molly saw Smiley McDeath wheel backward, grimacing in pain, clutching his shoulder. Then she turned and screamed Victor's name again as she saw the warrior sink to his knees. Blood was burbling out of a small, wicked, black hole smack in the middle of him.

The entire gunfight had taken a second, maybe two. Molly had watched it unfold from where she lay on the floor, propped on one arm. Now she saw the pistol drop from Victor One's slack hand. She saw him tilt to the side, flinching in pain. He fell over and rolled onto his back, blinking up weakly into the high lights.

Molly rushed to him.

This time, when she spoke his name, he turned his head and blinked at her weakly. He tried to smile but couldn't. He had to lick his lips before he could force out a whisper.

"Run."

Molly heard a footstep behind her. She turned and looked over her shoulder. There was Smiley McDeath. He was coming down the spiral stairs that led to the balcony. He was wounded, his shoulder bleeding. His steps were slow and uncertain. But he was still gripping his pistol in his hand.

Molly saw Victor's pistol where it had fallen on the floor. She swept it up. She had never held a loaded gun before and the weight of it surprised her.

"Run," Victor One urged her again, his whisper barely audible.

But Molly did not run. She stood up, facing Smiley McDeath.

The killer had now reached the bottom of the stairs. He was shuffling toward them. His eyes were bright with pain, but he was still smiling. He came closer and closer.

Molly lifted the weapon, holding it steady with both hands. She pointed it at Smiley McDeath.

"Stop right there," she said.

"Oh, put that down," said Smiley McDeath. He didn't even hesitate. He just kept coming toward them, carrying his gun.

"I'll shoot you," said Molly.

"No you won't. Stop talking like an idiot," he told her.

Molly kept the gun trained on him, but he continued to ignore her. He truly didn't believe she would shoot him. And, in truth, she herself didn't think she was going to be able to pull the trigger and destroy a living man.

Smiley McDeath limped toward her steadily. Now he was very close, very close to Molly and close to where Victor One lay wounded and helpless on the floor.

"Stop!" Molly pleaded with him, holding the gun on him unsteadily.

Smiley McDeath didn't even look at her. He lifted his gun and pointed it at Victor One's head. His smile flashed downward in a frown of hatred as his finger tightened on the trigger.

The sound of the gunshot filled the barn, louder it seemed than all the previous gunfire combined. The blast seemed to sweep away everything else until Molly's mind was filled with nothing but that echoing explosion.

When the noise faded away, Smiley McDeath lay dead at her feet.

The pistol was smoking in her trembling hands.

36. WATERSLIDE

RICK, IN THE heart of Kurodar's WarCraft, never saw what happened in the barn. He never saw Victor One kill the gunmen. He never saw Molly shoot Smiley McDeath. He was still standing under Kurodar's misty and thunderous presence, still looking up to watch his two friends in RL approaching the barn's open doorway, when a sound reached him. A voice. A whisper.

"Rick."

He blinked. Had someone just spoken his name? Startled, he tore his gaze from the scene in RL and looked down at the model of Washington, D.C., that stood before him.

"Come to me, Rick. Now."

Another moment passed as Rick, confused, afraid for Molly, unfocused, tried to puzzle out what was happening, where the voice was coming from.

Then he knew. The river. The model Potomac—made of real water flowing through the miniature city.

Rick let out a startled murmur: "Mariel!"

And her silver hand flashed up out of the water.

"Now!" she said.

Rick hesitated only a second. Something inside him

there. He wanted to be with Molly. He wanted to help Molly. But she was beyond his reach, in RL, another world. There was nothing he could do for her from here.

He had to go, get out. He had to stop the attack on the city. That's what he was here for.

And even in that single second of hesitation, his chance to escape had begun to slip away. The Cobra Guards stationed around the walls had also heard Mariel's voice. Puzzled by the sound at first, they were now alert, beginning to catch on. Rick could hear them hissing to one another.

"Whaaat wassss thaaaat?"

"Did you hear ssssssomething?"

He could see them coiling forward out of the darkness, coming toward him. Some were already slithering between him and the river, just about to block his way.

He focused. He flashed.

Like Favian, he became little more than a body of light, a meteoric streak over the white crosses of Arlington National Cemetery. His insubstantial hand extended toward Mariel's silver hand.

Above him, the pink presence of Kurodar thundered, "Stop him!"

The nearest Cobra reached for him. The others charged forward.

But he was already past them—that fast. He became solid again at the shore of the river and Mariel's hand grabbed his. Rick felt himself yanked down into the freezing depths of the water.

On the instant, Mariel was all around him and she carried him away. Her liquid-metal presence was strangely warm, and he knew from experience that he could breathe while under her protection. But in fact, they raced along the stream so swiftly there wasn't much chance to breathe anyway.

In the air above them, he heard Kurodar's raging shout: "Get him, get him now!"

Then he and Mariel were gone, racing through the heart of the model city, dashing into the water outlet on the far side so quickly it was as if they had *both* turned into a Favian-style flash of light. There was an instant of mindless motion, a sensation of hurtling through the dark.

Then with a splash they broke free, broke out into the open air.

Rick found himself up to his neck in a cistern full of the Realm's silver, mercury-like substance. All he could see was the water bubbling around him and an iron ceiling high above.

And then there was Mariel, rising out of the water beside him. As always the sight of her—her queenly presence—rocked him somehow, touched him deep down even now. He had a sense that she was almost a part of him, the other half of his soul . . .

"Go on!" she commanded, her voice taut with urgency. She gestured toward the cistern's rim. "They'll be here any second. Go, Rick."

"But how . . . ?" he said. "How did you get here?"

"I stowed away in the supply ships. In the water. There's no time to explain now. Go!"

He obeyed her. Swam to the edge of the cistern. Grabbed the rim. Hauled himself up, wrestled himself over, and tumbled down the other side to the floor. Dripping silver, he looked back. There she was, rising over the edge of the container, an imperious metallic spirit looking down at him.

"Mariel! I think I know who you are," he blurted out breathlessly.

But she only answered: "There—over there—quickly—go."

There was never any time with her, he thought bitterly. They were always under attack, always racing off somewhere. He never got a chance to really talk to her.

He stayed stubbornly where he was. "You were part of the MindWar Project, sent here like me," he said. "You were trapped here. You and Favian and someone else, the man who died."

"Please, Rick! Hurry! Once you're in the drains, keep to the right. It isn't far."

"I won't let you grow old again. I won't let you die, too."

"I'm not afraid. I'll be fine. Just do what you have to do."

"My father says if I can find your body, your real body, he might be able to bring you back. Favian too."

"Go on! Now!"

In spite of her words, Rick thought he saw something come into her eyes, something that softened that regal and distant face.

But she looked down at him, her frown dark. "If you don't go now, they'll get you. Through there. See it? Where that grate is. It will take you where you need to go. Quickly."

He glanced over his shoulder. He was in a cramped room full of pipes and wires and small turning cogs and wheels. From here, the water from the cistern was being recycled back to the model river, and some of the WarCraft's energy was being pumped through the lines into the main room.

And yes, he saw the grate on the floor. Some kind of drain. Runoff from the cistern was flowing into it.

He turned back to Mariel. The longing to be near her surged through him. He knew he had to go, but he couldn't.

"Listen to me, Mariel."

"No. Go. Now," she said.

He opened his mouth to speak again. He was about to tell her . . . what? He wasn't sure. But he heard the hisses and slithering noises of the Cobra Guards approaching out in the hall.

"This isn't over," he said.

She glanced at him. He thought—he hoped—she inclined her chin in a little nod of agreement. He wasn't sure.

He left her. He ran to the grate. He knelt. Wrapped his fingers through the crisscrossing metal bars. He thought it would be heavier than it was, and he pulled up hard. But the grate was light. It nearly flew up and out of his hands.

"Thisssss waaaaay," came a Cobra voice from the hallway beyond the door. Very close. Footsteps and slithering whispers were getting closer every second.

Rick glanced back toward Mariel, but she was already melting away, raining back down into the cistern. Gone.

He turned back to the opening before him. He worked his way into the drain and pulled the grate back into place on top of it.

Then he let go—and he was gone. The narrow passage descended sharply and was slick with water. It was like a slide at a water park. It carried him away. He slid on his back, sluicing this way and that. Above him, he heard voices and slithering and footsteps—but the noise of the Cobra Guards rapidly faded as he swooshed down.

There was a juncture up ahead. Keep right, Mariel had said. He turned his body, putting his weight on the right side of his butt. He hit the fork. He sluiced right—plummeted with breathless speed into the cold puddle at the bottom.

Crouched beneath a low ceiling, in freezing water to his knees, he saw a grate just above his eye level. He shoved it and out it went. He climbed up into it and tumbled out the other side.

He wheelbarrowed his way out onto a hard floor. Climbed to his feet. Looked around him.

He saw at once where he was. He knew at once what he had to do.

He had seen the drones in the barn in RL. They were here before him also. He was in another of the great ship's enormous bays. Fighter planes were lined up here just as the drones were lined up in the RL barn. The planes here were Realm bots, analog creations of Kurodar's imagination, responsive to Kurodar's mind. The terrorist would control these fighter planes here in the Realm, and the planes in turn would control the drones in RL. The real drones would do what the bot drones do. And so, using only his imagination, Kurodar would be able to launch his strike on the capital.

Rick knew he had to destroy the fighting machines before they took off. But how? With what? There were so many of them.

Forty? Fifty? He wasn't sure. And they were big, too. Not like drones, but like real planes.

Rick looked around for a weapon, for anything that would help him destroy the fleet. There was nothing. The room was just an enormous holding bay. He wondered: was there time to disassemble the fighting crafts one by one before they launched?

Even as the question went through his mind, the answer came: there was no time at all. There was a wrenching screech above him. Startled, he looked up and saw: the bay's enormous ceiling was coming open, parting in the center, the two halves slowly drawing away from each other. Beyond, Rick saw the living blackness of the night. He felt the draw of the darkness, felt it pulling him upward off the floor. His sneakers seemed to grow light beneath him.

The drones were about to be released.

37. FIRE ESCAPE

SMILEY MCDEATH DIED with a look of surprise on his face. He truly hadn't believed Molly would shoot him.

And the truth was: It sickened her to have done it. All this violence sickened her. Standing there in the barn, surrounded by corpses, guarding the badly wounded Victor One, she wanted nothing more than to get out of there, get home, and never have to fight again.

With God's help, she would, she thought. But not yet. There was still more to do.

She knelt next to Victor. She set the gun down on the floor beside him. Victor lay still. His eyes were closed. But when Molly spoke his name, they fluttered open.

He tried to shake his head at her. It barely moved, but Molly knew what he was trying to say. He wanted her to run, get out, escape, before McDeath's army of reinforcements arrived and she was captured again.

She wanted to do that, too. To run. To get away. But she couldn't.

She would not leave Victor One as long as he was still alive. If there was any chance of saving him, she would carry him out of the forest on her back if she had to.

But even before she could do that, she had to try to find a way to destroy these drones.

Victor One had guessed they were going to attack Washington. Tens of thousands of people would die, he had said. Molly couldn't allow that to happen. Not if there was even a slim possibility she might stop it.

She reached down and touched Victor One's shoulder gently, reassuringly. Then she stood up. She didn't know how much time she had before Smiley McDeath's army arrived. Not much, probably. She had to move fast.

She crouched down and took Victor One by his wrists. She expected him to cry out in pain when she started to drag him across the barn floor. But he didn't—which was even worse. He was hurt so badly he couldn't even scream. His eyes fell shut again. He made faint wheezing noises, barely breathing. As she dragged him, his body left a trail of blood on the stone floor.

Molly worked Victor One to the door of the barn and then dragged him out into the night. She dropped his arms and let him rest on the earth a small distance from the structure. She knelt beside him again.

"I'll be right back," she told him.

Victor One didn't answer. He never opened his eyes.

She hurried to the edge of the forest. Quickly, she began gathering wood—as many dry twigs and branches as she could carry in her arms. This being winter, there was plenty of kindling around, and she was almost staggering under her burden as she brought her armload of it back to the barn.

She stepped inside. It was eerie in there with all the dead bodies: the pistol man sprawled on his back, the machine gunner crumpled at the bottom of the balcony, and the fallen Smiley McDeath, whom Molly herself had destroyed.

She could not think about it now. She could not hesitate. She kicked her way past the drones, moving to the center of the array. She dumped the wood down on top of the drone at the center. She hurried to Victor One's backpack where it lay on the floor near the fallen pistol man. Ignoring the corpse—all the corpses—she fixed her concentration on the pack. Knelt down beside it. Unzipped it. Rummaged in it until she came out with what she needed: a plastic cigarette lighter.

She returned to the pile of wood and flicked the lighter's wheel. As she held the flame to one of the smaller twigs at the bottom of the pile, a tear fell on her hand and she realized she was crying. She didn't know why. Maybe it was grief over Victor One or terror at the oncoming army or sorrow that she'd had to act so violently or just exhaustion. She didn't know, but she couldn't make it stop.

The twig caught fire and Molly dragged her sleeve across her eyes, drying her tears. She stood a moment and watched as the fire rose up through the bundle of dry wood. She didn't know how the drones were powered, but there had to be some kind of fuel inside them. If she was lucky, the fuel would explode and consume as many of the drones as possible.

And she didn't want to be around when that happened. She had to go.

She had taken one step toward the door when a loud grinding noise startled her and stopped her in her tracks. As she turned toward the sound, she saw . . . well, she couldn't believe what she was seeing. It was beyond belief.

The wall in front of her seemed to be dissolving. In the next moment, she was looking right through it, right into the woods on the other side. The moment after that, the wall was gone completely. The winter chill of the forest was washing over her.

And now . . . more amazing still . . . the forest itself was vanishing. The trees, the swamps, the starry skies themselves were flickering and going out like images on a broken TV. In place of reality, there came a blackness, blacker and emptier than anything Molly had ever experienced. It seemed to go on forever. And it seemed to have a kind of life inside it that drew her to it, tried to draw her in.

At the same time the grinding noise continued. And when Molly looked up, she saw that the roof of the barn was rolling open. She felt a stirring at her feet and looked down. The drones were starting to shudder and come alive. One or two of them were starting to lift off the floor.

It's happening, Molly thought. *It's happening now.*

The fire she had started continued burning. Any minute now, the drone beneath the wood might explode. Any minute now, Smiley McDeath's reinforcements might arrive, an entire army intent on killing both her and Victor One.

She couldn't wait around to watch this happen. She had to get out of here.

As the bizarre blackness pulled at her, as the ceiling of the barn continued to open, as the drones bounced and lifted at her feet, Molly moved with long, swift steps to the door.

She stepped out into the night again, pulling the door shut behind her. She moved to where Victor One lay still in the dirt. As she hurried to him, she heard a loud *thump* inside the barn. The fire had done its job. A drone had exploded.

Good, she thought.

She hoped there would be more.

Molly knelt down by Victor One. He lay still and silent, barely breathing. She had had brave plans to get him out of the forest, but she knew now it was impossible. She could never move him. Even if she could, he wouldn't survive.

It was over. She had done everything she could do. Exhausted, she sank down to the earth and sat beside him.

The barn's ceiling continued to rumble open. There was another explosion inside: another drone down. The blue of the night sky grew red with the rising flames.

Molly took Victor One's head onto her lap. She stroked his hair with her hand. She looked down at his still face. All the vitality had gone out of the handsome, craggy features. He was dying, she knew.

Molly lifted her eyes again and looked at the barn. A new noise reached her over the grind of the opening roof and the snicker of flames. At first, she couldn't figure out what it was. Then she understood: it was the buzz of the drone propellers.

Molly's hand rested in Victor One's hair. She looked up to the top of the barn, its roof now opened wide, the light of the fire within flickering upward as another drone blew.

But it was not enough. Because now other drones began emerging from the flames. One and then another and another and another . . .

Molly watched as they rose into the night. Then they darted off across the sky on their mission of destruction.

38. WARBIRDS

THE CEILING WAS opening in the Great Bay of the WarCraft, too. Rick felt the blackness of space pulling at him. He saw the fighter planes beginning to rise, ready to launch.

Kurodar's attack was under way.

Rick could hear the Cobra Guards at the door. He knew he had just seconds before they burst in on him. He did the only thing he could think of. He rushed to the nearest plane. He pulled the cockpit door open. If he could take control of one of the fighters, maybe he could shoot some of the others out of the air. Not all of them. But some. He'd be able to save a few lives, at least.

He was about to step into the cockpit of the fighter when the craft burst into flames. He had no idea what caused it. It just seemed to happen. He didn't know what was going on in RL. He didn't know that Molly had set a fire and some of the drones in RL were burning.

Crying out in surprise, he reeled back from the blazing fighter plane, throwing his arm up to protect his face. As he did, the fighter gave a little cough and exploded. The blast knocked Rick backward onto his seat. The wreckage rose above him in a burgeoning fireball. Flinching at the heat on his face, Rick leapt up and moved quickly to the next drone—just as the next drone burst into flames as well.

Rick stood in the bay and looked around him. Everywhere the fighter planes were catching fire, one after another—an analogue of what was happening in the barn in RL.

But even as some of the planes burned, others were lifting up off the bay floor, tilting their noses upward, ready to head for space.

And now the bay doors slid open—and the Cobra Guards came charging in, some running on their short legs, others slithering with stunning speed straight at him across the floor.

More drones exploded. Flames were everywhere now. But there was no escaping the fire: behind him, the Cobra Guards were moving toward him from every side. One hurled a spear. Rick saw it and ducked. But the spear had eyes! It followed his movement. Rick had to spin away at the last minute, and even then he felt the wind of the spearhead cross his cheek.

Other Cobra Guards were drawing back their spears to throw.

Rick plunged into the midst of the blaze. Arms up to protect his face, he rushed past one burning craft—and then past another craft that burst into flames as he approached it. Spears were flying at him, but even with their eyes, they couldn't find him in the smoke. He went running past more fiery planes until he saw a small group of fighters that hadn't caught fire yet.

He wove his way through the flaming wreckage and reached a plane that was still intact. As he pulled the cockpit door open, two other planes beside it shot up into the air and headed toward the open roof.

Rick stepped into the low cockpit with one foot—but then his trailing foot was grabbed; held fast. Rick looked back, wide-eyed, and saw a Cobra coiling its thick body around his ankle, its black eyes trained on him, its tongue flickering, its fangs bared.

Rick punched the snake in the head. He felt cold, scaly skin retract under his knuckles. He hit the thing again. Then again. The snake went limp and fell off him in a jumbled coil.

Rick jumped into the fighter plane. He slammed the cockpit door behind him just as another spear hit the windshield, staring in at him. He settled into the seat. His eyes went quickly over the dashboard. At this point, he was not surprised to see that despite a lot of flashing lights and meters and electronic readouts, the flight controls themselves were ridiculously simple: a steering stick to move the ship up, down, left, and right; a gun stick to aim, with a trigger to fire; an accelerator pedal beneath his foot. It was this way throughout the Realm. Everything here was a cyberimitation of reality, but not very much like reality itself. With his mind flowing through the Internet, Kurodar needed only a digital analogue of the drones in order to fly them. He didn't actually need to know how to fly.

Rick looked out through the windshield and saw two, then three fighter planes leaving the bay floor to shoot up toward the open ceiling and into the blackness of space beyond. There were no pilots in the cockpits, so he knew that it was Kurodar who was flying them with his mind.

He looked down and saw three, then four more of the planes in the bay catching fire. If his plane went up next, there'd be no getting out of it. He'd burn alive—or, if he did manage to break away, the slithering Cobras would swarm him, a snake nightmare washing over him like a rising tide.

But now his own craft lifted, pulled by the gravity of the blackness. It rose slowly off the floor. Slowly, it turned its nose cone up toward the depths of the night beyond the bay. And then, with a sudden burst of awesome speed, it shot up out of the bay and into the dark, leaving the sea of fire and the writhing sea of Cobras below.

The craft emerged swiftly into the vast blackness. Rick looked around him and took in the scene.

Looming directly over him was the massive WarCraft and the gargantuan Octo-Guardian that seemed grafted onto it, its baleful eyes observing the scene. The Octo-Guardian's tentacles were waving in the blackness, their single red eyes burning, searching, examining whatever they passed. One tentacle was already moving his way.

To the left was the red horizon of the Lower Realm. Down there was the Golden City and the portals that could take Rick back to RL.

And up ahead? Four other fighter planes. Like him, they had escaped the burning bay. They were just out in front of him and speeding away into space. In the distance he could see something that looked like a gleaming planet, a glowing orb with shining silver buildings rising from its surface. That, he thought, was what the model inside the WarCraft was meant to represent: the true target, the Realm analogue of Washington, D.C. If the fighter planes reached the Washington planet and opened fire, even just these surviving four, they would do untold damage in RL. They would leave untold numbers of real people dead.

Rick had to give chase. He had to shoot those fighters down. He had to stop them.

But before he did he looked to his right. And he saw the Breach.

He didn't know what it was, of course. He didn't know that Kurodar had found a way to think straight from his cyber-created imagination into reality. All he knew was that in the midst of this infinite blackness, he could see Real Life in real time. There was a forest. There was a barn.

And there was Molly—Molly with Victor One.

She was sitting on the ground. She was holding Victor One's head on her lap. Rick felt a twinge of jealousy at the sight, but it was replaced at once with fear and concern. Victor was clearly hurt, hurt badly. And worse than that . . .

Much worse than that, Rick could see about a dozen men, men masked in balaclavas and carrying machine guns. They were spread out in the trees around but slowly closing in. Molly hadn't seen them yet, but any minute they would break out of the trees and encircle her. She would be a prisoner again, and they would carry her off to who-knew-where. That is, if they didn't simply shoot her dead.

Rick had to get to her if he could. He had to fly his fighter into that Breach and see if he could break through to RL and save her.

But if he did that . . . He turned to look ahead of him. If he did that, those fighters heading for Washington would reach their mark and launch their missiles.

For a moment, Rick froze, his fighter hovering motionless.

What did he do now? How did he decide? Should he save Molly? Or save the thousands who would die in the city?

The power of his feelings for Molly welled up inside him as never before. There was more between the two of them than he had really understood. He remembered thinking that Mariel was part of his soul, but Molly . . . was it possible she was even more than that?

It flashed through Rick's brain in that moment that his father had probably faced just the sort of choice he was facing now: stay with his family or fight the MindWar, cling to the people he loved or try to save the country.

What if you had to sacrifice everything you love to save everything you love?

That was the question his father had asked Molly's father before he'd left to battle Kurodar. Rick had been angry at him for choosing that battle over him and Raider and their mother, but now he understood: His father's love for him was in his sacrifice. His father's sacrifice was the face of his love.

He forced himself to turn his eyes away from the Breach, away from Molly. He pressed the fighter's stick forward and dropped his foot onto the accelerator. His craft shot off after the enemy planes.

The craft was swift. The row of enemy fighters ahead of him grew larger in his windshield. The Octo-Guardian's tentacles still surrounded them all. As Rick put on a burst of speed, the tentacles stiffened. They turned. Their red eyes burned as they stared at him.

Rick's craft shot past the watching tentacles toward the enemy ships. His right hand tightened on the trigger of the gun stick. He moved the stick and a green target display appeared on his windshield. He centered the target on the enemy ship farthest to his left. He squeezed the trigger.

He felt the fighter buck beneath him. A dotted line of brilliant blue light shot out of the guns under his wings. The light sliced through the darkness, tracking to the center of the target. A split second later, the light struck the enemy craft. It caught the thing midflight, bingo, right on the tail. Instantly, the plane exploded into a swiftly broadening ball of fire and debris.

"Yeah!" Rick heard himself shout. "Yeah! Yeah! Yeah!"

He shifted the target display to the next craft over. One down, three to go. Just like in a video game. Awesome!

He pulled the trigger again.

Three things happened simultaneously.

There was another stuttered blast of blue light from his guns, another dotted line of brilliance lancing the blackness toward another enemy fighter. The light hit the second ship and that ship exploded, sending red flames and silver garbage sailing through the depths of space.

But even as that happened, the other two enemies realized they were under attack from behind and started to turn around. Rick saw them in his windshield, one wheeling in a broad arc off to the left, one barrel-rolling wing over wing to the right. No way to catch them in his sights when they were dodging like that. And anyway, there was no time to try.

Because now, too, the Octo-Guardian came after him. The beast's malicious eyes seemed to flare with vengeful fire. Something like a mouth opened in him, and a noise came out of it that filled the vast empty blackness all around. It was a strange ragged roar, guttural and high-pitched at once, a sound that seemed full of both rage and satisfaction. He remembered the baleful eyes of the Troll who had taunted them in his video. That Troll—this creature—they were one being—one being eager to release its fury in a rampage of destruction.

Rick saw the tentacles all around him start to whip and wave. They curled toward him, each with a red eye glowing. At the same time the two remaining fighter planes were coming back toward him, each one rolling and diving in evasive maneuvers to keep Rick from getting his target display trained on them.

The scene was so insane, and so insanely deadly—giant octopus tentacles trying to snatch him out of space while fighter planes zipped in toward him—that for a moment Rick actually wondered if he might be in one of his post-Realm nightmares.

But no, this was real—or as real, at least, as anything in this crazy place. As real, at least, as death. There was no time to hesitate. The enemy craft to his left let out a blast of blue light. The fatal blast zipped toward him.

Rick jammed his foot down on the accelerator and yanked up on the stick. His fighter lifted and shot upward. The deadly burst of light passed under him harmlessly. But up above him, through the windshield, Rick saw two gigantic octopus tentacles spiraling around to lasso him. The Octo-Guardian roared again. And Rick roared back. All his video-game prowess came into play as his body reacted faster than his mind, working the fighter's stick so that his craft shot right through the spiraling loops of the tentacles and blasted out the other side before they could close around him.

And there—at the top of the tentacle spiral—was the second of the remaining two fighters, waiting for him. The moment Rick's plane emerged, the enemy opened fire. But even after all this time, Rick's athletic reflexes were too good. He fired back—and with the same speed that had once helped him spin out of the clutches of onrushing linemen, he hauled up on the fighter's stick—hauled up so hard that his craft somersaulted backward in midcareer. The windshield flashed as the enemy's shot went past it, missing by inches. Then space went red as his own shot hit home and the enemy craft exploded. And with that, Rick's fighter nosed down and plummeted through the unchartable dark.

One fighter left—and sure enough, the sudden loop-de-loop brought Rick onto an intersecting course with that last enemy ship. It was a piece of luck; a great shot. If he could aim fast and pull the trigger, he would hit the thing smack in the side and cut it in half.

But now another gigantic tentacle whiplashed through space and its red eye snapped toward him. Rick should have dodged it, but he had to take that shot at the enemy while he had it. He couldn't lose the chance. He waited just long enough to press the trigger—and then tilted the stick to the right to escape the tentacle. The last enemy fighter exploded and the flaming wreckage wheeled across his windshield as his craft barrel-rolled to avoid the Octo-Guardian's reach. But he hadn't moved fast enough. The Octo-Guardian's slithery arm couldn't grab him, but its tip smacked his fuselage and the blow sent his craft spinning out of control.

Rick fought the controls as the fighter tumbled through space, a nauseating roll. He gasped aloud as a tentacle flashed across his windshield. It missed him only because his craft was whirling away so wildly. The Octo-Guardian roared in frustration and the sound was deafening. The thunderous noise made Rick's craft shudder. But now the fighter's controls took hold. Rick wrestled the fighter upright and circled back around to face the WarCraft.

The WarCraft, bigger than a city, dwarfed his little plane. The roaring mouth of the Octo-Guardian could have swallowed his fighter easily. The eyes alone—those malignant eyes—were ten times larger than the craft. They glared at Rick with such sick hatred that Rick could feel the force of it in the pit of his stomach.

The Octo-Guardian roared one final time and as it did, it threw its tentacles wide in rage and then brought them snapping forward all at once to seize Rick out of the sky.

There was no way to avoid them. There were too many. They were too big. They were closing on him too fast. There was no chance to escape.

So instead Rick hit the accelerator and charged the beast. With the tentacles ripping toward him, he flew straight for the Octo-Guardian's black open maw, the gaping hole hovering above the mighty WarCraft.

As he flew forward, he centered his target display on the beast's right eye and started pressing the trigger. He fired again and again. In his peripheral vision, he could see the tentacles whisking at him from the right and the left, from above and below. Another instant and he knew they would grab his fighter craft and tear it to pieces like an evil child ripping the wings off a fly.

But he didn't change course. He kept zooming toward the Octo-Guardian. He kept pressing the trigger. The dotted lines of blue light kept shooting from his guns, one barrage after another. They flashed to the center of the target display—the center of the Octo-Guardian's vicious stare.

Just as the tentacles reached Rick's fighter, the blasts struck home. The Octo-Guardian's right eye erupted in a mushroom cloud of red gore. The Octo-Guardian's scream of agony blew every thought out of Rick's mind, even the thought of death. Something hit his craft—a tentacle?—and again his fighter spun away wildly wing over wing. But even as it did, he saw the Octo-Guardian lose its hold on the WarCraft and tumble backward, its tentacles trailing after it in a chaotic and slithery train.

The Octo-Guardian roared and flew back and back into the darkness of space. Without the WarCraft to anchor it, the gravity of that blackness sucked the beast in. In a second, it was pulled into the depths of nothingness. In another second, it was lost in the dark entirely and forever. Its furious roar echoed for another moment and then died away completely. The beast was gone.

But the black space of the Realm was far from peaceful then. The violence of the Octo-Guardian's release had set the immense WarCraft twirling. As Rick got his fighter under control, he saw the vast ship tumbling past his windshield. It was an awesome sight, like watching an entire island go flying end over end. Rick looked on, wide-eyed, as the monstrous craft spun away from him toward the red surface of the Lower Realm. It spun and fell and fell and spun, growing smaller as it dropped toward the red surface of MindWar. Rick could only sit and stare at its long, long fall.

And when the WarCraft struck the surface of the Realm, the impact shook cyberspace itself. The explosion lit the very core of the blackness, the flames opening like the petals of a hellish flower—rising so high off the Lower Realm's surface that Rick thought they would engulf his own craft out here in space and burn it to a cinder. But no, the flower of flame touched the blackness for only a second and then closed in on itself and winked out, leaving the blackness even blacker still.

Dazed in the vast silence of the aftermath, Rick looked around him. It was over. The WarCraft was destroyed. The fighters were gone. The city was safe and . . .

Molly.

He had to crane his neck to see her, but there she still was. Looking around now as she heard the masked gunmen moving out of the forest to close in a half circle around her and Victor. There was nowhere for her to run, no way for her to run without leaving the wounded Victor One behind, which Rick knew she would never do.

One last time he wheeled his fighter round. He did not know what would happen if he flew straight into the Breach. Would he somehow cross the divide between the Realm and RL, or would he smack into a cyberwall and explode?

It didn't matter. For Molly? He was more than willing to chance it. He had to reach her if he could.

He drove the stick forward and jammed his foot down on the accelerator and flew full speed at the Breach.

39. WHITE KNIGHT CHRONICLES

MOLLY SAW THE last drone explode in the sky above the night forest. Her heart felt big with triumph. It was Rick who had done that. She knew it somehow. It was Rick.

She bowed her head over Victor One. Her tears fell on the soldier's face. He lay still, his head in her lap, his eyes closed, his breath coming hard and slow. She did not know if he could hear her, but she whispered to him anyway.

"We did it, Victor. Us and Rick. It's over."

Then, in the woodland silence, she heard the footsteps of the approaching killers. She knew at once who it was: Smiley McDeath's army of reinforcements, coming to get her, to take her to their leader. Or maybe they would just kill her here.

She stroked Victor One's hair to give him comfort and to give herself comfort. What happened next was going to be terrible, she knew. More terrible than anything that had happened before. They would hate her for what she had done. Burning their drones, helping to stop their attack. They would hate her for it and they would take their hate out on her. But whatever they did, whatever happened, no matter how bad it got, she would always know that she had beaten them. She and Victor One. And Rick, wherever he was.

She drew a deep breath and lifted her head. She could see them now, dark masked figures moving out of the trees, their machine guns at the ready, pointed at her. Guns on every side.

She bowed her head. She closed her eyes. She prayed.

Quieted in her heart, she looked up. The killers were so close to her now, she could see their eyes, even in the dark. What dead things they were, those eyes. How full of darkness.

When the first shot was fired, it was incomprehensible to her. She had never seen anything like it before. What blue streak of light flashes through the air like that? What makes such a weird whisking *whoosh* of a sound? What sort of weapon sets off such an explosion?

She had no idea. All she knew was that the next instant there was utter chaos on every side of her. The masked killers were flying into the air like toys tossed off a blanket. The earth was erupting upward all around, clods of dirt exploding through the night. Another blue flash cut the dark, then another, each one making that same *whoosh*. Now the killers' voices were shouting, screaming. The masked men were running in a panic, escaping back into the woods.

Stunned, Molly turned, looked up—and saw the fighter craft hovering above the open roof of the barn. No mere drone, a full-fledged aircraft, and such an aircraft as she had never seen, as no one had ever seen in real life. It looked like something out of a science-fiction movie, an impossible multiwinged beast of a warship, firing its deadly blue rays as if from another world into this one.

Now, as Molly stared openmouthed, the fighter edged forward over the barn. The air stirred all around her, making her hair blow wildly around her face. The fighter craft slowly lowered out of the darkness and settled gently onto the earth beside her.

The cockpit sprang open and Molly's cry of surprise and delight caught in her throat.

Oh boy! she thought. *Oh, boy oh boy!*

That face. How well she remembered the look on that face. That grin and those bright, fiery, triumphant eyes. It was the look of a football star after a victory. It was the look of a hometown hero in his moment of glory. It was the look of Number 12, the quarterback of her high school team. His aspect seemed strange, not wholly real, a sort of electronic presence, overbright and staticky on the surface of the night. But that didn't matter. It was him, all the same. It was Number 12, all right, his old self. Cocky, hilarious, and so bright with spirit and life you had to love him.

She had to love him, anyway.

"Climb aboard, sweetheart," Rick told her, still grinning. "I'm taking you out of here."

Molly felt Victor One stirring in her lap. Roused from unconsciousness by the blasts from the fighter, he managed to open his eyes a little. He managed to whisper up at her: "What . . . ? What . . . ?"

Molly was still crying, but she was laughing now, too. "It's Rick," she said to him. "It's Rick come to rescue us. Like a knight in shining armor."

Victor One smiled up at her weakly. "Love those," he said.

And he closed his eyes again.

40. FINAL FANTASY

RICK FLEW HIS fighter craft low over the Realm. His eyes scanned the surface, searching for a portal. He passed above the crash site of the great WarCraft. There was wreckage everywhere: flaming black metal debris, splintered blue-green trees, seared earth, fuming craters. A thick pall of smoke.

Just as he flew to the edge of the central crater—the place where the main body of the WarCraft had landed—Rick spotted the floating purple diamond he was looking for: the way back to RL. He brought the fighter craft around in a broad half circle and slowly headed in for a landing.

He had wanted to stay with Molly and Victor One, but he couldn't. He had transported them out of the forest in his fighter craft, but then he had to leave them by the side of the road, waiting for the police cars that were already rushing to the scene. He wished he could have gone home with them, but it wasn't possible. The timer on his hand was ticking down to zero, and his mind was beginning to dissolve, reality coming apart into pixels and a nauseating blur.

Because even though he had broken through the Breach, he was still embedded in the Realm. He had flown his fighter into Real Life, but he was not real himself, not yet. The complex process his father had invented that would bring him out through the portal would also restore him to his real body where it lay in the glass coffin in the MindWar complex. Until he went through that process, he was not fully a part of RL. He had to return, alone, and find his way out.

Now the fighter touched down. Rick stepped out of the cockpit. The Realm seemed dead to him at first. Nothing moving but the drifting smoke, the flickering fires, the rising sparks. No sound but the hiss of dying machinery and the crackle of flame.

He glanced at his palm. His final minute was ticking away. The portal was only a few steps off. He would make it easily.

Still, he stood there another moment. He looked over the scene of the disaster anxiously.

He thought: *Mariel.*

He knew she wasn't dead. He could still feel her. He could feel her energy in the sword at his side. More than that, he could feel her presence inside him. If she were dead, he would know it. She was part of him somehow. He knew she was still alive.

He hated to leave without seeing her, without telling her again that he would find her body in RL, that he would bring her out. So he hesitated, and after a moment, a noise reached him, a quiet sound that was almost drowned out by the snickering flames and the sizzling electronics all around him.

It was the sound of water. A steady drip of it. Rick turned, searching for the source. There it was: in the midst of the gray smoke and the black burned-out woods, a little trail of silver was leaking from a broken vessel to form a puddle on the wounded ground.

A small hope rising in him, Rick moved toward the gleam of silver. He peered into its surface.

Sure enough, she traveled by water—and there she was.

He saw her face floating just beneath the surface of the silver liquid. Already, he saw, age and exhaustion were creeping back into her features. Already, the energy that had revived her was leaking away. If he couldn't come back here soon, she would sink back into that haggard decrepitude in which he'd first found her. She would be lost forever.

He reached his hand down toward her. He opened his mouth to speak. He wanted to promise her he would return, swear that he would save her. But before he could say anything, she smiled at him very gently. She spoke very softly.

She said, "Don't be afraid."

And she faded away.

Rick moved to the portal . . .

LEVEL FIVE: AFTERMATH

THIS TIME, THERE were no alarms. There was no one chasing him. The flash drive his father had given him had helped him hack into the compound's security system. It had taught the system to regard Rick as a thing invisible, a non-threat. No one even knew he was there.

Rick dragged himself through the air vents quickly. No Miss Ferris barking at him now. No security men chasing him. And Victor One was still in the hospital. There was no one to stop him. He smiled at the thought.

He paused for a moment, catching his breath. He worked his phone out of his pocket and held it up in front of him. He checked the map his father had given him. He put the phone away and continued to drag himself through the vents.

After another fifteen minutes or so, he found what he was looking for: he looked down and saw the room hidden at the heart of the MindWar compound. He could hear the refrigeration units humming. He could feel the chill seeping up to him through the grate.

He brought out his Swiss army knife. He worked quickly to loosen the grate's screws. He removed the grate and lowered himself down into the room.

333

The room was small and windowless. The walls were painted black. A band of fluorescent lights ran around the base of them, bathing the place in a cool, dim, purple glare.

And at the center of the room, there stood the two glass coffins.

Rick approached them slowly, his heart beating hard. He had not been this nervous during the worst of it: out there in Realm space with the fighters escaping him and the tentacles closing in. Even then, he hadn't been this tense.

He reached the side of the first box and looked in. Through the swirling mist of refrigeration he saw the man lying inside. He was a small, broad-shouldered black man maybe a few years older than Rick. He had a round face under close-cropped hair. He was unconscious, but he was breathing steadily. One corner of Rick's mouth turned up at the sight of him. He knew at once that this was Favian. It didn't look like him exactly, but somehow Favian's anxious, good-hearted, and resourceful personality was written on the man's face.

He lifted his eyes to the second coffin.

Mariel.

He stepped away from the sleeping Favian and moved to the other box. He tried to prepare his mind for what he would see: what she would look like here in RL. He drew a deep breath and then he looked down through the glass.

Rick's mouth opened in shock and his eyes went wide.

He thought: *But that's impossible!*

READING GROUP GUIDE

1. Molly's father thinks religion is unscientific, while Rick's father believes that science makes no sense without God. What do you think? Are the two compatible? If so, in what ways?

2. Both Rick and Molly use prayer to gain strength during their trials and challenges. Have you turned to prayer when facing difficulties in your life? Do you think it has made a difference?

3. At one point in the story Molly says that everyone has a conscience and can be reasoned with. Do you think this is true? What about the character Kurador? Do you think he has a conscience?

4. Rick has a fiery temper that often lands him in trouble, but this quality has a positive side: it makes him immovable when he sets his mind to something, which served him well during his fight in the Realm. Can you think of any other character traits that may appear negative but can actually be qualities of strength?

5. Both Rick and Molly develop feelings for their rescuers—Mariel and Victor One. When people undergo stressful or life-threatening experiences, do you think it is common for them to form a strong emotional attachment? Why? Can those feelings be real and lasting?

6. At the end of *Hostage Run* Rick faces a tremendously diffi-
cult decision: save Molly or try to abort Kurador's attack on
Washington, DC? Do you think he made the right decision?
Why or why not?

7. Rick's mother has faith in her husband even after he leaves the
family under the suspicion that he is going to be with a former
girlfriend. How do you develop that kind of trust and faith in
another person? Do you have that kind of trust in anyone?

8. Commander Mars is the very powerful man in charge of the
MindWar Project. Do you think his power is corrupting him?
How can a person possess a great amount of power without
letting it corrupt them?

9. Do you think there is a traitor within the ranks of the
MindWar Project? If so, who is it and why do you believe this
person could possibly be a traitor?

10. What do you think about Lawrence Dial's statement, "If you
let your spirit get poisoned and dark . . . like all darkness it
wants to turn you into itself"? Do you think evil is like that?
What are some things you would want to avoid in order to
keep darkness from invading your spirit? Do you think faith
in God will protect your spirit from darkness?

HE'S **EMERGED** FROM THE REALM **VICTORIOUS** TWICE.

IS HIS LUCK ABOUT TO RUN OUT?

GAME OVER

AVAILABLE JANUARY 2016

CHARLIE WEST JUST WOKE UP IN SOMEONE ELSE'S NIGHTMARE.

THE HOMELANDERS SERIES

AVAILABLE IN PRINT AND E-BOOK

CHAPTER ONE

The Torture Room

Suddenly I woke up strapped to a chair.

"What . . . ?" I whispered.

Dazed, I looked around me. I was in a room with a concrete floor and cinder block walls. A single bare lightbulb hung glaring from a wire above me. Against the wall across from me was a set of white metal drawers. A tray was attached to it. There were instruments on the tray—awful instruments—blades and pincers and something that looked like a miniature version of those acetylene torches welders use. The instruments lay on a white cloth. The cloth was stained with blood.

The sight of the blood jolted me into full consciousness. I tried to move my arms and legs. I couldn't. That's when I saw the straps. One on each wrist holding me to the chair's metal arms. One on each ankle holding me to its metal legs. And there was blood here too. More blood. On the floor at my feet. On my white shirt, on my black slacks, on my arms. And there were bruises on my arms, dark purple bruises. And there were oozing burn marks on the backs of my hands.

I hurt. I kind of just realized it all at once. My whole body ached and stung inside and out. My shirt was soaking wet. My skin felt clammy with sweat. My mouth tasted like dirt. I smelled like garbage.

Have you ever had a nightmare, a really bad one, where you woke up and you could feel your heart hammering against the bed and you couldn't catch your breath? Then, as you started to understand that the nightmare wasn't real, that it was all a dream, your heart slowed down again and your breathing got deeper and you relaxed and thought, *Whew, that sure seemed real.*

Well, this was exactly the opposite. I opened my eyes expecting to see my bedroom at home, my black-belt certificate, my trophies, my poster of *The Lord of the Rings.* Instead, I was in what should have been a nightmare, but wasn't. It was real. And with every second, my heart beat harder. My breath came shorter. Panic flared up in me like a living flame.

Where was I? Where was my room? Where were my parents? What was happening to me? How did I get here?

Terrified, I racked my brain, trying to think, trying to figure it out, asking myself in the depths of my confusion and fear: what was the last thing I remembered . . . ?

The adventure continues in *The Last Thing I Remember*
by Andrew Klavan.

ABOUT THE AUTHOR

ANDREW KLAVAN is a bestselling, award-winning thriller novelist whose books have been made into major motion pictures. He broke into the YA scene with the best-selling Homelanders series, starting with *The Last Thing I Remember.* He is also a screenwriter and scripted the innovative movie-in-an-app *Haunting Melissa.*

Website: www.andrewklavan.com
Twitter: @andrewklavan
Facebook: aklavan